OBASAN

ALSO BY JOY KOGAWA

NOVEL
Itsuka

POETRY
The Splintered Moon
A Choice of Dreams
Jericho Road

OBASAN

Joy Kogawa

Anchor Books
A DIVISION OF RANDOM HOUSE, INC.
NEW YORK

FIRST ANCHOR BOOKS EDITION, January 1994

*Although this novel is based on historical events, and many of the
persons named are real, the main characters are fictional.*

Library of Congress Cataloging-in-Publication Data
Kogawa, Joy.
    Obasan / Joy Kogawa — 1st Anchor Books ed.
        p.   cm.
    Sequel: Itsuka.
    1. Japanese—Canada—Evacuation and relocation, 1942–1945—
Fiction. 2. World War, 1939–1945—Canada—Fiction. I. Title.
PR9199.3.K6302 1994
813'.54—dc20   93-26081
                                                            CIP

ISBN 0-385-46886-5

Book design by Claire Naylon Vaccaro

www.anchorbooks.com

PRINTED IN THE UNITED STATES OF AMERICA

25   24   23   22

To him that overcometh
will I give to eat
of the hidden manna
and will give him
a white stone
and in the stone
a new name written.

THE BIBLE

I wish to thank Ed Kitagawa, Grace Tucker, Jean Suzuki, Gordon Nakayama and the Public Archives of Canada for permission to use documents and letters from the files of Muriel Kitagawa, Grace Tucker, T. Buck Suzuki and Gordon Nakayama.

This book is dedicated to my mother and father and to those amazing people, the Issei—the few who are still with us and those who have gone.

Joy Kogawa

OBASAN

There is a silence that cannot speak.

There is a silence that will not speak.

Beneath the grass the speaking dreams and beneath the dreams is a sensate sea. The speech that frees comes forth from that amniotic deep. To attend its voice, I can hear it say, is to embrace its absence. But I fail the task. The word is stone.

I admit it.

I hate the stillness. I hate the stone. I hate the sealed vault with its cold icon. I hate the staring into the night. The questions thinning into space. The sky swallowing the echoes.

Unless the stone bursts with telling, unless the seed flowers with speech, there is in my life no living word. The sound I hear is only sound. White sound. Words, when they fall, are pockmarks on the earth. They are hailstones seeking an underground stream.

If I could follow the stream down and down to the hidden voice, would I come at last to the freeing word? I ask the night sky but the silence is steadfast. There is no reply.

1

9:05 P.M., AUGUST 9, 1972.

The coulee is so still right now that if a match were to be lit, the flame would not waver. The tall grasses stand without quivering. The tops flop this way and that. The whole dark sky is bright with stars and only the new moon moves.

We come here once every year around this time, Uncle and I. This spot is half a mile from the Barkers' farm and seven miles from the village of Granton, where we finally moved in 1951.

"Nothing changes ne," I say as we walk toward the rise.

"Umi no yo," Uncle says, pointing to the grass. "It's like the sea."

The hill surface, as if responding to a command from Uncle's outstretched hand, undulates suddenly in a breeze, with ripple after ripple of grass shadows, rhythmical as ocean waves. We wade through the dry surf, the flecks of grass hitting us like spray. Uncle walks jerkily as a baby on the unsure ground, his feet widespread, his arms suddenly out like a tightrope walker's when he loses his balance.

"Dizzy?" I ask, grabbing him as he wobbles unsteadily on one leg.

His lips make small smacking sounds as he sucks in air.

"Too much old man," he says, and totters back upright.

When we come to the top of the slope, we find the dip in the ground where he usually rests. He casts around to make sure there are no wild cactus plants, then slowly folds down onto his haunches, his rootlike fingers poking the grass flat in front of him.

Below us the muddy river sludges along its crooked bed. He squats and I stand in the starlight, chewing on bits of grass. This is the closest Uncle ever gets to the ocean.

"Umi no yo," he always says.

Everything in front of us is virgin land. From the beginning of time, the grass along this stretch of prairie has not been cut. About a mile east is a spot which was once an Indian buffalo jump, a high steep cliff where the buffalo were stampeded and fell to their deaths. All the bones are still there, some sticking right out of the side of a fresh landslide.

Uncle could be Chief Sitting Bull squatting here. He has the same prairie-baked skin, the deep brown furrows like dry riverbeds creasing his cheeks. All he needs is a feather headdress, and he would be perfect for a picture postcard—"Indian Chief from Canadian Prairie"—souvenir of Alberta, made in Japan.

Some of the Native children I've had in my classes over the years could almost pass for Japanese, and vice versa. There's something in the animal-like shyness I recognize in the dark eyes. A quickness to look away. I remember, when I was a child in Slocan, seeing the same swift flick-of-a-cat's-tail look in the eyes of my friends.

The first time Uncle and I came here for a walk was in 1954, in August, two months after Aunt Emily's initial visit to Granton. For weeks after she left, Uncle seemed distressed, pacing back and forth, his hand patting the back of his head. Then one evening, we came here.

It was a quiet twilight evening, much like tonight. His agitation seemed to abate as we walked through the waving grass, though his eyes still stabbed at the air around him and occasionally at me.

When we reached the edge of the hill, we stopped and looked down at the coulee bottom and the river with the tree clumps and brush along its edge. I felt apprehensive about rattlesnakes and wanted to get back to the road.

"Isn't it dangerous?" I asked.

Uncle is almost never direct in his replies. I felt he was chiding me for being childishly afraid when he said abruptly, "Mo ikutsu? What is your age now?"

"Eighteen," I said.

He shook his head as he scuffed the ground. He sighed so deeply that when he exhaled, his breath was a groan.

"What is the matter, Uncle?"

He bent down and patted the grass flat with his hands, shaking his head slowly. "Too young," he said softly. "Still too young." He smiled the gentle half-sad, half-polite smile he reserves for small children and babies. "Someday," he said.

Whatever he was intending to tell me "someday" has not yet been told. I sometimes wonder if he realizes my age at all. At thirty-six, I'm hardly a child.

I sit beside him in the cool of this patch of prairie and immediately I am hidden with him in a grass forest. My hands rest beside his on the knotted mat of roots covering the dry earth, the hard untilled soil.

"Uncle," I whisper, "why do we come here every year?"

He does not respond. From both Obasan and Uncle I have learned that speech often hides like an animal in a storm.

My fingers tunnel through a tangle of roots till the grass stands up from my knuckles, making it seem that my fingers are the roots. I am part of this small forest. Like the grass, I search the earth and the sky with a thin but persistent thirst.

"Why, Uncle?"

He seems about to say something, his mouth open as he stares straight ahead, his eyes wide. Then, as if to erase his thoughts, he rubs his hands vigorously over his face and shakes his head.

Above and around us, unimaginably vast and unbroken by silhouette of tree or house or any hint of human handiwork, is the prairie sky. In all my years in southern Alberta, I have not been able to look for long at this. We sit forever, it seems, in infinite night while all around us the tall prairie grasses move and grow, bending imperceptibly to the moon's faint light.

Finally, I touch his arm. "Wait here awhile," I say as I stand up and walk to the edge of the hill. I always pick at least one flower before we go home. I inch my way down the steep path and along the stretch where the side of the slope oozes wet from the surface seepage of the underground stream. Wild rose bushes, prickly and profuse with green, cluster along the edges of the trickle. I can smell them as I descend. At the bottom of the coulee I can hear the gurgling of the slowly moving water. I stand for a long time watching as the contours of the coulee erode slowly in the night.

2

SEPTEMBER 13, 1972.

In the future I will remember the details of this day, the ordinary trivia illuminated by an event that sends my mind scurrying for significance. I seem unwilling to live with randomness.

This afternoon, when the phone call comes, it is one month after my last visit to Granton and I am standing in front of my grades five and six class at Cecil Consolidated, defending myself.

The town of Cecil, Alberta, is one hundred and fifty-odd miles northeast of Granton and I have been teaching in the

same room now for the last seven years. Every month or so, I
try to drop in to see my uncle and my aunt, Obasan, who are
both now in their eighties. But at the beginning of the school
year, I'm quite busy.

It usually takes me at least two weeks to feel at home with
a new class. This year there are two Native girls, sisters,
twelve and thirteen years old, both adopted. There's also a
beautiful half-Japanese, half-European child named Tami.
Then there's Sigmund, the freckle-faced redhead. Right
from the beginning, I can see that he is trouble. I'm trying to
keep an eye on him by putting him at the front of the
class.

Sigmund's hand is up, as it usually is.

"Yes, Sigmund."

"Miss Nah Canny," he says.

"Not Nah Canny," I tell him, printing my name on the
blackboard: NAKANE. "The *a*'s are short as in 'among'—Na Ka
Neh—and not as in 'apron' or 'hat.' "

Some of the children say "Nah Cane."

"Naomi Nah Cane is a pain," I heard one of the girls say
once.

"Have you ever been in love, Miss Nakane?" Sigmund
asks.

"In love? Why do you suppose we use the preposition 'in'
when we talk about love?" I ask evasively. "What does it
mean to be 'in' something?"

Sigmund never puts his hand up calmly but shakes it
frantically like a leaf in the wind.

I am thinking of the time when I was a child and asked
Uncle if he and Obasan were "in love." My question was out
of place. "In ruv? What that?" Uncle asked. I've never once
seen them caressing.

"Are you going to get married?" Sigmund asks.

The impertinence of children. As soon as they learn I'm no disciplinarian, I lose control over classroom discussions.

"Why do you ask?" I answer irritably and without dignity.

"My mother says you don't look old enough to be a teacher."

That's odd. It must be my size: five feet one, 105 pounds. When I first started teaching sixteen years ago, there were such surprised looks when parents came to the classroom door. Was it my youthfulness or my oriental face? I never learned which.

"My friend wants to ask you for a date," Sigmund adds. He's aware of the stir he's creating in the class. A few of the girls gasp and put their hands up to their mouths. An appropriate response, I think wryly. Typically Cecil. Miss Nakane dating a friend of Sigmund's? What a laugh!

I turn my back to the class and stare out the window. Every year the question is asked at least once.

"Are you going to get married, Miss Nakane?"

With everyone in town watching everything that happens, what chance for romance is there here? Once a widower father of one of the boys in my class came to see me after school and took me to dinner at the local hotel. I felt nervous walking into the Cecil Inn with him.

"Where do you come from?" he asked as we sat down at a small table in a corner. That's the one surefire question I always get from strangers. People assume when they meet me that I'm a foreigner.

"How do you mean?"

"How long have you been in this country?"

"I was born here."

"Oh," he said, and grinned. "And your parents?"

"My mother's a Nisei."

"A what?"

"N-i-s-e-i," I spelled, printing the word on the napkin. "Pronounced 'knee-say.' It means 'second generation.'" Sometimes I think I've been teaching school too long. I explained that my grandparents, born in Japan, were Issei, or first generation, while the children of the Nisei were called Sansei, or third generation.

The widower was so full of questions that I half expected him to ask for an identity card. The only thing I carry in my wallet is my driver's license. I should have something with my picture on it and a statement below that tells who I am. Megumi Naomi Nakane. Born June 18, 1936, Vancouver, British Columbia. Marital status: Old maid. Health: Fine, I suppose. Occupation: Schoolteacher. I'm bored to death with teaching and ready to retire. What else would anyone want to know? Personality: Tense. Is that past or present tense? It's perpetual tense. I have the social graces of a common housefly. That's self-denigrating, isn't it?

The widower never asked me out again. I wonder how I was unsatisfactory. I could hardly think of anything at all to ask him. Did he assume I wasn't interested? Can people not tell the difference between nervousness and lack of interest?

"Well," I say, turning around and facing the general tittering, "there are many questions I don't have answers for."

Sigmund's hand is waving still. "But you're a spinster," he says, darting a grin at the class. More gasps from the girls.

"Spinster?" I grimace and have an urge to throttle him. "What does the word mean?"

"Old maid," Sigmund says impudently.

Spinster? Old maid? Bachelor lady? The terms certainly apply. At thirty-six, I'm no bargain in the marriage market. But Aunt Emily in Toronto, still single at fifty-six, is even more old-maidish than I am and yet she refuses the label. She says if we laundered the term properly she'd put it on, but it's too covered with cultural accretions for comfort.

"I suppose I am an old maid," I say glumly. "So is my aunt in Toronto."

"Your aunt is an old maid too? How come?"

I throw up my hands in futility. Let the questions come. Why indeed are there two of us unmarried in our small family? Must be something in the blood. A crone-prone syndrome. We should hire ourselves out for a research study, Aunt Emily and I. But she would be too busy, rushing around Toronto, rushing off to conferences. She never stays still long enough to hear the sound of her own voice.

"What's her name, Teacher?"

"Emily Kato," I say, spelling it. "That's 'Cut-oh,' not 'Cat-oh' or 'Kay-toe.' Miss E. Kato." Is there some way I can turn this ridiculous discussion into a phonics lesson?

Someone is sure to ask about her love life. Has Aunt Emily ever, I wonder, been in love? Love no doubt is in her. Love, like the coulee wind, rushing through her mind, whirring along the tips of her imagination. Love like a coyote, howling into a "love 'em and leave 'em" wind.

There is an urgent knock on the door and I'm glad for the interruption.

"Would you answer the door, please," I ask, nodding to Lori, the Native girl who sits at the back and never says anything.

The secretary's smiling face pokes in the doorway and she says, "There's a phone call for you, Miss Nakane, from Granton."

I tell the class to carry on. It's one of my more useful orders. "Carry on, class." And I walk down the hallway to the principal's office, leaving a hubbub behind me.

The principal is standing with his back to me, his almost bald head looking like a faceless face. His soft hands are behind his back and he is pulling on his fingers one after another. It reminds me of the time I tried to milk cows.

The phone is off the hook and an operator's voice answers me.

"Miss" . . . scratch . . . scratch. "Go ahead, please."

The connection is full of static sounds and I press the receiver hard against my ears.

"Hello? Pardon me? Who is it?"

It's Dr. Brace from the hospital in Granton. His voice in my ear has the quality of an old recording. I can't believe what he is saying.

"Who? My uncle?"

There is an odd sensation like an electrical jolt but not so sharp—a dull twitch simultaneously in the back of my head and in my abdomen. And then a rapid calming.

"Be still," the voice inside is saying. "Sift the words thinly." I am aware that I cannot speak.

I don't know if I have said goodbye to Dr. Brace. I am holding the receiver in my lap and the principal puts his hand on my shoulder.

"Bad news, Naomi?" he asks.

I stare blankly at him.

"Your uncle?" His brow is furrowed sympathetically.

I nod.

He lifts his hands in a gesture of offering but I cannot respond. My mind is working strangely, as if it has separated and hovers above me, ordering me to action from a safe distance, like a general.

What must I do now? Call Stephen. It's 3:15 P.M. What time is it in Montreal? I don't have his number here. Nor Aunt Emily's. I'll phone them later. Must go back to the classroom and make notes for the substitute. How many days' absence should I take? Normally we're allowed a week off. . . .

When I return to the classroom, I am in time to see Sigmund dashing for his desk from the blackboard, where something has been erased. I assign the class free reading till bell time.

By five-thirty I am on the road for Granton. Driving conditions are rather poor this evening. There's a drizzle of rain that is making the road slippery in places. It's taking me longer to drive down than it usually does. But I'm not in a great hurry to see Obasan.

3

She's sitting at the kitchen table when I come in. She is so
deaf that my calling doesn't rouse her and when she sees me
she is startled.

"O," she says. The sound is short and dry as if she has no
energy left. She begins to stand but falters, and her hands,
outstretched to greet me, fall to the table. She says my name
as a question.

"Naomi-san?"

I remove my muddy shoes and put on the slippers at the
door before stepping in.

"Oba," I say loudly, and take her hands. My aunt is not one for hugs and kisses.

She peers into my face. "O," she says again.

I nod in reply.

Her head is tilted to the side as if it's all too heavy inside, and her lower jaw moves from side to side.

I open my mouth to ask, "Did he suffer very much?" but loud talking feels obscene.

"Everyone someday dies," she says eventually. Her voice is barely audible. She turns aside, pivoting in shuffles, and goes to the stove, picking up the large aluminum kettle with both hands. It's been made heavy over the years by the mineral deposits from the hard water. She twists the knob and the gas flame flares blue and red.

I hang my jacket on a coat peg, then sit on a stool beside the table. Uncle's spot.

The house is in its usual clutter. Nothing at all has changed. The applewood table is covered with a piece of discolored plastic over the blue-and-white tablecloth. Along one edge are Uncle's African violets, profusely purple, glass salt and pepper shakers, a soy sauce bottle, a cracked radio, an old-fashioned toaster, a small bottle full of toothpicks.

She pours the tea. Tiny twigs and bits of rice puffs circle in the cups.

"Thank you," I say loudly, lifting the cup in both hands and nodding my head in thanks.

Her eyes are unclear and sticky with a gumlike mucus. She told me years ago her tear ducts were clogged. In all this time I've never seen her cry.

She takes a fold of toilet paper from her sleeve and rubs her lips, which are flaked with dry skin. Her mouth is plagued with a gummy saliva and she drinks the tea to loosen her tongue sticking to the roof of her false plate.

We sit in silence sipping and turning the cups around on the tips of our fingers.

Behind her on the counter is a black loaf of Uncle's stone bread, hefty as a rock. It's too big to be a bun but much smaller than regular "store-boughten" bread. The fact that it's uncovered means that it was made either yesterday or to-day. Was making this bread Uncle's last act?

I can remember the first time he attempted baking. It must have been around 1946 or 1947, when I was about ten years old, shortly after we came to southern Alberta. The fat woman in the Granton general store was giving everyone handwritten recipes for bread with every purchase of flour that day. I begged Obasan to let me try. In the end, it was Uncle who made it.

"Burreddo," Uncle said as he pulled it from the oven. "Try. Good."

"How can you eat that stone?" I asked, poking it. "It'll break your teeth. Shall I get the ax?"

"Stone burreddo. Oishi," Uncle said. "Taste beri good."

He carved a piece off and held it out to me.

"Here," my brother Stephen said. Stephen, three years older than me, was always ordering me around. He plopped a spoonful of hand-yellowed margarine onto the slab. He called margarine "Alberta," since Uncle pronounced Alberta "aru bata," which in our Japanese English means "the butter that there is." "Try some Alberta on it."

"No ten kyou," I said irritably.

Uncle had baked the bread too long. I refused to eat it, but Uncle kept making it that way over the years, "improv-ing" the recipe with leftover oatmeal and barley. Sometimes he even added carrots and potatoes. But no matter what he put in it, it always ended up like a lump of granite on the counter.

When Obasan eats it, she breaks her slice into tiny pieces and soaks them in the homemade "weed tea." The "weedy tea," as Stephen and I named it, was better on cold rice with salted pickles, especially late at night.

Once I took the stone bread in my fists and tried to break it in half but I couldn't. "If you can't even break it, it's not bread," I said. "It's all stone."

"That's not how," Stephen said. He speared the loaf with the sharp knife point and handed me a clump. "Matches your complexion."

"What! Bristleface!"

Stephen was an early beginner when it came to hair on his face. He was the first boy in his class to shave.

With Uncle gone now there will be no more black bread and black bread jokes.

Obasan is rolling a bit of dried-up jam off the plastic tablecloth as she sips her tea. When she speaks, her voice is barely a whisper. Uncle, she says, woke up this morning and called her but she couldn't hear what he had to say.

"There was no knowing," she says. She did not understand what was happening. The nurses at the hospital also did not understand. They stuck tubes into his wrists like grafting on a tree but Death won against the medical artistry. She wanted to stay beside him there, but, again, "There was no knowing." The nurses sent her home. The last she saw of him, his head was rolling backward and he was looking at the ceiling through the whites of his eyes.

What, I wonder, was Uncle thinking those last few hours? Had the world turned upside down? Perhaps everything was reversing rapidly and he was tunneling backward top to bottom, his feet in an upstairs attic of humus and memory, his hands groping down through the cracks and walls to the damp cellar, to the water, down to the underground sea. Or back to his fishing boats in B.C. and the skiffs moored along the shore. In the end did he manage to swim full circle back to that other shore and his mother's arms, her round moon face glowing down at her firstborn?

"Nen nen korori—lullaby, lullaby . . ." Uncle was a child of the waves. Was he rocked to sleep again by the lap-lap of the sea?

Obasan taps her wrist with her thumb. "Here," she says, "medicine was put in, but—oso katta—it was too late."

She leans her head back to look up at me and her cheeks sink into the cavity of her mouth, making her face resemble a skull. The pulse is a steady ripple in her wrinkled neck. Such an old woman she is. She opens her mouth to say more, but there is no further sound from her dry lips.

The language of her grief is silence. She has learned it well, its idioms, its nuances. Over the years, silence within her small body has grown large and powerful.

What will she do now? I wonder.

What choices does she have?

My brother will be of little help. Stephen, unable to bear the density of her inner retreat and the rebuke he felt in her silences, fled to the ends of the earth. From London, he went to New York, to Montreal. Stephen has always been a ball of mercury, unpredictable in his moods and sudden rages. Departure, for him, is as necessary as breath.

Obasan keeps his infrequent letters in her jewel box.

"Oba, are you all right?" I ask as she struggles to stand up. I put my hands over hers, feeling the silky wax texture.

"Now old," she says. "Too old."

She totters as she moves to the door and squats beside the

boot tray, picking up my shoes weighted by the heavy clay. Granton gumbo adheres like tar.

"It is late now," I say to her. "Should you not rest?"

She is deaf to my concern and begins to gouge out the black sticky mud wedged against the heel. Beside her on the shoe shelf are Uncle's boots and overshoes scraped clean and ready for the next rain. She takes a sheet of newspaper from the pile that is kept beside the entrance and the mud drops down in clumps. In a tin can are a blunt knife and a screwdriver. Everything else is in its place. She is altogether at home here.

Could she, I wonder, come to live with me? I cannot imagine her more comfortable in any other house.

"This house," Obasan says as if she has read my mind. "This body. Everything old."

The house is indeed old, as she is also old. Every homemade piece of furniture, each pot holder and paper doily is a link in her lifeline. She has preserved on shelves, in cupboards, under beds—a box of marbles, half-filled coloring books, a red, white, and blue rubber ball. The items are endless. Every short stub pencil, every cornflakes box stuffed with paper bags and old letters is of her ordering. They rest in the corners like parts of her body, hair cells, skin tissues, tiny specks of memory. This house is now her blood and bones.

Squatting here with the putty knife in her hand, she is every old woman in every hamlet in the world. You see her on a street corner in a village in southern France, in a black dress and black stockings. Or bent over stone steps in a Mexican mountain village. Everywhere the old woman stands as the true and rightful owner of the earth. She is the bearer of keys to unknown doorways and to a network of astonishing tunnels. She is the possessor of life's infinite personal details.

"Now old," Obasan repeats. "Everything old."

She pushes Uncle's overshoes to the side and places my shoes neatly beside them.

"Let us rest now, Obasan," I say once more. "You must be tired. Mo nemasho."

4

From my many years with Obasan, I know that no urging on my part will persuade her of anything. She will do what she will do. She will rest when she is ready to rest.

I have come to the living room to wait for her.

"Too old," I hear her saying to herself again.

I can imagine that my grandmother said much the same thing those dark days in 1942, as she rocked in her stall at the Vancouver Hastings Park prison. Grandma Nakane, Uncle's mother, was too old then to understand political expediency, race riots, the yellow peril. She was told that a war was on. She understood little else.

One of the few pictures we have of Grandma Nakane is in the silver-framed family photograph hanging above the piano, taken when my brother Stephen, the first grandchild on either side, was born.

The Nakanes and Katos are posed together, the four new grandparents seated in front like an advance guard, with their offspring arranged behind them. What a brigade! Square-faced Dr. Kato, my mother's father, sits upright in his chair with his short legs not quite touching the floor. The toes of his black boots angle down like a ballet dancer's. A black cape hangs from his shoulders and his left hand clutches a cane and a pair of gloves. Beside him, stiff and thin in her velvet suit, is Grandma Kato, her nostrils wide in her startled bony face. And there's gentle round-faced Grandma Nakane, her hair rolled back like a wreath, her plump hands held tightly in her soft lap. The last of the quartet is Grandpa Nakane with his droopy mustache, his high-collared shirt, and his hand, like Napoleon's, in his vest. They all look straight ahead, carved and rigid, with their expressionless Japanese faces and their bodies pasted over with *Rule Britannia*. There's not a ripple out of place.

Grandpa Nakane, "number one boatbuilder" Uncle used to say, was a son of the sea that tossed and coddled the Nakanes for centuries. The first of my grandparents to come to Canada, he arrived in 1893, wearing a Western suit, a round black hat, and platformed geta on his feet. When he left his familiar island, he became a stranger, sailing toward an island of strangers. But the sea was his constant companion. He understood its angers, its whisperings, its generosity. The native Songhies of Esquimalt and many Japanese fishermen came to his boatbuilding shop on Saltspring Island, to barter and to buy. Grandfather prospered. His cousin's widowed wife and her son, Isamu, joined him.

Isamu, my uncle, born in Japan in 1889, was my father's older half brother. Uncle Isamu—or Uncle Sam, as we called him—and his wife, Ayako, my Obasan, married in their thirties and settled on Lulu Island, near Annacis Island, where Uncle worked as a boatbuilder.

"How did you and Uncle meet?" I asked Obasan once. "Was it arranged?"

Her answers are always oblique and the full story never emerges in a direct line. She was, I have learned, the only daughter of a widowed schoolteacher and was brought up in private schools. When she came to Canada, she worked as a music teacher and became close friends with Grandma Nakane, who was an accomplished koto player and singer. She married Uncle, she told me with a chuckle, to please Grandma Nakane.

Their first child, a boy, was born dead. He looked, Obasan told me, like Grandpa Nakane. Exactly the same outline of the face.

"Fushigi," Uncle said, "a marvel." Not being Grandpa Nakane's son, he traced the resemblance back through his father's line and concluded finally that the pointed chin and wide jaw of his stillborn child came from his father's and Grandpa Nakane's grandmother. The baby had long paper-thin fingernails and white skin and was perfectly formed. Sometime during birth, the umbilical cord got wrapped around his neck and he was strangled. Three years later the next child also died during birth, but this time there was no explanation. Obasan refused to see or talk about the second child and doesn't know if it was a boy or girl. After that, there were no more. Aunt Emily gave them a springer spaniel pup in the fall.

In the back row, Uncle and Obasan stand behind

Grandma and Grandpa Nakane. There is an exquisite tenderness in Obasan's slanted eyes, her smile more sad than de-
mure. She would be forty-two years of age when this picture
was taken in 1933.

In the center of the picture, in the place of honor, is the
new grandchild held for display in my father's arms. Stephen's face is a freshly baked bun and his tiny mouth is puck-
ered. His marshmallow fists pop out from the long sleeves of a
white lacy christening gown. Father, in a black suit with his
hair slicked back like Mandrake the Magician's, holds Stephen
up like a rabbit in a hat. Father's eyebrows are in a high arch,
as if he is surprised and pleased at the trick he has managed.
"Lo, my son."

To the left are Aunt Emily and Mother, the two Kato
sisters, their heads leaning slightly toward each other. I have
examined this picture often, looking for resemblances. The
sisters are as dissimilar as a baby elephant and a gazelle. Aunt
Emily, a pudgy teenager, definitely takes after Grandpa Kato
—the round open face and the stocky build. She isn't wearing
glasses here, though I've never seen her without them. The
carved ridges of her short waved hair stop abruptly at her
cheeks. She is squinting so that the whites show under the
iris, giving her an expression of concentration and determina-
tion. Not a beauty but, one might say, solid and intelligent-
looking. Beside her, Mother is a fragile presence. Her face is
oval as an egg and delicate. She wears a collarless straight-up-
and-down dress and a long string of pearls. Her eyes, Obasan
told me, were sketched in by the photographer because she
was always blinking when pictures were being taken.

Every once in a while, Obasan catches me looking at this
photograph and she says, "Such a time there was once."

Grandma and Grandpa Kato look fairly severe in the picture. They all look rather humorless, but satisfied with the attention of the camera and its message for the day that all is well. That for ever and ever all is well.

But it isn't, of course. Even my eleven-year-olds know that you can't "capture life's precious moments," as they say in the camera ads.

From a few things Obasan has told me, I wonder if the Katos were ever really a happy family. When Mother was a young child, Grandma Kato left Grandpa Kato, who was a medical student at the time, and returned to Japan. I don't know how many times Grandma went to Japan, but each time she took Mother and left Aunt Emily and Grandpa Kato behind.

"No, the families were not fragmented," Aunt Emily said once when I asked her. She insisted the Nakanes and Katos were intimate to the point of stickiness, like mochi. (Sometimes, instead of buying mochi ready-made in white balls, we cook the special dense mochi rice, then pound it with a small wooden bat over and over till it is stickier than glue. Obasan eats it without her false teeth, ever since the time the mochi clamped her teeth together so tight she had to soak them in hot water for hours.)

The marriage between Father and Mother was the first nonarranged marriage in the community, Aunt Emily said. Grandpa Kato opposed it at first, until his frail daughter became ill. But then when Stephen was prematurely born, it was Grandpa Kato who spent the most time ogling his tiny red face looking for evidence of himself. A male child at last.

My parents, like two needles, knit the families carefully into one blanket. Every event was a warm-water wash, drawing us all closer till the fiber of our lives became an impenetrable mesh. Every tiny problem was discussed endlessly. We were the original "togetherness" people. There were all the picnics at Kitsilano, and the concerts at Stanley Park. And the Christmas concert in the church at Third Avenue when tiny Stephen sang a solo. And I was born. And after that?

After that—there was the worrying letter from Grandma Kato's mother in Japan—and there were all the things that happened around that time. All the things . . .

If we were knit into a blanket once, it's become badly moth-eaten with time. We are now no more than a few tangled skeins—the remains of what might once have been a fisherman's net. The memories that are left seem barely real. Gray shapes in the water. Fish swimming through the gaps in the net. Passing shadows.

Some families grow on and on through the centuries, hardy and visible and procreative. Others disappear from the earth without a whimper.

"The rain falls, the sun shines," Uncle used to say.

Aunt Emily, after graduating at the top of her class in Normal School, was unable to get a teaching position and stayed home to help Grandpa Kato with his medical practice. Father, at the time this picture was taken, was a university student. Later he helped Uncle, designing and building boats.

One snapshot I remember showed Uncle and Father as young men standing full front beside each other, their toes pointing outward like Charlie Chaplin's. In the background were pine trees and the side view of Uncle's beautiful house. One of Uncle's hands rested on the hull of an exquisitely detailed craft. It wasn't a fishing vessel or an ordinary yacht, but a sleek boat designed by Father, made over many years and many winter evenings. A work of art.

"What a beauty," the RCMP officer said in 1941 when he saw it. He shouted as he sliced back through the wake, "What a beauty! What a beauty!"

That was the last Uncle saw of the boat. And shortly

thereafter, Uncle too was taken away, wearing shirt, jacket, and dungarees. He had no provisions, nor did he have any idea where the gunboats were herding him and the other Japanese fishermen in the impounded fishing fleet.

The memories were drowned in a whirlpool of protective silence. Everywhere I could hear the adults whispering, "Kodomo no tame. For the sake of the children . . ." Calmness was maintained.

Once, years later on the Barker farm, Uncle was wearily wiping his forehead with the palm of his hand and I heard him saying quietly, "Itsuka, mata itsuka. Someday, someday again." He was waiting for that "someday" when he could go back to the boats. But he never did.

And now? Tonight?

Nen nen, rest, my dead uncle. The sea is severed from your veins. You have been cut loose.

5

It is past midnight when I waken to see Obasan enter the bedroom with a flashlight in her hand.

"What is it?" I ask, switching on the bedside lamp and frowning against the sudden light.

"It was in the attic, surely," she says. An open stairway to the attic is built along the inside wall of my bedroom and she grasps the railing.

"What was in the attic?" I ask, rubbing my eyes and sitting up.

I put my slippers on and follow her as she climbs the narrow stairs one step at a time.

"At this hour, Obasan?"

The best position is behind her, holding the railing with my left hand, my right arm poised to catch her if she stumbles.

"Slow can go," I say.

At the top of the stairs, I push open the square ceiling door carefully. A pencil line of dust drops through the crack. The light from the bedroom is just enough to show the outlines of a number of cardboard boxes, a small trunk, piles of magazines and newspapers. I arc the flashlight along the floor where there are some glass kerosene lamps covered in thick dust. In the nearest corner by the eaves is a dead sparrow on its back, its feet straight back like a high diver's.

"What are you looking for?" I ask, breaking off the web dangling from the steep-angled rough ceiling.

"Somewhere here," she says.

She squats in front of a pile of cardboard boxes. Her hands, pulling, pushing, tugging, are small weak fists. They remind me—these hands that toil but do not embrace—of the wings of a wounded bird, battering the ground in an attempt at balance.

"Lost," she says occasionally. The word for "lost" also means "dead."

She turns to face me in the darkness.

"Eyes can no longer see."

My shoulder brushes against a canvas bag hanging from a nail in a beam. The lumps protruding here and there are the tools Grandfather Nakane brought when he came to this country—chisels, a hammer, a mallet, a thin pointed saw, the handle extending from the blade like that of a kitchen knife. I can feel the outline of the plane with a wooden handle which he worked by pulling it toward him. There is a fundamental difference in Japanese workmanship—to pull with control rather than push with force.

Obasan is searching through bundles of old letters and papers. She picks up a yellow wallet-size ID card. I shine the flashlight on it and there is Uncle's face, young and unsmiling, in the bottom right-hand corner. Isamu Nakane #00556. Beside the picture is a signature which looks like "McGibbons"—Inspector, RCMP.

She lifts the thick glasses from around her neck and her magnified eyes are as blurry as the sea. She stares at the picture a long time. Finally, she puts the ID card in her apron pocket. This is not what she is looking for. She squats beside a pile of magazines—*Life, New Liberty, Mechanix Illustrated*—mostly from the fifties. As she pushes a box aside, she stretches the corner of a spider's web, exquisitely symmetrical, balanced between the box and the magazines. A round black blot, large as a cat's eye, suddenly sprouts legs and ambles across the web, shaking it. It pauses and another spider of a different variety comes scuttling up. It is lighter in color, its legs more muscular, striped and tapered. Its antennae are short knobs that protrude like eyes from its head. Sidling aggressively, it reaches its long pincer legs out toward the first. The tips touch. In a burst of speed, the first spider leaps down the roadway of webs and disappears into the floorboards.

Its flight is so sudden I recoil, jerking my arm up, sending the beam of light over the ceiling and a whole cloudy scene of carnage. Ugh! What a sight! A graveyard and feasting ground combined. Shredded rag shapes thick with dust hang like evil laundry on a line. A desperate wash day. Spiders, I would say, are indelicate.

"Give you the creeps," the children say.

I wish Obasan would find what she's looking for.

The dust, light-winged as soot, is swarming thickly across the flashlight beam. I sneeze and the specks pummel across the light. Everything, I suppose, turns to dust eventually. A man's memories end up in some attic or in a Salvation Army bin. His name becomes a fleeting statistic and his face is lost in fading photographs, the clothing quaint, the anecdotes gone.

All our ordinary stories are changed in time, altered as much by the present as the present is shaped by the past. Potent and pervasive as a prairie dust storm, memories and dreams seep and mingle through cracks, settling on furniture and into upholstery. Our attics and living rooms encroach on each other, deep into their invisible places.

Obasan shuffles to the trunk and stoops to lift the lid. The thick dust slides off like chocolate icing sugar—antique pollen. Black fly corpses fall to the floor. She pushes aside the piles of old clothes—a 1920s nightgown, a peach-colored woolen bathing suit. A whiff of mothballs wafts up. The odor of preservation.

"Shall I help you?" I ask, not knowing what she seeks.

"Everyone someday dies," she answers.

I scan the contents of the trunk, zigzagging the flashlight beam over the old clothes. The thin flowery patchwork quilt Mother made for my bed when I was four years old is so frayed and moth-eaten it's only a rag. I remember standing by the sewing machine, watching as her hands, quick as birds, matched and arranged the small triangles of colored cloth. I would like to drop the lid of the trunk, go downstairs and back to bed. But we're trapped, Obasan and I, by our memories of the dead—all our dead—those who refuse to bury themselves. Like threads of old spiderwebs, still sticky and hovering, the past waits for us to submit, or depart. When I least expect it, a memory comes skittering out of the dark, spinning and netting the air, ready to snap me up and ensnare me in old and complex puzzles. Just a glimpse of a worn-out patchwork quilt and the old question comes thudding out of the night again like a giant moth. Why did my mother not return? After all these years, I find myself wondering, but with the dullness of expecting no response.

"Please tell me about Mother," I would say as a child to Obasan. I was consumed by the question. Devoured alive. But Obasan gave me no answers. I did not have, I have never had, the key to the vault of her thoughts. Even now, I have no idea what urgency prompts her to explore this attic at midnight.

"Is it enough, Obasan? Shall we go downstairs?"

She turns to face me. Her glasses, thick as marbles, dangle from the chain around her neck.

"Lost," she says.

The light from the flashlight grazes her forehead as I sweep it in a final arc around the attic. Her hair is so fine that her scalp shows through, the texture of skin, hair, and net almost translucent.

"What is lost?"

She seems to have forgotten her reason for coming up here. I notice these days, from time to time, how the present disappears in her mind. The past hungers for her. Feasts on her. And when its feasting is complete? She will dance and dangle in the dark, like small insect bones, a fearful calligraphy—a dry reminder that once there was life flitting about in the weather.

She laughs a short dry sound like clearing her throat. "Everything is forgetfulness," she says.

It's a long journey to her bedroom, and near the end she stumbles. "Thank you, thank you," she says as I hold her small body upright. She crawls into her bed fully dressed. She lies in exhaustion, half awake, half asleep—almost, it seems to me, half alive.

After all these many earth years, where is she now? My arms are suffused with an urge to hold, but a hug would startle her. I can only sit quietly beside her and wait for small signs of her return.

6

Early in the still gray morning I can hear Obasan emptying her chamber pot in the toilet. I wait until she returns to her bed before I drift off again. Haze. Cloud. Again the descent.

I was dreaming just now, was I not? I drift back down into white windless dream. The distance approaches and the roots of trees are prayers descending. Fingers tunneling. Wordlessness.

The mist in the dream swarms like the foam of dry ice on the weatherless mountainside. Together, from out of another dream or from nowhere, the man and woman arrive. Their arrival is as indistinct as the fog. There is no language. Everything is accepted. It is not yet known that I am the woman.

They also are here, the other man and woman. They have been here before us, forever in the forest. At what point we notice them is not clear. It is too strong to say we become aware of them. They move on a heavily treed slope that rises sharply to our right. The woman's back is bent. Slow and heavy as sleep, her arms sway and swing, front to back, back to front. For a flickering moment, she appears as she once was, naked, youthful, voluptuous.

But the mirage fades. Her face is now harsh again and angular as quartz—square, a coarse golden brown. Her body, a matching squareness, is dense as earth. With a sickle she is harvesting the forest's debris, gathering the branches into piles.

The man is taller, thinner and precise—a British martinet. It is evident that he is in command. With his pruner's shears, he is cutting the trees.

They may be trying to make a clearing or gather brush or search for food. Basic survival activities. We do not know what the effort is.

We do not greet them but the man looks at us. We are to help in the work at hand. His glance is a raised baton. Like an orchestra of fog we join them and toil together in the timelessness. We move without question or references in an interminable unknowing without rules, without direction. No incident alerts us to an awareness of time. But at some subtle hour, the white mist is known to be gray, and the endlessness of labor has entered our limbs.

Weariness.

The mist is, is not, is a mist—a smoky curtain continuously rising.

It happens here, in the heart of the forest. One instant.

One fraction of an instant, and a realization is airborne. There is the startle effect of a flock of birds in sudden flight.

"Look!" The shouting inside me communicates to everyone.

There is in the forest a huge gentle beast—a lion or a dog or a lion dog. It belongs to the man. Its obedience is phenomenal.

My electrifying discovery occurs just as the animal yawns. Its yawn is frozen a bare sliver of a second longer than a natural yawn should be and in that moment I see that the inside of the mouth is plastic. The animal is a robot!

In the moment of the too long yawn, when the mechanism that hinges the jaws has proven faulty, a house of cards silently collapses. Instantly in our telepathic world, the knowing spreads and the great boulder enclosing change splits apart.

The square woman farther down the slope moves up toward me from under the curly-branched trees. One of her arms is now connected to her shoulder by four hooks locked to make a hinge. It dangles there as she approaches. She begins to speak but the words are so old they cannot be understood. There is a calmness in her face as she recites an ancient mythical contract made between herself and the man so long ago the language has been forgotten.

The dream changes now and Uncle stands in the depth of the forest. He bows a deep ceremonial bow. In his mouth is a red red rose with an endless stem. He turns around slowly in a flower dance—a ritual of the dead. Behind him, someone— I do not know who—is straining to speak, but rapidly, softly, a cloud overtakes everything. Is it the British officer with his pruning shears disappearing to the left? He is wearing an army uniform.

． ． ．

The waking is white and perfectly still, without sensation and without haste. Some mornings it isn't clear at all where the edge of the forest or the dust storm is. Daybreak blends in all directions.

What time is it and how am I back in my low-ceilinged bedroom with the ladder stairs along the wall? And a late-season mosquito here as well. Yesterday the phone call came. Yesterday seems an age ago.

Obasan is shuffling in the kitchen. The rattle of the fridge shudders to a halt, making way for other sounds—the kettle boiling, the high rhythmical whine of a truck in the distance. The dream recedes like a tiny asterisk star at dawn, a footnote disappearing in the morning sky.

Obasan is folding toilet-paper squares and filling a Kleenex box with them as I enter the kitchen.

"Good morning," I say loudly. "Were you able to sleep?" She lifts her head to look up at me. "Good morning," I repeat.

On the stool is a thick parcel tied in twine. She makes a short apologetic "eh" sound as I pick up the parcel.

"That was thought to be in the attic," she says, "but . . ." She points to a mandarin orange box under the table and makes her embarrassed sound again. "Everything is forgetfulness. The time of forgetting is now come."

A package from Aunt Emily, I note.

7

The parcel is as heavy as a loaf of Uncle's stone bread. Someone, I see, has already opened it and the Scotch tape wings stretch out unstickily from the two end flaps.

"When did this arrive?" I ask Obasan.

"What is it?"

"When did this arrive?" I have to shout everything two or three times.

"Sa," Obasan says wearily, "around when . . ."

The answer doesn't so much matter.

There are several packages here—an old scrapbook full of newspaper clippings, a brown manila envelope, one gray cardboard folder, a three-ring-binder-size hardcover book full of Aunt Emily's handwriting. I untie the loose twine from around the middle of the envelope and a note falls loose and drops to the floor.

Aunt Emily's writing is as wispy and hard to decipher as the marks of a speed skater on ice.

"Write the vision and make it plain. Habakkuk 2:2."

Dear Aunt Em is crusading still. In seven canonical words, she exhorts, cajoles, commands someone—herself? me?—to carry on the fight, to be a credit to the family, to strive onward to the goal. She's the one with the vision. She believes in the Nisei, seeing them as networks and streamers of light dotting the country. For my part, I can only see a dark field with Aunt Emily beaming her flashlight to where the rest of us crouch and hide, our eyes downcast as we seek the safety of invisibility.

Write the vision and make it plain? For her, the vision is the truth as she lives it. When she is called like Habakkuk to the witness stand, her testimony is to the light that shines in the lives of the Nisei, in their desperation to prove themselves Canadian, in their tough and gentle spirit. The truth for me is more murky, shadowy and gray. But on my lap, her papers are wind and fuel nudging my early-morning thoughts to flame.

The hardcover book, I see, is a journal. The private words of Y. Emily Kato. Dear Diary, Christmas 1941. Last May, during a fly-by-night stopover between conferences, Aunt Emily told me she'd be sending me "the works." I expected the conference papers, perhaps documents—not a diary.

She was on her way home to Toronto from a conference in California called "The Asian Experience in North America," and from the moment we met, I was caught in the rush-hour traffic jam of her nonstop conference talk.

How different my two aunts are. One lives in sound, the other in stone. Obasan's language remains deeply underground but Aunt Emily, BA, MA, is a word warrior. She's a crusader, a little old gray-haired Mighty Mouse, a Bachelor of Advanced Activists and General Practitioner of Just Causes.

Since her first visit to Granton in 1954, there have been, let me see, seven, or is it eight, more. There was the summer of 1958 and a week in 1960, another week or so the following year, then a Christmas visit. There have been a few others. So counting that last fast visit, there have been nine trips in all. And in between visits, there's the army, the navy, the air force of letters—all the Aunt Emily correspondence jamming up our small metal box in the Granton PO.

The May morning of her last visit, the sky by 10 A.M. was already yawning open like a great oven door. It was a premature furnace day. In southern Alberta, spring weather is unpredictable—a blizzard one moment and midsummer the next. The only thing that is constant is the wind.

She led the small string of passengers filing out of the Time Air plane at the Lethbridge airport. Her traveling bag dangled from her shoulders. Clutching her briefcase and her small-brimmed hat, she lowered her head like a bull against the wind. She's about the same height as I am, five feet one or so, but much chunkier and with "daikon ashi" as we used to say—legs as shapely as Japanese radishes. A small tank of a woman with a Winston Churchill stoop. Apart from a deeper puffiness under her eyes and more gray hair, she seemed unchanged from her visit the year before. With her mind and her hair leaping wildly in the gusts, she was Stephen Leacock's horseman riding off in all directions at once.

I hurried behind her as she marched ahead to the car.

"What a conference! You should have been with me, Nomi," she said. "There was so much to learn. I had no idea how much I still hurt. Just read some of these papers." She flung open her briefcase and took out a bundle of conference notes and papers as I searched for the car keys.

"Ever read this?" she asked, punctuating the air with a pamphlet entitled "Racial Discrimination by Orders-in-Council."

I held the pages down on the steering wheel and scanned the sheets as the edges flittered in the gusts. There it was in black and white—our short harsh history. Beside each date were the ugly facts of the treatment given to Japanese Canadians. "Seizure and government sale of fishing boats. Suspension of fishing licenses. Relocation camps. Liquidation of property. Letter to General MacArthur. Bill 15. Deportation. Revocation of nationality."

Wherever the words "Japanese race" appeared, Aunt Emily had crossed them out and written "Canadian citizen."

"What this country did to us, it did to itself," she said.

I handed the pamphlet back to her and started the car. The very last thing in the world I was interested in talking about was our experiences during and after World War II. But Aunt Emily was full of her California weekend and the outspoken people she'd met who obviously didn't share my reluctance.

"I hate to admit it," she said, "but for all we hear about the States, Canada's capacity for racism seems even worse."

"Worse?"

"The American Japanese were interned as we were in Canada, and sent off to concentration camps, but their property wasn't liquidated as ours was. And look how quickly the communities reestablished themselves in Los Angeles and San Francisco. We weren't allowed to return to the West Coast like that. We've never recovered from the dispersal policy. But of course that was the government's whole idea—to make sure we'd never be visible again. Official racism was blatant in Canada. The Americans have a Bill of Rights, right? We don't."

Injustice enrages Aunt Emily. Any injustice. Whether she's dealing with the Japanese-Canadian issue or women's rights or poverty, she's one of the world's white blood cells, rushing from trouble spot to trouble spot with her medication pouring into wounds seen and not seen. For her, the injustice done to us in the past was still a live issue.

She thumbed through her pile of papers as we drove down the Mayor Magrath Highway and onto Highway 3. Occasionally she would hold up a paper and shake it excitedly in front of me as if she expected me to drive and read at the same time.

"Now look at this one," she said. "Here's a man who was looking for the source of the problem in the use of language. You know those prisons they sent us to? The government called them 'Interior Housing Projects'! With language like that you can disguise any crime."

The conference had obviously been a meeting ground for a lot of highly charged energy. Looking at her wildly gesticulating hair caught in the windows' drafts, I felt she should have electrocuted me. But I was curiously numb beside her.

People who talk a lot about their victimization make me uncomfortable. It's as if they use their suffering as weapons or badges of some kind. From my years of teaching I know it's the children who say nothing who are in trouble more than the ones who complain.

For a few moments I was afraid she was about to attack me for my lack of enthusiasm about the conference and I tried to muster up some intelligent comments. Talking to

Aunt Emily is sometimes like walking through a minefield. I never quite know when she'll explode.

There were a number of people at the conference, she said, who were cautioning against "rocking the boat." "All they're opting for is 'the good life.' " She threw up her hands and sighed. "You'd think, after all we've been through—you'd think there'd be some collective social conscience."

She stared out the open window as she talked about one man at the conference who quite openly applauded the whole-sale imprisonment of Canadian and American Japanese.

"He knows the war was just an excuse for the racism that was already there. We were rioted against back in 1907, for heaven's sakes! We've always faced prejudice. He knows we were no military threat. So what is he saying? That the inno-cent should be made to suffer for the guilty?" She was almost spluttering. "That's scapegoatism. As long as we have politi-cians and leaders and media people who feast on people's fears, we'll continue making scapegoats."

"Maybe," I said feebly, "he's trying to be conciliatory and see the point of view of the other side. Or maybe he believes the welfare of the whole is more important than the welfare of the part and the fears of the collective can only be calmed by the sacrifice of a minority. Isn't that the way it's always been?"

"Some people," Aunt Emily answered sharply, "are so busy seeing all sides of every issue that they neutralize con-cern and prevent necessary action. There's no strength in see-ing all sides unless you can act where real measurable injus-tice exists. A lot of academic talk just immobilizes the oppressed and maintains oppressors in their positions of power."

For the rest of the car ride home I kept quiet while Aunt Emily bulldozed on. I could see that we were in for an eve-

ning of marathon talking, whether anyone else felt up to it or
not.

Even before the supper dishes were cleared away, Aunt Emily
was shuffling and sorting documents and conference papers
on the kitchen table.

"Read this, Nomi," she said from time to time, handing
me papers as if they were snapshots. I sometimes managed to
catch half a paragraph on a page before she gave me something else. She must have thought I was speed-reading and
listening to her at the same time, like switching back and
forth between movies on television. A good way to stay agi-
tated.

"Give you something to chew on," she said. She was eating a slice of Uncle's stone bread with a slab of raw onion.

You're the one with the strong teeth, I thought to myself.
She did have strong teeth. And a tough digestion.

"Not like woman," Uncle said as he sat at the table and
watched her working. "Like that there can be no marriage."

He waved a toothpick at the documents spread in front of
him. "For what purpose, this?"

"We're gluing our tongues back on," Aunt Emily said. "It
takes a while for the nerves to grow back."

Uncle shook his head. "Nisei muzukashi," he said. "Difficult people."

"We have to deal with all this while we remember it. If we
don't we'll pass our anger down in our genes. It's the children
who'll suffer," Aunt Emily said.

"Children?" Uncle asked. "Too late for Emiri-san, isn't
it?" He held up a form letter and started reading it slowly,
sucking in air between the words.

I leaned over and read it out loud for him. I was being

more polite than genuinely interested. ". . . While it is not necessary that this title be available in order to complete the sale it is preferred that it be surrendered to the Registrar of Land Titles. Will you be good enough therefore . . ." It was obviously a form letter sent to all of us back in the forties asking us to hand over the titles to our properties but advising us that, whether we did or not, our houses would be taken from us.

"The power of print," Aunt Emily interrupted. "The power of government, Nomi. Power. See how palpable it is? They took away the land, the stores, the businesses, the boats, the houses—everything. Broke up our families, told us who we could see, where we could live, what we could do, what time we could leave our houses, censored our letters, exiled us for no crime. They took our livelihood . . ."

The muscle in Uncle's jaw moved back and forth as he put the form letter down. I nodded, not wanting to aggravate the atmosphere further.

My eyes caught a brief official-looking letter from someone signed B. Good to Aunt Emily. B. Good? I noticed that he was the custodian in charge of all the property that was supposedly being kept safe for us. I read through the short note while she talked on.

Dear Madam
    This will acknowledge your letter of the 31st ultimo.
    This will also advise you that as Mrs. T. Kato is a Japanese National living in Japan at the outbreak of war, all property belonging to her in Canada vests in the Custodian.

Yours truly,
B. Good

A toneless form letter. I wondered what Aunt Emily's letter to the Custodian had been. "Tell me what happened to my mother's tiny house—the house where my sister was born, with the rock garden in front and the waterfall and goldfish. Tell me what has happened."

The Custodian's reply to Aunt Emily must have been the same to anyone else who dared to write. "Be good, my undesirable, my illegitimate children, be obedient, be servile, above all don't send me any letters of inquiry about your homes, while I stand on guard (over your property) in the true north strong, though you are not free. B. Good."

What did Mr. Good feel, I wondered, as he signed his letters—as he read Aunt Emily's questions, or perhaps the more timid letters of the others? Did he even read them? He must have had similar form letters ready to send out automatically. Did he experience a tiny twinge of pleasure at the power his signature must represent? Did B. Good sometimes imagine himself to be God? Or was it all just a day's mindless job?

Aunt Emily, seeing me reading the B. Good letter, started talking of Grandpa Kato's Cadillac. She said it was sold by the government for $33. Handling charges came to $30 and the amount Grandpa finally received was $3.00 and a few pennies.

"Next thing we expected was to owe the Custodian money for the services done in relieving us of all we owned," Aunt Emily said. "What a bunch of sheep we were. Polite. Meek. All the way up the slaughterhouse ramp. Why in a time of war with Germany and Japan would our government seize the property and homes of Canadian-born Canadians but not the homes of German-born Germans?" she asked angrily.

"Racism," she answered herself. "The Nazis are everywhere."

Obasan was standing at the sink with her mouth set the way it always is whenever there is agitation. She surrounds herself with a determined kind of stillness and a certain slow concentration on anything her hands are doing.

I picked up a folder of Uncle's documents. One was a mimeographed sheet signed by an RCMP superintendent, authorizing Uncle to leave a Registered Area by truck for Vernon, where he was required to report to the local Registrar of Enemy Aliens, not later than the following day.

It was hard to think of Uncle as anyone's enemy. One Sunday when Uncle went to church, the clergyman turned him away from the communion rail. But there was no enemy there.

Aunt Emily was searching through her briefcase. She brought out a yellowing manuscript sewn together with thread.

"Here. This was my biggest effort," she said. "Read this, Nomi." I held it gingerly on my lap. In the center of the title page in capital letters was printed: THE STORY OF THE NISEI IN CANADA: A STRUGGLE FOR LIBERTY—by Emily Kato.

The opening words of the manuscript were "I understand the Nisei." So she does, I thought. She certainly knows them better than I do or Uncle does. None of my friends today are Japanese Canadians.

I read the first paragraph.

I understand the Nisei, I know them well. Better than do Mr. Green or Mrs. Ralston. [Who, I wondered, were they that she singled them out?] I have seen the Nisei in anger, in exuberant spirits, enthusiasm and despair, in the quiet stillness of resignation or renunci-

ation—I've worked beside them in canneries, on
farms, in Red Cross groups—I've seen them in poverty
and in luxury, in cabins and stuccoed residences,
struggling for higher education on meager earnings, or
cushioned through college by a parent's wealth—I've
known them as mill hands, lumberjacks, clerks, dressmakers, stenos, domestic servants—I've watched them
waltz and jitterbug, play baseball, tennis, rugby, golf,
and Ping-Pong—I've known them in sickness and in
health, at weddings and births and face to face with
death. In short, I know the Nisei in every mood and
circumstance, and because of this intimacy with them,
I shall discuss some of the accusations brought against
us.

The entire manuscript was sixty pages long. I skimmed
over the pages till I came across a statement underlined and
circled in red: *I am Canadian.* The circle was drawn so hard
the paper was torn. Three lines of a poem were at the top of
the page.

> *Breathes there the man with soul so dead*
> *Who never to himself hath said:*
> *This is my own, my native land!*

The tanned brown edges of the page crumbled like autumn leaves as I straightened the manuscript.

The exact moment when I first felt the stirrings of
identification with this country occurred when I was
twelve years old, memorizing a Canto of "The Lay of
the Last Minstrel."

So many times after that, I repeated the lines: sadly, desperately, and bitterly. But at first I was proud, knowing that I *belonged*.

This is my *own*, my native land.

Then as I grew older and joined the Nisei group taking a leading part in the struggle for liberty, I waved those lines around like a banner in the wind:

This is my own, my *native* land.

When war struck this country, when neither pride nor belligerence nor grief had availed us anything, when we were uprooted, and scattered to the four winds, I clung desperately to those immortal lines:

This *is* my own, *my* native land.

Later still, after our former homes had been sold over our vigorous protests, after having been re-registered, fingerprinted, card-indexed, roped and restricted, I cry out the question:

Is this my own, my native land?

The answer cannot be changed. Yes. It is. For better or worse, *I am Canadian*.

While I was reading, Uncle was leaning his head back and exercising his neck muscles. "Nisei, not very Japanese-like," he said.

"Why should we be?" Aunt Emily said. "We're Canadian."

All her life, it seemed to me, Aunt Emily toiled to tell of the lives of the Nisei in Canada in her effort to make familiar, to make knowable, the treacherous yellow peril that lived in the minds of the racially prejudiced. I pictured her as a young woman in Toronto, gradually getting more hunched as she sat over her typewriter, growing gray over the years, erasing, rewriting, underlining, trying to find the right mix that strikes home. Like Cupid, she aimed for the heart. But the heart was not there.

Before I could finish more than a few pages of her manuscript she handed me an old scrapbook full of brown and brittle clippings. The headlines crackled as I read them aloud.

"Bar Japs from B.C."

"Claim Deportation of Japs Violates International Law."

Some of the statements were underlined in faded blue-black ink.

June 21, 1944. It seems highly disturbing that without debate and with agreement by all parties, the House of Commons adopted a clause in the new bill dealing with elections which will disenfranchise men and women of Canadian birth. This is Bill 135. . . . No other democratic country has such legislation.

Words of Stanley Knowles (CCF Winnipeg North Centre) were circled.

What is at stake here today is not so much the rights of Japanese Canadians who have moved from British Columbia to other parts of Canada, but rather the basic concept of democracy and our belief as a nation so far as our belief in the franchise is concerned.

Mackenzie King's words were also marked.

. . . There would have been riots at the polls at the time of the election when any of those Japanese presented themselves for that purpose [to vote] and certainly it was taking the part of wisdom to see that nothing of the kind should take place. . . .

The thin wafers of paper were fragile with old angers. Crimes of history, I thought to myself, can stay in history. What we need is to concern ourselves with the injustices of today. Expedience still demands decisions which will one day be judged unjust. Out loud I said, "Why not leave the dead to bury the dead?"

"Dead?" she asked. "I'm not dead. You're not dead. Who's dead?"

"But you can't fight the whole country," I said.

"We are the country," she answered.

Obasan was not taking part in the conversation. When pressed, finally she said that she was grateful for life. "Arigatai. Gratitude only."

Uncle, who had been listening tensely up to this point, relaxed his jaws and slapped his lap with both hands. "In the world, there is no better place," he said. "This country is the best. There is food. There is medicine. There is pension money. Gratitude. Gratitude."

He was right, I thought. If Aunt Emily with her billions of letters and articles and speeches, her tears and her rage, her friends and her committees—if all that couldn't bring contentment, what was the point?

"What energy," Uncle said good-humoredly and yawned aloud. "Genki ga ii ne."

"Have to keep trying," Aunt Emily said.

Uncle shuffled off to bed, leaving us in the kitchen. "A time to work. A time to talk. Now time to sleep," he said.

"Good night, Uncle," I said. I would have gone to bed as well, but Aunt Emily was not sleepy.

"Life is so short," I said, sighing, "the past so long. Shouldn't we turn the page and move on?"

"The past is the future," Aunt Emily shot back.

8

Just at the last minute, before Aunt Emily walked out to the plane, she asked me if I really wanted to "know everything."

"I'll send you some of my correspondence and stuff. Would you like that?" she asked.

"Sure," I lied.

Now here I am this autumn morning, five months later, with her heavy package on my lap. Many of the conference papers she showed me last May are here as well as her diary and a bulging manila envelope full of letters. The side seam of the envelope is slightly torn and it bursts apart as I try to take out the contents. The pile cascades over my lap, falling onto the floor and into the plastic bleach bottle wastebasket beside me. Obasan bends over to pick up the letters and hands them open to me one at a time.

There's a copy of a letter to Mackenzie King; one to Mr. Glen, Minister of Mines and Resources; one from General Headquarters of the Supreme Commander for the Allied Powers; another from H. L. Keenleyside, Deputy Minister of Mines and Resources. . . .

What, I wonder, was Aunt Emily trying to accomplish through all this correspondence? She was no doubt keeping the home fires burning and shouting "Democracy" to keep the enemy at bay. But all of this belongs to yesterday and there are so many other things to attend to today. All the details of death that are left in the laps of the living.

Obasan is sitting on a mandarin box at my feet winding the twine from Aunt Emily's package onto a twine ball she keeps in the pantry. Obasan never discards anything. Besides the twine ball, there's a ball of string full of knots, a number of balls of wool bits, and even short bits of thread twirled around popsicle sticks that are stacked up like soldiers in a black woven box. The twine ball is larger than a baseball and slips off her lap, rolling a short distance along the floor.

I glance at the electric clock above the stove. Unlike the faithful grandfather clock that stopped when its owner died, this one whirrs and hiccups on and on. Eight A.M. Some children from the farms will be getting ready for the buses. I hope the substitute doesn't overwater the plants the way the last one did.

I can hear the scratch slap of the tree's fingers by the kitchen window this morning. The tree's outline is blurred through the plastic covering the pane. Ever since Obasan's operation for cataracts, she's lived in a darkened house. The branches of the tree are as elastic as whips in the gusts—slap clatter clatter, insistent as a drummer.

Obasan has picked up the twine ball again and her fingers move along the hemisphere of the globe, carefully forming and re-forming the shape. All her movements this morning are in a different dimension of time. When she is finished, she stands up. Slow as pyramid blocks rising one by one, her leg muscles, thigh muscles, her hands resting on the box, will her upright.

She takes the twine to the pantry, then shuffles to the kitchen sink. She never wipes her dishes, saying it's un-hygienic. Her way is to hold them under a trickling tap, rins-ing each one without soap, then setting it aside to drain dry. Now, with her bad eyesight, she doesn't see the dark stains in the plastic cups and in the grooves of the plates and saucers. Every so often, I give the plastic kitchen things a bleach bath.

"Everyone someday dies," she is saying with a sigh as she clears the table. She takes half a piece of leftover toast and puts it away in a square plastic container. The refrigerator is packed with boxes of food bits, a slice of celery, a square of spinach, half a hard-boiled egg. She orchestrates each remain-der of a previous dinner into the dinner to come, making every meal like every meal, an unfinished symphony. Our Lady of the Leftovers.

There are some indescribable items in the dark recesses of the fridge that never see the light of day. But you realize when you open the door that they're there, lurking, too old for mold and past putrefaction.

Some memories, too, might better be forgotten. Didn't Obasan once say, "It is better to forget"? What purpose is served by hauling forth the jar of inedible food? If it is not seen, it does not horrify. What is past recall is past pain. Questions from all these papers, questions referring to turbu-

lence in the past, are an unnecessary upheaval in the delicate
ecology of this numb day.

Another item of Aunt Emily's package is a gray cardboard
folder. I have seen this folder before, though I can't quite
remember where or when. It's complete with dime-size red
circle tabs, one on each of the two flaps that meet in the
middle. A short red string is twirled around the tabs as a
fastener.

Inside the folder are two envelopes about as narrow and
long as bank checks, and inside each envelope are blue-lined
rice-paper sheets with Japanese writing which I cannot read.

"What is this about, Obasan?" I ask.

She wipes her hands on her apron as I hold the slippery
sheets out to her and she shuffles past me to the sideboard
where she keeps one of several magnifying glasses. Then, putting on her glasses and holding the magnifying glass about
two inches from the sheets, she reads the words. Her head
moves in a long slow fall, top to bottom and up again.

"Who are the letters from?" I ask loudly.

She does not respond. Her face is expressionless. After a
while she puts down the magnifying glass.

"Everyone someday dies," she says again.

By repeating this so often, I suppose she is trying to make
realizable what is real. Surely that is task enough for her today. But I ask once more, "Who are the letters from?"

She stares steadily at the table. The greater my urgency to
know, the thicker her silences have always been. No prodding
will elicit clues.

Her hand moves on the table like an electrocardiograph
needle, delicate and unreadable. Then, with her back bent
forward, she stands up and shuffles out of the room.

Today is not, I repeat, reprimanding myself—today is not
the day for unnecessary questions.

The last item in the package is Aunt Emily's diary. It is written, I see, in the form of letters to my mother. The book has obviously suffered from moisture. Its edges are crinkly and the covers are sprung apart by a stiff clump of wavy pages.

"Dearest Nesan," her diary entries begin. The sight of the word "Nesan" cuts into me with a peculiar sensation of pain and tenderness. It means "older sister," and was what Aunt Emily always called Mother. Grandma Kato also called Mother "Nesan" from time to time, especially if she was talking to Aunt Emily. I remember one time I called Mother "Nesan" and Grandma Kato laughed and laughed.

The book feels heavy with voices from the past—a connection to Mother and Grandma Kato I did not know existed. I feel a strong urge to put everything aside and read the journal, but right now it is Uncle's absent voice that speaks even more urgently and that I must attend. I can hear Obasan rummaging in the next room. "Care for Obasan," Uncle is saying. "Odaiji ni—keep her safe."

I put the diary and letters aside on a clear spot on the sideboard. By the time Obasan returns, I have finished cleaning the counter and cupboards.

In her hands is a familiar photograph. I am about two or three years of age and clinging to my mother's leg with one arm. My mother's face is childlike and wistful. Her head leans shyly to the side and her hair is tucked under her wide-brimmed hat.

"Yasashi desho," Obasan says. She has often spoken of my mother's "yasashi kokoro," her tender, kind, and thoughtful heart. She places the picture in my hand. "Here is the best letter. This is the best time. These are the best memories."

When would this be? I turn the photo around to see if there is any identification on the back, but there is none.

9

In the picture I am clinging to my mother's leg on a street

corner in Vancouver. A small boy is standing hugging a lamp-

post and is staring at us. His thumb is in his mouth. I am

mortified by the attention. I turn my face away from everyone.

My mother places her cool hand on my cheek, its scent light

and flowery. She whispers that the boy will laugh at me if I

hide. Laugh? There is no worse horror. Laughter is a cold

spray that chills the back of my neck, that makes the tears

rush to my eyes. My mother's whisper flushes me out of my

hiding place behind the softness of her silk dress. Only the

sidewalk is safe to look at. It does not have eyes.

Who is it who teaches me that in the language of eyes a stare is an invasion and a reproach? Grandma Kato? Obasan? Uncle? Mother? Each one, raised in Japan, speaks the same language; but Aunt Emily and Father, born and raised in Canada, are visually bilingual. I too learn the second language.

My mother and I are on a streetcar. She boosts me up on the seat and I reach for the cord. We will be getting off soon. As I scramble down to the floor, I see a man sitting hunched forward, his elbows on his knees. He is looking around quizzically, one dark eyebrow higher than the other. When our eyes meet, he grins and winks. I turn away instantly, startled into discomfort again by eyes. My mother's eyes look obliquely to the floor, declaring that on the streets, at all times, in all public places, even a glance can be indiscreet. But a stare? Such lack of decorum, it is clear, is as unthinkable as nudity on the street.

On the other hand, nudity at home is completely thinkable. Grandma Kato is in the bathtub with me. The water is so hot the skin reddens instantly. When I lift my foot up it looks as though I am wearing red socks.

"Samui, samui," she says jokingly. "Cold, cold." The hot-water tap is on full blast.

"Atsui," I screech. The comic books are right. We yell words like that.

She urges me down deeper into the liquid furnace and I go into the midst of the flames, obedient as Abednego, for lo, Grandma is an angel of the Lord and stands before me in the midst of the fire and has no hurt, neither is a hair of her body singed nor has the smell of fire passed on her. She is sitting directly beside the gushing boiling hot-water tap and the steaming froth plunges around her bony buttocks.

"You can sit down." She nods, placing a steaming

facecloth wrung to dampness on my knees and again on my
back.

I squat slowly at the other end of the tub. This is sweet
torture, with Grandma happy and approving and enjoying the
heat I cannot endure. I am more brave, more praiseworthy
than Stephen. He will not bathe with Grandma. But I will
suffer endless indignities of the flesh for the pleasure of my
grandmother's pleasure.

When the tub is full, Grandma lies down on her back, her
head up against the taps.

"Ah, such a good feeling," she murmurs. "Rest your
shoulders fully under the water."

My body is extended beside hers and she makes waves to
cover my shoulders. Once the body is fully immersed, there is
a torpid peace. We lie in this state forever.

At some point, Grandma has opened her eyes and rolled
her washcloth into a tight damp fist. I stand beside her and
over the redness of my body she scrubs vigorously, like an
eraser over a dirty page. The dead skin collects in little rolls
and falls off into the water. She exclaims at the rolls.

"Look at this!" Her voice is full of curiosity and amuse-
ment at this cleansing and she makes mock cries of alarm at
my dirtiness. She rubs each of my fingers, my hands, arms,
chest, belly and abdomen, neck, back, buttocks, thighs, legs,
ankles, the lines behind the ankles, the soles of the feet, between the toes. Then I soak again, watching as Grandma tow-
els herself the same way. She rinses the cloth, makes another
fist, and hands it to me. Although I use all my strength to rub
her back, it is not really quite hard enough, I know. Grandma,
however, is content.

"Is there much aka?" she asks. That is the word for the
little rolls I rub off. She always wishes to know how much
there is.

While I lie back again to soak, I play with my washcloth, wringing it out and resting it on the water, then thrusting it up like a tent with two fingers and thumbs. This makes an air bubble which can be captured like a balloon if I squeeze the edges and corners together in my fist. I squash the bubble into my face and feel its moist airiness oozing out with a wet wheeze.

So many uses for one piece of cloth. Grandma rubs the bar of soap over it until it is spongy with lather. The cloth, once it is soaped, must not enter the water. She soaps me thoroughly and I am rinsed off before she soaps herself.

The bathroom is steaming and I am languid as I am hoisted out, my body limp and capable of no objections. I am dressed in a nemaki, a sleeping garment of purple-and-white cotton which Grandma has sewn by hand. It has rectangular envelope-shaped sleeves with openings at the armpits and two ties meeting in a bow at the back. I am supremely safe in my nemaki, under the heavy bright-colored futon in my house.

The house in which we live is in Marpole, a comfortable residential district of Vancouver. It is more splendid than any house I have lived in since. It does not bear remembering. None of this bears remembering.

"You have to remember," Aunt Emily said. "You are your history. If you cut any of it off you're an amputee. Don't deny the past. Remember everything. If you're bitter, be bitter. Cry it out! Scream! Denial is gangrene. Look at you, Nomi, shuffling back and forth between Cecil and Granton, unable either to go or to stay in the world with even a semblance of grace or ease."

All right, Aunt Emily, all right! The house then—the house, if I must remember it today, was large and beautiful. It's still there on West 64th Avenue in Vancouver. Phone

Langara 0938-R. I looked it up once in the November 1941 inch-thick Vancouver telephone directory. I wrote to the people who live there and asked if they would ever consider selling the house but they never replied. I don't know their names. I don't know what they've done to the house. It used to have a hedge and rose bushes and flowers and cactus plants lining the sidewalk, and the front iron gate had a squeeze latch. The backyard had a sandbox and an apple tree and a swing, and I could dangle by my knees from a branch thicker than my father's arms.

If I search the caverns of my mind, I come to a collage of images—somber paintings, a fireplace, and a mantel clock with a heavy key like a small metal bird that fits in my palm.

The living room is the darkest room, the walls of dark wood lit with dim lights. On the floor is a deep blue Indian rug with a complex border of multicolored designs and a ribbon of rectangles and roads that can be traversed like a maze by Stephen's toy train. We line the lead soldiers in their bright red coats along the edges, march them around the sofa legs on their flat bases, leap them upward to land them off balance on the soft velvet frieze of the sofa. The sofa is a mountain to climb, a valley for sleeping in, a place of ambush for surprise attacks on passing parents.

Beside the sofa is a large record player with a shiny handle on the left-hand side which I can just reach. Below are thick wine-colored albums with silver rings on the back. Some of the records have flags or pictures of a dog, some have only gold or black printed letters. The ones with Japanese writing have green labels.

The music room beside the living room is full of windows and plants and a round goldfish bowl with two goldfish. A piano, a violin, another stringed instrument that is half constructed, a piccolo, and a shakuhachi with its eerie wail are in this room. My father plays every instrument by ear. My mother and Stephen play the piano.

Here they are in the music room in the evening, before dark, Mother in her chair beside Stephen, who sits on the piano stool with its eagle-claw feet clutching three glass globes.

"And one, and two, up and one, and duh two and . . ."

Stephen's practice time each night is half play. Father, with his violin bow raised dramatically, bobs in time to the music, sometimes making a correction on his violin when Stephen hits a wrong note. Father's sleek hair angles away sharp as a knife's edge from his shiny face. With a pencil held by the tips of his long thin fingers, Father makes tiny pencil marks on Stephen's music book. Everything about Father is precise and graceful as the milk-white porcelain crane, its beak pointing straight up from its long smooth neck.

I am sitting in my nemaki on the wicker chair beside the fern, eating a tea biscuit and watching the goldfish with their little round mouths puckering open and closed endlessly. We three, the goldfish and I, are the listeners in the room, as Mother sings and Stephen and Father play. Mother's voice is yasashi, soft and tender in the dimming daylight. She is altogether yasashi. She is singing a kindergarten song to entice me to join in.

> *How did you, Miss Daffodilly,*
> *Get your pretty dress?*
> *Is it made of gold and sunshine?*
> *Yes, child, yes.*

Beside me on its carved wooden pedestal is another silent listener, the Ninomiya Kinjiro statue. My fingers slide over its

head, down over the lump on its back, to the porcelain books
in its porcelain hands.

Father, seeing my reluctance to join in, comes and sits
beside me on the wicker chair.

"See how he carries the wood on his back?" Father asks,
lifting the statue and placing it on my lap. He shows me the
green and red and golden twigs strapped to its back like a
knapsack. Dangling from its side is a parcel of books.

Stephen stops playing and comes over to us, leaving
Mother at the piano, still humming kindergarten songs.

"He's studying," Father tells us. The statue has clear
white arms and hands and his little white-and-gold book lies
open to some black squiggles I cannot read. His feet are
spread apart in full stride.

Father tells us the story often. "Up early to the mountains
for wood before the rooster calls 'ko-ke-kok-ko!' He studies
and works every day every day to feed his baby brother and his
mother. That is how he becomes the great teacher, Ninomiya
Sontaku of Odawara, Japan."

Father also studies every day every day. His rolltop desk
sits in my memory in the center of the basement with a heavy
iron lamp bent over like his head. Along the walls are shelves
of books.

Behind Father's study is the huge sawdust furnace and
behind the furnace room is the playroom with the back door
at ground level leading to the backyard. The playroom has two
bronze baby cribs and a black carriage in the corner. These
seem untidy to me, sitting there useless and unattended. Stephen and I have light wooden blocks with crinkly red celluloid
windows and pointed roofs for building houses and gateways
and castles. There are scissors, folding paper, Plasticine, huge
picture books, a Meccano set, doll dishes, and a rocking horse
with its mouth open wide in laughter.

My dolls are not in this room but upstairs in a large bin in the kitchen. Later, it was the family of dolls I missed more than anything else—the representatives of the ones I loved.

My bedroom with its long white-lace-curtained window looks out over the neighbor's yard. A peach tree is directly outside the window. Above my bed with the powdery blue patchwork quilt is a picture of a little girl with a book in her lap, looking up into a tree where a bird sits. One of the child's hands is half raised as she watches and listens, attending the bird. The picture is entirely in muted shades of green.

These are the bits of the house I remember. If I linger in the longing, I am drawn into a whirlpool. I can only skirt the edges after all.

"This was a long time ago," I say to Obasan, returning the photograph to her.

The woman in the picture is frail and shy and the child is equally shy, unable to lift her head. Only fragments relate me to them now, to this young woman, my mother, and me, her infant daughter. Fragments of fragments. Parts of a house. Segments of stories.

10

"Mukashi mukashi o-o mukashi . . . ," Obasan says, holding the photograph. "In ancient times, in ancient times, in very very ancient times . . ."

She places the picture on the sideboard, propping it against a tin can filled with old pens.

Seeing Obasan now, older than the grandmother I knew as a child, older than any person I know today, I feel that each breath she takes is weighted with her mortality. She is the old woman of many Japanese legends, alone and waiting in her ancient time for the honor that is an old person's reward.

"Mukashi mukashi . . ."

Each night from the very beginning, before I could talk, there were the same stories, the voices of my mother or my father or Obasan or Grandma Kato, soft through the filter of my sleepiness, carrying me away to a shadowy ancestry.

"Tonight, which story? Momotaro again?"

Night after night I asked for Momotaro. What remains as I remember the story, beyond the rhythm of the words and the comfort and closeness, is our transport to the gray-green woods where we hover and spread like tree spirits, our ears and our eyes, raindrops resting on leaves and grass stems.

The mountainside, hazy as Vancouver fog, is so far away that distance is blurred. The old old man and the old old woman of the Momotaro story, white-haired and bent double with age, move with slow tiny steps in the whispery rice-paper house. The haze makes everything one color. Even the morning glories that cluster around the well are the same green-gray. A bamboo bucket hangs from a rope. Wooden wind chimes clatter softly.

My mother's voice is quiet and the telling is a chant. I snuggle into her arms, listening and watching the shadows of the peach tree outside my window. "Early every morning," she murmurs, "Grandfather goes to the mountain to gather firewood. Grandmother goes to the stream to wash clothes.

"One day as Grandmother is washing the clothes—pound and dip, pound and dip—down over the waterfall comes a big peach bouncing over the foam toward her. 'What a fine peach,' she says, and takes it home for Grandfather. All day she waits for him to come home. When Grandfather arrives— ah—when Grandfather arrives . . ."

"What then, what then?" I say as Mother pauses in this delicious moment. "So-re kara?"

The story never quite recovers from the excitement of Grandfather's homecoming.

"Grandmother shows him the huge peach. 'Ah, such a fine momo,' Grandfather says. And carefully they lift it up, feeling its ripe lush flesh in their hands."

Whenever I bite into peaches, I wonder as my lips touch the slippery cool tang how it must have been. I wonder as I stare at the peaches in the peach tree outside the window, changing from buds to blossoms to small green balls.

" 'Momotaro, Momotaro, what a fine young man, what a gift from heaven.' "

The little boy, golden and round as a peach, leaps onto the table from the heart of the fruit before their astonished eyes. The delight of it. And the wonder. Simply by existing a child is delight.

The story could end here, but Mother offers the whole telling before she rolls up the tale once more, round and complete as an unopened peach ready for a fresh feasting.

Secretly, I realize I am more fortunate than Stephen because I am younger and will therefore be a child for a longer time. That we must grow up is an unavoidable sadness.

My arms are flung around my mother as she lies beside me and I breathe in her powdery perfume as she continues her chant.

The time comes when Momotaro must go and silence falls like feathers of snow all over the rice-paper hut. Inside, the hands are slow. Grandmother kneels at the table forming round rice balls, pressing the sticky rice together with her moist fingertips. She wraps them in a small square cloth and, holding them before her in her cupped hands, she offers him the lunch for his journey. There are no tears and no touch. Grandfather and Grandmother are careful, as he goes, not to weight his pack with their sorrow.

Alone in the misty mountains once more, the old folk wait. What matters in the end, what matters above all, more than their loneliness or fears, is that Momotaro behave with honor. At all times what matters is to act with a fine intent. To do otherwise is shameful and brings dishonor to all.

To travel with confidence down this route the most reliable map I am given is the example of my mother's and Grandma's alert and accurate knowing. When I am hungry, and before I can ask, there is food. If I am weary, every place is a bed. No food that is distasteful must be eaten and there is neither praise nor blame for the body's natural functions. A need to urinate is to be heeded whether in public or visiting friends. A sweater covers me before there is any chill and if there is pain there is care simultaneously. If Grandma shifts uncomfortably, I bring her a cushion.

"Yoku ki ga tsuku ne," Grandma responds. It is a statement in appreciation of sensitivity and appropriate gestures.

I cannot remember that I was ever reprimanded or punished for anything, although that seems strange and unlikely now. The concept that a child could do wrong did not seem to exist. There was no need for crying.

"Surely I cried sometimes," I said to Aunt Emily when she told me what a quiet child I'd been.

She shook her head. "I can't remember that you ever did. You never spoke. You never smiled. You were so 'majime.' What a serious baby—fed on milk and Momotaro."

"Milk and Momotaro?" I asked. "Culture clash?"

"Not at all," she said. "Momotaro is a Canadian story. We're Canadian, aren't we? Everything a Canadian does is Canadian."

11

It isn't true, of course, that I never speak as a child. Inside the house in Vancouver there is confidence and laughter, music and mealtimes, games and storytelling. But outside, even in the backyard, there is an infinitely unpredictable, unknown, and often dangerous world. Speech hides within me, watchful and afraid.

One day, I am standing alone in the backyard. Beside the garage is a wire cage placed high above the ground, at about the level of a table. I can barely see the floor of the cage. A white hen struts in here, its head jerking as it scatters the hay looking for grain—claw scratch, claw scratch—jerking as it starts up in alarm, cocking its head sideways, its neck feathers fluffing in and out. Where its chin should be, a rubbery tongue flaps and jiggles. It seems constantly surprised, ready to utter its gurgles and squawks, its limited language of exclamation and alarm.

My mother and father have bought a dozen cotton-batting-soft yellow chicks, a light boxful of jostling fluff. Their feet are scratchy as twigs. If I stand on a stool, I can lift the wire gate. Carefully, I take the babies and put them into the cage one by one, the trembling bodies filling the palms of my hands.

In the corner of the cage where I place them, they are a clump of yellow puffballs, a piccolo orchestra. The white hen stops scratching and cocks her head at them. The chicks begin to leave the cluster, hopping, cheeping, their shiny round eyes black as apple seeds. One chick reaches the hen's feet. Without warning, the hen's sharp beak jabs down on the chick, up again and down, deliberate as the needle on the sewing machine. A high trilling squeal and the chick spreads its short wings like a fan as it flops forward. Again and again the hen's beak strikes and the chick lies on its side on the floor, its neck twisted back, its wings, outstretched fingers. The hen lifts a scaly leg, the claws collapsing and clutching as it struts around the cage, bayoneting the chicks darting past her feet, their wings outspread.

I climb down from the stool and run up the back stairs into the house, where my mother is sitting in the music room with Mrs. Sugimoto.

"Mama . . ."

Without a word and without alarm, she follows me quickly to the backyard. The arena is punctuated by short piercing trills as the hen keeps pecking and the chicks squeal and flutter, squeal and fall.

With swift deft fingers, Mother removes the live chicks first, placing them in her apron. All the while that she acts, there is calm efficiency in her face and she does not speak. Her eyes are steady and matter-of-fact—the eyes of Japanese motherhood. They do not invade and betray. They are eyes that protect, shielding what is hidden most deeply in the heart of the child. She makes safe the small stirrings underfoot and in the shadows. Physically, the sensation is not in the region of the heart, but in the belly. This that is in the belly is honored when it is allowed to be, without fanfare, without reproach, without words. What is there is there.

But even a glance, if it is not matter-of-fact, is a betrayal.

Mrs. Sugimoto has followed us. Although it is a warm day, she is wearing a fur collar around her neck and a tiny animal head with sharp teeth looks over her shoulder. Mrs. Sugimoto's teeth are also sharp and protrude and a slight spittle is on her lower lip. When she talks she breathes in audibly through her front teeth, making "ff" sounds. Mrs. Sugimoto reminds me of the white hen, always fussing over her boys, telling them to put sweaters on even when the weather is warm. Her face is not matter-of-fact like Mother's. Her eyes search my face. Her glance is too long. She notes my fear, invades my knowing.

I look away from Mrs. Sugimoto to my mother's face. She is examining the wounded chicks in her apron, holding them upside down even as they peep in alarm.

And suddenly, the yard is full of boys, clambering and exclaiming and jostling.

"What happened? What happened?" I am pushed aside by Ralph, the boy who lives at the end of the alley. He bangs his fist on the cage and the hen squawks as its wings flap once.

Mrs. Sugimoto's eyes are wide with alarm and she steps

backward. Although her knowing is an invasion, I stand close to her and away from the other children. Given a yard full of enemies, the most familiar enemy is a friend.

"Hey, Nome, whassa matter?" Ralph says. "Cat gotcher tongue?"

"No."

"What's a matter with the chicks, eh?"

I do not answer.

Mother takes all the chicks, the dead as well as the wounded and the unharmed ones, into her apron and goes to the garage filled with sawdust.

Later, when all the children and Mrs. Sugimoto have gone, Mother and Stephen and I are in the kitchen, where the chicks are now kept in a box beside the stove.

"It was not good, was it?" Mother says. "Yoku nakatta ne." Three words. Good, negation of good in the past tense, agreement with statement. It is not a language that promotes hysteria. There is no blame or pity. I am not responsible. The hen is not responsible. My mother does not look at me when she says this. She squats beside the box and we watch the trembling chicks together. "Kyotsuke nakattara abunai," she says. "If there is not carefulness, there is danger." She has waited until all is calm before we talk. I tell her everything. There is nothing about me that my mother does not know, nothing that is not safe to tell.

Except there is the one secret thing that emerges even now, curious as an infant fern, a fiddlehead question mark asking with its unformed voice for answers still hidden from me.

His name is Old Man Gower. He lives next door. I can see his house beyond the peach tree from my bedroom window. His belly is large and soft. His hair is thin and brown and the top of his head is a shiny skin cap. When he lifts me up in his arms, I smell something dank and unpleasant. His breathing is noisy and too close to my face. He has a mustache, scratchy as a Christmas tree. I do not wish him to lift me up but I do not know what it is to struggle. Every time he carries me away, he tells me I must not tell my mother. He asks me questions as he holds me but I do not answer.

It is not an isolated incident. Over and over again, not just Old Man Gower—but years later there is Percy in Slocan, pressing me against the cave wall during hide-and-go-seek, warning me against crying out. The sharp stone cuts into my shoulder. I try to move but he holds me harder. The other children are running past on their way back to home base. We will be the last ones unless we go. He says we will fool them and hide there. I am filled with a strange terror and exhilaration. When does this begin—this fascination and danger that rockets through my body?

Two weeks ago, the day of our first staff meeting at Cecil Consolidated, there was that dream again. The dream had a new and terrible ending. In earlier versions, there was flight, terror, and pursuit. The only way to be saved from harm was to become seductive. In this latest dream, three beautiful oriental women lay naked in the muddy road, flat on their backs, their faces turned to the sky. They were lying straight as coffins, spaced several feet apart, perpendicular to the road like railway ties. Several soldiers stood or shuffled in front of them in the foreground. It appeared they were guarding these women, who were probably prisoners captured from a nearby village.

The woman closest by made a simpering coy gesture with her hands. She touched her hair and wiggled her body slightly —seductively. An almost inaudible whimper or sob was drowned in her chest. She was trying to use the only weapon she had—her desirability. This is what a punished dog feels—

this abject longing, wretchedness, fear, and utter helplessness. She lay on the edge of nausea, stretched between hatred and lust.

The soldiers lifted their rifles, aiming across the bodies of the women. This was sport. A game to play with animals in the forest. Power. The rush of release from the rifle barrels. The puffs of blue smoke.

Crack!

The first shots were aimed at the toes of the women, the second at their feet. A few inches from the body, the first woman's right foot lay like a solid wooden boot neatly severed above the ankles. It was too late. There was no hope. The soldiers could not be won. Dread and a deathly loathing cut through the women.

Does Old Man Gower still walk through the hedges between our houses in Vancouver, in Slocan, in Granton and Cecil?

I am a small girl being carried away through the break in the shrubs where our two yards meet. Old Man Gower is taking me to the edge of his garden on the far far side away from the street. His backyard is a jungle of bushes, flowering trees, weeds, and flowers. Near the farthest corner is a thick arch of vines. He stoops to enter the arch. The ground here is covered with pebbles and a wooden slab across two stones forms a bench. If I reach up I can touch the small green grapes that cluster in bunches across the vine roof. But I do not move.

When he sits on the bench, no one can see us. The vines are so thick I cannot see my house or his. He does not release me. When I make the faintest move he puts his hand on my skirt. He offers me a toffee. I neither wish nor do not wish to have the candy, but it is more polite to refuse.

He thrusts it into my hands.

I sit still on his lap.

"Would you like me to tell you a story?" he asks.

I do not respond. If I am still, I will be safe.

Is this where the terror begins?

I am four years old. His hands are large and demanding. He caresses my head as if I were a small animal. My short black hair straight across my forehead like a broom is blown aside as he puts his mouth on my face.

Another day I am in the garage, behind the huge pile of sawdust. I have arranged a bed for my dolls out of baby blankets. I have many many dolls, and stuffed animals. Baby dolls with breakable hard heads and straw-filled bodies, children dolls, grown-up dolls, a rabbit, a bear, a furry mouse. I have tea sets and doll shoes and socks and dresses.

Mr. Gower is standing beside me and looking down. I cannot play because he is watching. I wait for him to go away. He squats down. I wish to go to my mother. His hand holds my skirt as I get up to go. The soft elastic around the waist pulls at the straps crisscrossing over my shoulders. I cannot move. I cannot look at his face. It is unthinkable to be held by force.

He lifts me up saying that my knee has a scratch on it and he will fix it for me. I know this is a lie. The scratch is hardly visible and does not hurt. Is it the lie that first introduces me to the darkness?

The room is dark, the blind drawn almost to the bottom. I am unfamiliar with such darkness. The bed is strange and pristine, deathly in its untouched splendor. I have never seen his wife. Does she not live here? Is this where they sleep?

"Don't be afraid," he says. "I know another little girl just like you and she isn't afraid."

He tells me her name is Veronica and she talks to him. She is also four years old. I cannot imagine Veronica actually talking to Old Man Gower. If I speak, I will split open and spill out. To be whole and safe I must hide in the foliage, odorless as a newborn fawn. But already the lie grows like a horn, an unfurled fiddlehead fist, through the soft fontanelle of my four-year-old mind.

He stands me on the bathroom toilet and opens the medicine cabinet. He begins to undress me. I do not resist. One does not resist adults. But I know this is unnecessary for my knee. He is only pretending to fix my scratch.

From outside the bathroom window I can hear Stephen calling for me, his high voice singing the two-tone chant "O-mi".

"Sh," Mr. Gower says. One finger is on his lips and the other hand on my mouth.

Mr. Gower closes the bathroom door, locking me in.

I hear him calling Stephen from the kitchen door. "She's hurt her knee," he says, "I'm fixing it."

He is giving Stephen a penny to go and buy some candy. My mother never does this. I know he only wants to send Stephen away so we will be safe. I want Stephen to rescue me from this strange room. But I do not wish him to see me half undressed. I am not permitted to move, to dress, or to cry out. I am ashamed. If Stephen comes he will see my shame. He will know what I feel and the knowing will flood the landscape. There will be nowhere to hide.

"Run away, little girl. Hide. Hide," he says, putting me down in the bathroom. I am Snow White in the forest, unable to run. He is the forest full of eyes and arms. He is the tree root that trips Snow White. He is the lightning flashing through the dark sky.

We are in the movie theater in a torrent of sound. I am transfixed by the horror. Old Man Gower lifts me onto his lap.

"Don't tell your mother," he whispers into my ear. This is what he always says. Where in the darkness has my mother gone?

I am clinging to my mother's leg, a flesh shaft that grows from the ground, a tree trunk of which I am an offshoot—a young branch attached by right of flesh and blood. Where she is rooted, I am rooted. If she walks, I will walk. Her blood is whispering through my veins. The shaft of her leg is the shaft of my body and I am her thoughts.

But here in Mr. Gower's hands I become other—a parasite on her body, no longer of her mind. My arms are vines that strangle the limb to which I cling. I hold so tightly now that arms and leg become one through force. I am a growth that attaches and digs a furrow under the bark of her skin. If I tell my mother about Mr. Gower, the alarm will send a tremor through our bodies and I will be torn from her. But the secret has already separated us. The secret is this: I go to seek Old Man Gower in his hideaway. I clamber unbidden onto his lap. His hands are frightening and pleasurable. In the center of my body is a rift.

In my childhood dreams, the mountain yawns apart as the chasm spreads. My mother is on one side of the rift. I am on the other. We cannot reach each other. My legs are being sawn in half.

12

It is around this time that Mother disappears. I hardly dare to think, let alone ask, why she has to leave. Questions are meaningless. What matters to my five-year-old mind is not the reason that she is required to leave, but the stillness of waiting for her to return. After a while, the stillness is so much with me that it takes the form of a shadow which grows and surrounds me like air. Time solidifies, ossifies the waiting into molecules of stone, dark microscopic planets that swirl through the universe of my body waiting for light and the morning.

. . .

SEPTEMBER 1941.

The harbor is crowded with people. It is altogether bewildering. Aunt Emily is here and Aya Obasan, Grandpa Kato, Uncle, Father and his friend Uncle Dan, Grandma and Grandpa Nakane. The whole family. Stephen is wearing his short gray pants and gray suit top and gray knee socks and I am wearing the blue woolen knit dress that mother made and likes best. It has delicate five-petaled white flowers with red-dot centers stitched in wool and spaced all around the border of the skirt. I have short white socks and shiny black shoes with a single strap.

Father is holding my hand and asking foolishly if I can see my mother. There is nothing to be seen but legs and legs. All I know is that Mother and Grandma are at the other end of a long paper streamer I clutch in my fist. Father picks me up in his arms and points but I can see nothing except thousands of colorful paper streamers stretched between the people below and the railing of the ship. Stephen is gathering spools of streamers that lie here and there unused on the ground.

"She'll be back soon," my father says.

I do not doubt this.

Uncle Dan winks at me and smiles. Uncle Dan is almost always smiling or laughing, his mouth wide open and his head thrown back like the junkman's horse, showing his large straight teeth.

"Obaa-chan [the old grandmother] only needs to see their faces," Aya Obasan says, "then they will come back." She tells me that though Mother was born in Canada she was raised in Japan by her grandmother. "Obaa-chan is very ill," Aya Obasan says. My great-grandmother has need of my mother. Does my mother have need of me? In what marketplace of the universe are the bargains made that have traded my need for my great-grandmother's?

The boat pulls away and I cannot see my mother's face, though Father keeps pointing and waves.

When we get home, Stephen gives me three of the spools he's retrieved, and I put them in the top left-hand drawer of my mother's sewing-machine cabinet for a surprise homecoming present for her. I put my fluffy Easter chicks in there as well, their feet three wire prongs. Last Easter I found them in a wicker basket sitting on top of candy and chocolate eggs.

There is a scene I imagine in which I am my mother come home and am sitting at the treadle machine. My hand is poised at the round wooden knob carved into the ornate drawer, my fingers feeling around the smooth curves. With my eyes averted, I am my mother pulling the drawer open to look for the black darning knob, or a spool of thread, or scissors. To my mother's surprise, she finds the colorful paper streamer rolls and her fingers touch the soft fluff of the Easter chicks. She lifts them up one at a time. "Ah," I say in my mother's voice. Two small Easter chicks. Who would not cry out?

Everything we have ever done we do again and again in my mind. We take the streetcar to Kitsilano beach and buy potato chips in cardboard baskets. We go with Aunt Emily and Grandpa Kato in his shiny black car, across the Lions' Gate Bridge and along the Dollarton Highway to visit Uncle Dan, who is staying in the small house that Grandma and Grandpa Kato own. Or to New Westminster and the island where Aya Obasan and Uncle Isamu live in their beautiful house full of plants by the sea. I play with the dog they call "Puppy" though he is not a puppy at all, romping around the pond full of goldfish with the waterfall and the rock garden surrounding it. We go to the zoo at Stanley Park and sit on the grass by the dome of the outdoor theater, listening to the symphony concerts in the dusk. I rehearse the past faithfully in preparation for her return.

Aya Obasan is in the house every day now. She is gentle and quiet like Mother. She sleeps in my room on an extra bed that has been brought upstairs from the basement. The first morning she is here, I am surprised to see her long black hair, a thick braid thinning out to a few tassels that reach to her buttocks. Normally her hair is coiled around and around in a braided bun at the back of her head.

Stephen and I watch her as she sticks countless hairpins in to keep the bun in place above the nape of her neck.

"Long legs, crooked thighs, no head, and no eyes," Stephen chants.

Obasan takes a while to understand the hairpin riddle.

She has an ivory brush with soft useless bristles and a comb with teeth as thick as chopsticks. I hold the matching hand mirror with its curved edges as she powders her face. A fold of her long velvet dressing gown rests on my arms, soft and fluid and heavy as dry water. Many of Aya Obasan's things are soft against my cheek. Her fur coat, the fluffy quilt on her bed, and especially Obasan herself. She is plump, unlike Grandma Kato, whose knees are like bed knobs.

But even with Obasan's warmth and constant presence, there is an ominous sense of cold and absence—a darkness that has crept into the house as stealthily as Mrs. Sugimoto's dead animal fur piece she sometimes leaves on the living-room sofa.

One night I waken frightened. There is no light anywhere —in the hallway, in the streets, in the neighbors' houses. This night I remember we are not to turn on any lights. We are doing what Stephen calls a "blackout." I feel my way along the walls into the living room, where there are voices.

Old Man Gower is here. He has never come into our house before and it is strange that he should be sitting in the darkness with Father.

"Yes, yes," he is saying, his large soft hands rubbing together. The light from his pipe glares and fades. I don't know what he is agreeing to as he sits in the armchair. Even in the darkness, I can tell that Father's eyes are not at ease.

"I'll keep them for you, Mark. Sure thing." Old Man Gower's voice is unlike the low gurgling sound I am used to when he talks to me alone. "The piano. Books. Garden tools. What else?"

Although I am in the room, he acts as if I am not here. He seems more powerful than Father, larger and more at home even though this is our house. He sounds as if he is trying to comfort my father, but there is a falseness in the tone. The voice is too sure—too strong.

Father is as if he is not here. If my mother were back, she would move aside all the darkness with her hands and we would be safe and at home in our home.

I am relieved when Old Man Gower leaves but when I turn to my father, the safety has not returned to him. I clamber onto his lap and put my arms around his neck.

"Naomi-chan," he whispers, "could you not sleep?"

I understand later what it is about. The darkness is everywhere, in the day as well as the night. It threatens us as it always has, in the streetcars, in the stores, on the streets, in all public places. It covers the entire city and causes all the lights to be turned out. It drones overhead in the sounds of airplanes. It rushes unbidden from the mouths of strangers and in the taunts of children. It happens to Stephen even more terrifyingly than it does to me.

One day he comes home from school, his glasses broken, black tear stains on his face. Obasan is hanging up clothes on the line from the back porch. When she sees him, she does not cry out but continues hanging up the laundry, removing the pegs from her mouth one at a time.

"What happened?" I whisper as Stephen comes up the stairs.

He doesn't answer me. Is he ashamed, as I was in Old Man Gower's bathroom? Should I go away?

"What happened?" It is Obasan asking this time and her voice is soft.

He still does not reply and Obasan takes him by the hand into the kitchen and wipes his face. I stand hesitantly in the doorway, watching.

"I told you," Stephen says at last.

I am encouraged that he is speaking to me. "Oh," I say, wishing to show that I understand, but I do not.

"You know, Nomi."

Stephen is in grade three at David Lloyd George School. There are "air-raid drills" at school, he tells me, which means that when a loud alarm sounds, all the children line up and file out of the classrooms as quickly as possible. They lie flat on the ground, crouch by hedges or in ditches, to hide from the bombs which may drop on us all—not just on the school, but anywhere at any time out of enemy aircraft overhead. We may be killed or maimed, blinded for life or burnt. We may lose an arm, or a finger even. To be safe, we must hide and be still so they will not see us.

The girl with the long ringlets who sits in front of Stephen said to him, "All the Jap kids at school are going to be sent away and they're bad and you're a Jap." And so, Stephen tells me, am I.

"Are we?" I ask Father.

"No," Father says. "We're Canadian."

It is a riddle, Stephen tells me. We are both the enemy and not the enemy.

13

Riddles are hard to understand. Only Stephen knows what they mean. Neither Aya Obasan nor Grandma and Grandpa Nakane understand the jokes in Stephen's riddle book. But Grandpa Nakane pats Stephen on the head and laughs when Stephen does.

When Grandpa Nakane walks, he bends forward from his waist and his right arm dangles loose from his shoulder close to his knees like some of the monkeys at Stanley Park. The monkeys are swift and hop and swing acrobatically from wall to ceiling and around in great arcs. But Grandpa Nakane is no leaping dancer and lopes along at his own pace.

During the Christmas concert, I look up and see Grandpa Nakane coming down the aisle of the church to sit in front, his hoary white eyebrows lifted high so he can see better.

Under his left arm he is carrying a present wrapped in rustly white tissue paper. He is watching intently as Stephen and I stand around the manger singing carols with the other white-robed cherubs, our hands folded like church steeples and our eyes gazing down at the little Lord flashlight Jesus asleep in the hay. Nakayama-sensei, the round-faced minister, is standing beside the organ smiling widely and nodding in time to the music. When I peek up at the audience, I can see short Grandpa Kato sitting in the aisle near the back, his round belly like a ball with his gold watch chain draped in front. I know Aunt Emily and Uncle Dan are somewhere in the crowded church watching and I am filled with a need to hide but there is nowhere to go. If the wooden manger in front were bigger I could dive into the hay and be buried from view.

All the lights except for the flashlight in the hay go out and the room is suddenly so still and dark that it seems almost to have disappeared. In a moment a candle appears high up in the air in the middle of the aisle at the back and I can hear Father's high clear notes on his wooden flute, playing the *Gloria in Excelsis Deo*. After this, Father's voice, rich and tender, sings the beginning of the hymn and candle after candle comes through the archway from the hall, around to the back and, in a steady advancing stream of light and song, up to the front, engulfing us.

All of Christmas is like this. A mixture of white lights and colored twinkling lights in the dark, surprises, songs, and streams and streams of people, up and down the escalators, in the crowded stores and on the green and red decorated sidewalks.

Even on New Year's, Stephen and I are so showered with gifts that our rooms bulge with new toys. I have a wonderful set of entirely red things—an apple-fat shiny red purse that clicks open and shut like Aunt Emily's with a shiny red change purse inside, a red bead necklace, bracelet, comb, brush, and a gold-and-red kitten brooch with green jewel eyes. Stephen has a Meccano set and a wine-colored encyclopedia —*The Book of Knowledge*—which Aunt Emily exclaims over and reads aloud with excitement.

"Look, Nomi," she says, pointing to the picture of a little girl carrying a candle and walking in the dark to get a secret message to her father in a dungeon. It's a story in a part of the encyclopedia called "The Book of Golden Deeds," which is filled with tales of martyrs and brave children and people going through torment and terror. Could I, I wonder, ever do the things that they do? Could I hide in a wagon of hay and not cry out if I were stabbed by a bayonet?

Mother, it seems to me, could. So could Grandma Kato or Obasan. But not, I think, Aunt Emily, though perhaps that is not so. She is too often impatient and flustered, her fingers jerking her round wire-rimmed glasses up her short nose. And Stephen? Who among us would last the longest in a torture chamber without betraying the rest? Sometimes, in the dark, I send my finger digging deep into my arm or chest, imagining the bayonet's bloody stab.

At night I lie awake thinking of dangerous people wielding hooks and prongs, but during the day there is another danger, another darkness, soft and mysterious. I know it as whispers and frowns and too much gentleness. Then, one spring evening, the two shadows of day and night come together in a white heavy mist of fear.

I am in the basement playroom making folding paper cranes, each one tinier than the one before. I can hear Father coughing lightly in his study, over and over. He coughs almost all the time and he sits in his study writing at night. When I talk to him he smiles but he stares away as if I am not there. He is never cross. He is alone these days. Where has everyone gone? There used to be friends visiting us and staying for meals. They brought me little toys or toffee. Uncle Dan was almost always here in the evenings, his horsey face flung back in laughter and his shoulders pumping up and down. Where is he now? No one ever visits us in the evenings anymore.

But tonight Aunt Emily is here. I hear a groan and a thump as someone pounds—what? The wall? The desk?

I tiptoe out of the playroom and past the furnace to the door of the study. The room now has a cot in it since Father sleeps down here. Aunt Emily is pacing back and forth, her arms folded tightly and her black skirt swishing. No one sees me standing by the door and I take my smallest paper crane and crawl under the bed. From there, lying on my belly, I can see one of Father's legs crossed at the knees, moving back and forth like a pendulum. His black boot with the hooks lined up along either side of the tongue kicks the leg of his rolltop desk —tick, tick, tick, like a clock.

Then suddenly the crash again of a fist against the wall and I hear their voices speaking as I have never heard before —tight, low, dark. I half thought I would shout "boo" and jump up at them, but now I am afraid to move. I wish I had not thought to hide.

"What next, Mark?" Aunt Emily is whispering in a hoarse voice.

Father's fit of coughing begins again. When he speaks, his voice is thin as the wind. "It can't be helped. It can't be helped."

"But we can get them out. I'm sure we can," Aunt Emily

says. I have never heard such urgency. "Your father won't last in the Sick Bay. And he'll be left behind after the rest of us are gone. He'll be alone. The orders are to leave everyone in the Sick Bay behind. It's a death sentence for the old ones."

Grandpa Nakane at Sick Bay? Where, I wonder, is that? And why is it a cause of distress? Is Sick Bay near English Bay or Horseshoe Bay? When we go to Stanley Park we sometimes drive by English Bay. Past English Bay are the other beaches, Second and Third Beach, where I once went to buy potato chips and got lost. Grandpa Nakane came ambling out of all the crowd that day and took my hand in his one strong hand without saying a word and I fed him my potato chips one by one as if he were one of the animals at the zoo. If Grandpa Nakane is at the beach now, could he be lost the way I was? Should we not go to find him?

"They must have rounded up everyone on Saltspring Island and shipped the whole lot of them to the Pool," Aunt Emily says. "Where will it end?"

I have seen my Nakane grandparents only once since Christmas. Obasan told me Grandma and Grandpa went to visit friends and their old boat shop on Saltspring Island as they do every year. They have still not come back to their house in New Westminster. When Mother was with us we used to visit Grandma and Grandpa Nakane often and go to see Aya Obasan and Uncle Isamu who lived not far from them. I haven't seen Uncle for a long time either.

Aunt Emily treads back and forth across the wine-colored carpet, her black pointed shoes with the single strap coming straight toward me, then abruptly away. The round black fastener wobbles with every step.

"Your mother won't survive it either, Mark. We really have to get them out. We'll go together to the Security Commission tomorrow. I've met the woman there."

"You think she can help? In all this mess would there be time to listen to one story?"

"They'll have to. Oh, if Grandma and Grandpa had only stayed at home this year. We'll have to explain that your parents don't live in Saltspring. No one else from Vancouver or New Westminster has been shoved into that place."

"Is it so bad there?" Father speaks so softly I can barely hear.

Aunt Emily sits down on the bed and the wire slats suddenly form a rounded bulge above my head. I push back farther under the bed and my leg brushes against a red, white, and blue ball that Uncle Dan gave me. It's covered in a layer of fine dust.

"It's a nightmare," Aunt Emily whispers.

The black coils at the ends of the slats squeal as Aunt Emily shifts restlessly. "All those little kids. And the old women like Grandma—totally bewildered. Fumi and Eiko can't take any more. They're so thin." Aunt Emily's voice is shaking.

Fumi and Eiko are Aunt Emily's closest friends. I have seen them often at Aunt Emily's place laughing and talking and teasing each other.

Father's fist thuds against his knees for a long time. Then, in a halting voice I've never heard him use before, he says, "I have to leave it all in your hands, Emily. My time is up."

There is a jump from the bed and the round bulge disappears instantly as the smooth metal slats lie straight and flat again.

"Mark, it can't be. Listen to your cough. You're not well enough. We'll get an extension—for health reasons."

"No—no. It's my turn. Others have been filling the quota and going in my place."

All this talk is puzzling and frightening. I cradle the rubber ball against my cheek and stare up at the white tufts like tiny rabbit tails stuck all over the bottom of the mattress.

I am thinking of Peter Rabbit hopping through the lettuce patch when I hear Stephen's lopsided hop as he comes galloping down the stairs.

"The curfew, Auntie!" he is calling. "Look how dark it is. Hurry! The police!"

There is a sudden jump and Aunt Emily runs to the door. "Damn this mess," she says in a panicky voice. "I'll have to go down the back alleys." She pauses at the doorway briefly, then she is gone. I can hear her feet running through the playroom and out the open door. In a few seconds I hear the click of the latch at the back gate.

14

The ball I found under the cot that day was never lost again.

Obasan keeps it in a box with Stephen's toy cars on the bottom shelf in the bathroom. The rubber is cracked and scored with a black lacy design, and the colors are dull, but it still bounces a little.

Sick Bay, I learned eventually, was not a beach at all. And the place they called the Pool was not a pool of water, but a prison at the exhibition grounds called Hastings Park in Vancouver. Men, women, and children outside Vancouver, from the "protected area"—a hundred-mile strip along the coast— were herded into the grounds and kept there like animals until they were shipped off to roadwork camps and concentration camps in the interior of the province. From our family, it was only Grandma and Grandpa Nakane who were imprisoned at the Pool.

Some families were able to leave on their own and found homes in British Columbia's interior and elsewhere in Canada. Ghost towns such as Slocan—those old mining settlements, sometimes abandoned, sometimes with a remnant community—were reopened, and row upon row of two-family wooden huts were erected. Eventually the whole coast was cleared and everyone of the Japanese race in Vancouver was sent away.

The tension everywhere was not clear to me then and is not much clearer today. Time has solved few mysteries. Wars and rumors of wars, racial hatreds and fears are with us still.

The reality of today is that Uncle is dead and Obasan is left alone. Weariness has invaded her and settled in her bones. Is it possible that her hearing could deteriorate so rapidly in just one month? The phone is ringing but she does not respond at all.

Aunt Emily is calling from the airport in Calgary, where she's waiting for Stephen's flight from Montreal. They'll rent a car and drive down together this afternoon.

"Did you get my parcel?" she asks.

The airport sounds in the background are so loud she can hardly hear me. I shout into the receiver but it's obvious she doesn't know what I'm saying.

"Is Obasan all right? Did she sleep last night?" she asks. It's such a relief to feel her sharing my concern.

Obasan has gone into the bathroom and is sweeping behind the toilet with a whisk made from a toy broom.

"Would you like to take a bath?" I ask.

She continues sweeping the imaginary dust.

"Ofuro?" I repeat. "Bath?"

"Orai," she replies at last, in a meek voice. "All right."

I run the water the way she prefers it, straight from the hot-water tap. It's been a while since we bathed together. After this, perhaps she'll rest. Piece by piece she removes her layers of underclothes, rags held together with safety pins. The new ones I've bought for her are left unused in boxes under her bed. She is small and naked and bent in the bathroom, the skin of her buttocks loose and drooping in a fold.

"Aah," she exhales deeply in a half groan as she sinks into the hot water and closes her eyes.

I rub the washcloth over her legs and feet, the thin purple veins a scribbled maze, a skin map, her thick toenails, ancient rock formations. I am reminded of long-extinct volcanoes, the crust and rivulets of lava scars, crisscrossing down the bony hillside. Naked as prehistory, we lie together, the steam from the bath heavily misting the room.

"Any day now is all right," she says. "The work is finished." She is falling asleep in the water.

"It will be good to lie down," I shout, rousing her and draining the tub. I help her to stand and she moves to her room, her feet barely leaving the floor. Almost before I pull the covers over her, she is asleep.

I am feeling a bit dizzy from the heat myself.

Aunt Emily said she and Stephen would be here by four this afternoon. I should clear up the place as much as I can before they arrive. Find a safe place for all the papers.

This diary of Aunt Emily's is the largest I have ever seen. The hard cover is gray with a black border and "Journal" is written in fancy script in the middle. What a crackling sound old paper makes.

It has no page numbers and most of the entries begin

"Dear Nesan." It's a journal of letters to my mother. "Merry Christmas, Dearest Nesan, 1941" is printed in a rectangular decorated box on the first page.

Should I be reading this? Why not? Why else would she send it here?

The handwriting in blue-black ink is firm and regular in the first few pages, but is a rapid scrawl later on. I feel like a burglar as I read, breaking into a private house only to discover it's my childhood house filled with corners and rooms I've never seen. Aunt Emily's Christmas 1941 is not the Christmas I remember.

The people she mentions would be my age, or younger than I am now: her good friends Eiko and Fumi, the student nurses; Tom Shoyama, the editor of the *New Canadian;* Kunio Shimizu, the social worker, my father, Tadashi Mark; Father's good friend Uncle Dan; and Father's older brother, Isamu, Sam for short, or Uncle as we called him. Obasan is fifty years old in 1941.

In the face of growing bewilderment and distress, Aunt Emily roamed the landscape like an aircraft in a fog, looking for a place to land—a safe and sane strip of justice and reason. Not seeing these, she did not crash into the oblivion of either bitterness or futility but remained airborne.

The first entry is dated December 25, 1941.

Dearest Nesan,

In all my 25 years, this is the first Christmas without you and Mother. I wonder what you are doing today in Japan. Is it cold where you are? Do your neighbors treat you as enemies? Is Obaa-chan still alive?

When you come back, Nesan, when I see you again, I will give you this journal. It will be my Christmas present to you. Isn't it a sturdy book? It's one of Dan's Christmas gifts to me.

I'm sitting in the library, writing at the desk which has the picture of you and me beside the ink bottle. There are so many things to tell you. How different the world is now! The whole continent is in shock about the Pearl Harbor bombing. Some Issei are feeling betrayed and ashamed.

It's too early yet to know how the war will affect us. On the whole, I'd say we're taking things in our stride. We're used to the prejudice by now after all these long years, though it's been intensified into hoodlumism. A torch was thrown into a rooming house and some plate-glass windows were broken in the west end—things like that.

The blackouts frighten the children. Nomi had a crying bout a few nights ago. I don't tell you this to worry you, Nesan, but I know you will want to know. There was a big storm during the last blackout. Nomi woke up. That peach tree is too close to her window. When the wind blows, it sways and swings around like a giant octopus trying to break in. Aya had the spare bed in Nomi's room just as you arranged before you left, but since she's had to stay so much longer, she's moved into the main bedroom and Mark sleeps in the study downstairs. Aya slept through the whole storm but Mark woke up to find Nomi sitting on his pillow, hitting the Japanese doll you gave her. He tried to take the doll away from her and she started to cry and wouldn't stop. He said it's the first time she's ever really cried. She doesn't understand what's going on at all. Stephen does, of course. He went through a phase of being too good to be true but now he's being surly. He told Aya to "talk properly."

All three Japanese newspapers have been closed down. That's fine as far as I'm concerned. Never needed so many anyway. It's good for the *New Canadian,* which is now our only source of information and can go ahead with all the responsibility. Our December 12 headline is "Have Faith in Canada." Thank God we live in a democracy and not under an officially racist regime. All of us Nisei are intent on keeping faith and standing by. We were turned down for the Home Defense training plan but we're doing Red Cross work, buying War Savings bonds, logging for the war industries and shipyards, benefit concerts—the regular stuff.

There have been the usual letters to the editor in the papers. Rank nonsense, some of them. The majority are decent, however. The RCMP are on our side. More than anyone else, they know how blameless we are. When the City Fathers proposed canceling all our business licenses they said we did not rate such harsh treatment. Isn't that encouraging? But now the North Vancouver Board of Trade has gone on record to demand that all our autos be confiscated. What would doctors like Dad and the businessmen do? If they take something that essential away from 23,000 people the rest of British Columbia will feel some of the bad side effects. Remember the boat that Sam and Mark finished last winter with all the hand carvings? It was seized along with all the fishing boats from up and down the coast, and the whole lot are tied up in New Westminster. Fishing licenses were suspended a couple of weeks ago as well. The dog-salmon industry, I hear, is shorthanded because the Japanese cannot fish anymore. But the white fishermen are confident that they can make up the lack in the next season, if they can use the Japanese fishing boats.

There was one friendly letter in the *Province* protesting the taking away of the right to earn a living from 1,800 people. Said it wasn't democracy. But then there was another letter by a woman saying she didn't want her own precious daughter to have to go to school with the you-know-who's. Strange how these protesters are so much more vehement about Canadian-born Japanese than they are about German-born Germans. I guess it's because we look different. What it boils down to is an undemocratic racial antagonism —which is exactly what our democratic country is supposed to be fighting against. Oh well. The egg man told me not to worry.

It's the small businesses that are most affected— the dressmakers, the corner store, etc.—because the clientele are shy of patronizing such places in public. Lots of people have been fired from their jobs. Business on Powell Street is up slightly since most of us who usually go to the big department stores like Woodward's don't anymore.

A couple of Sundays ago the National President of the Imperial Order of Daughters of the Empire, who obviously doesn't know the first thing about us, made a deliberate attempt to create fear and ill will among her dominion-wide members. Said we were all spies and saboteurs, and that in 1931 there were 55,000 of us and that number has doubled in the last ten years. A biological absurdity. Trouble is, lots of women would rather believe their president than actual RCMP records. It's illogical that women, who are the bearers and nurturers of the human race, should go all out for ill will like this.

Are you interested in all this, Nesan?

I've knit Dad and Mark a couple of warm sweaters. Dad is back in full-time service in spite of his heart. When gas rationing starts he won't be able to use the car so much. It's so sleek it's an affront to everyone he passes. I wish he'd bought something more modest, but you know Dad.

He has to report every month to the RCMP just because he didn't take time to be naturalized, and didn't look far enough ahead to know how important it was. Politics doesn't seem to mean a thing to him. I feel so irritated at him.

But worse than my irritation, there's this horrible feeling whenever I turn on the radio, or see a headline with the word "Japs" screaming at us. So long as they designate the enemy by that term and not us, it doesn't matter. But over here, they say "Once a Jap always a Jap," and that means us. We're the enemy. And what about you over there? Have they arrested you because you're a Canadian? If only you'd been able to get out before all this started. Oh, if there were some way of getting news.

The things that go on in wartime! Think of Hitler shiploading people into Poland or Germany proper to work for nothing in fields and factories far from home and children—stealing food from conquered people—captive labor—shooting hundreds of people in reprisal for one. I'm glad to hear that the Russian army is taking some of the stuffing out of Hitler's troops. War

breeds utter insanity. Here at home there's mass hatred of us simply because we're of Japanese origin. I
hope fervently it will not affect the lives of the little
ones like Stephen and Nomi. After all, they are so
thoroughly Canadian. Stephen and the Sugimoto boy
are the only nonwhite kids in their classes. Mark says
Nomi thinks she's the same as the neighbors, but Stephen knows the difference. Came crying home the
other day because some kid on the block broke his
violin. Children can be such savages.

There is a lapse of over a month until the next entry.

February 15, 1942.
Dearest Nesan,
    I thought I would write to you every day but, as
you see, I haven't managed that. I felt so sad thinking
about what the children are having to experience I
didn't want to keep writing. But today I must tell you
what's happening.
    Things are changing so fast. First, all the Japanese
men—the ones who were born in Japan and haven't
been able to get their citizenship yet—are being
rounded up, one hundred or so at a time. A few days
ago, Mark told me he felt sure Sam had been carted
off. I took the interurban down as soon as I could.
Isamu couldn't have been gone too long because not
all the plants were parched though some of the delicate ones had turned to skeletons in the front window.
I tried to find the dog but she's just nowhere. I looked
and called all through the woods and behind the
house.
    Grandma and Grandpa Nakane will be so upset

and confused when they find out he's gone. You know how dependent they are on him. They went to Saltspring Island a couple of weeks ago and haven't come back yet. I know they're with friends, so they must be all right.

We know some people who have left Vancouver. Dad says we should look around and get out too, but we just don't know any other place. When we look at the map it's hard to think about all those unknown places. We were thinking of going to Kamloops, but that may be too close to the boundary of the "protected area."

It's becoming frightening here, with the agitation mounting higher. It isn't just a matter of fear of sabotage or military necessity anymore, it's outright race persecution. Groups like the "Sons of Canada" are petitioning Ottawa against us and the newspapers are printing outright lies. There was a picture of a young Nisei boy with a metal lunch box and it said he was a spy with a radio transmitter. When the reporting was protested the error was admitted in a tiny line in the classified section at the back where you couldn't see it unless you looked very hard.

March 2, 1942.

Everyone is so distressed here, Nesan. Eiko and Fumi came over this morning, crying. All student nurses have been fired from the General.

Our beautiful radios are gone. We had to give them up or suffer the humiliation of having them taken forcibly by the RCMP. Our cameras—even Stephen's toy one that he brought out to show them

when they came—all are confiscated. They can search
our homes without warrant.

But the great shock is this: we are all being forced
to leave. All of us. Not a single person of the Japanese
race who lives in the "protected area" will escape.
There is something called a Civilian Labour Corps and
Mark and Dan were going to join—you know how
they do everything together—but now will not go near
it as it smells of a demonic roundabout way of getting
rid of us. There is a very suspicious clause "within and
without" Canada, that has all the fellows leery.

Who knows where we will be tomorrow, next
week. It isn't as if we Nisei were aliens—technically or
not. It breaks my heart to think of leaving this house
and the little things that we've gathered through the
years—all those irreplaceable mementos—our books
and paintings—the azalea plants, my white iris.

Oh, Nesan, the Nisei are bitter. Too bitter for
their own good or for Canada. How can cool heads
like Tom's prevail when the general feeling is to stand
up and fight? He needs all his levelheadedness and
diplomacy, as editor of the *New Canadian,* since that's
the only paper left to us now.

A curfew that applies only to us was started a few
days ago. If we're caught out after sundown, we're
thrown in jail. People who have been fired—and
there's a scramble on to be the first to kick us out of
jobs—sit at home without even being able to go out
for a consoling cup of coffee. For many, home is just a
bed. Kunio is working like mad with the Welfare Soci-
ety to look after the women and children who were left
when the men were forced to "volunteer" to go to the
work camps. And where are those men? Sitting in un-

heated bunk cars, no latrines, no water, snow fifteen feet deep, no work, little food if any. They were shunted off with such inhuman speed that they got there before any facilities were prepared. Now other men are afraid to go because they think they'll be going to certain disaster. If the snow is that deep, there is no work. If there is no work, there is no pay. If there is no pay, no one eats. Their families suffer. The *Daily Province* reports that work on frames with tent coverings is progressing to house the 2,000 expected. Tent coverings where the snow is so deep? You should see the faces here—all pinched, gray, uncertain. Signs have been posted on all highways—"Japs Keep Out."

Mind you, you can't compare this sort of thing to anything that happens in Germany. That country is openly totalitarian. But Canada is supposed to be a democracy.

All Nisei are liable to imprisonment if we refuse to volunteer to leave. At least that is the likeliest interpretation of Ian Mackenzie's "Volunteer or else" statement. He's the Minister of Pensions and National Health. Why do they consider us to be wartime prisoners? Can you wonder that there is a deep bitterness among the Nisei who believed in democracy?

And the horrors that some of the young girls are facing—outraged by men in uniform. You wouldn't believe it, Nesan. You have to be right here in the middle of it to really know. The men are afraid to go and leave their wives behind.

How can the Hakujin not feel ashamed for their treachery? My butcher told me he knew he could trust me more than he could most whites. But kind people like him are betrayed by the outright racists and op-

portunists like Alderman Wilson, God damn his soul.
And there are others who, although they wouldn't per-
secute us, are ignorant and indifferent and believe
we're being very well treated for the "class" of people
we are. One letter in the papers says that in order to
preserve the "British way of life," they should send us
all away. We're a "lower order of people." In one
breath we are damned for being "unassimilable" and
the next there's fear that we'll assimilate. One reporter
points to those among us who are living in poverty
and says, "No British subject would live in such conditions." Then if we improve our lot, another says,
"There is danger that they will enter our better neigh-
borhoods." If we are educated, the complaint is that
we will cease being the "ideal servant." It makes me
choke. The diseases, the crippling, the twisting of our
souls is still to come.

March 12.

Honest, Nesan, I'm just in a daze this morning.
The last ruling forbids any of us—even Nisei—to go
anywhere in this wide dominion without a permit
from the Minister of Justice, St. Laurent, through
Austin C. Taylor of the Commission here. We go
where they send us.

Nothing affects me much just now except rather
detachedly. Everything is like a bad dream. I keep telling myself to wake up. There's no sadness when
friends of long standing disappear overnight—either
to Camp or somewhere in the Interior. No farewells—
no promise at all of future meetings or correspondence

—or anything. We just disperse. It's as if we never existed. We're hit so many ways at one time that if I wasn't past feeling I think I would crumble.

This curfew business is horrible. At sundown we scuttle into our holes like furtive creatures. We look in the papers for the time of next morning's sunrise when we may venture forth.

The government has requisitioned the Livestock Building at Hastings Park, and the Women's Building, to house 2,000 "Japs pending removal." White men are pictured in the newspaper filling ticks with bales of straw for mattresses, putting up makeshift partitions for toilets—etc. Here the lowly Jap will be bedded down like livestock in stalls—perhaps closed around under police guard—I don't know. The Nisei will be "compelled" (news report) to volunteer in Labor Gangs. The worse the news from the Eastern Front, the more ghoulish the public becomes. We are the billy goats and nanny goats and kids—all the scapegoats to appease this blindness. Is this a Christian country? Do you know that Alderman Wilson, the man who says such damning things about us, has a father who is an Anglican clergyman?

I can't imagine how the government is going to clothe and educate our young when they can't even get started on feeding or housing 22,000 removees. Yet the deadline for clearing us out seems to be July 1st or 31st—I'm not sure which. Seems to me that either there are no fifth columnists or else the Secret Service men can't find them. If the FBI in the States have rounded up a lot of them you'd think the RCMP could too and let the innocent ones alone. I wish to goodness they'd catch them all. I don't feel safe if there are any on the loose. But I like to think there aren't any.

March 20.

Dearest Nesan,

Stephen has been developing a slight limp. Dad's not sure what's wrong with the leg. He suspects that the fall he had last year never healed properly and there's some new aggravation at the hip. Stephen spends a lot of time making up tunes on the new violin Dad got him. The old one, I told you, was broken. It's lucky our houses are so close, as I can get to see the children fairly often, even with the miserable curfew.

Your friend Mina Sugimoto takes her boys to play with Stephen a fair amount but she's acting like a chicken flapping about with her head cut off since her husband left.

Last night over a hundred boys entrained for a road camp at Schreiber, Ontario. A hundred and fifty are going to another camp at Jasper. The Council (United Nisei) has been working like mad talking to the boys. The first batch of a hundred refused to go. They got arrested and imprisoned in that Immigration building. The next batch refused too and were arrested. Then on Saturday they were released on the promise that they would report back to the Pool. There was every indication they wouldn't but the Council persuaded them to keep their word. They went finally. That was a tough hurdle and the Commission cabled Ralston to come and do something.

On Thursday night, the confinees in the Hastings Park Pool came down with terrible stomach pains. Ptomaine, I gather. A wholesale company or something is contracted to feed them and there's profiteering. There are no partitions of any kind whatsoever and the people are treated worse than livestock, which at least had their own pens and special food when they were there. No plumbing of any kind. They can't take a bath. They don't even take their clothes off. Two weeks now. Lord! Can you imagine a better breeding ground for typhus? They're cold (Vancouver has a fuel shortage), they're undernourished, they're unwashed. One of the men who came out to buy food said it was pitiful the way the kids scramble for food and the slow ones go empty. God damn those politicians who brought this tragedy on us.

Dan has to report tomorrow and will most likely be told when to go and where. A day's notice at most. When will we see him again? Until all this happened I didn't realize how close a member of the family he had become. He's just like a brother to me. Nesan, I don't know what to do.

The Youth Congress protested at the ill treatment but since then the daily papers are not printing a word about us. One baby was born at the Park. Premature, I think.

If all this sounds like a bird's-eye view to you, Nesan, it's the reportage of a caged bird. I can't really see what's happening. We're like a bunch of rabbits being chased by hounds.

You remember Mr. Morii, the man who was teaching judo to the RCMP? He receives orders from the Mounties to get "a hundred to the station or else and here's a list of names." Any who are rich enough, or who are desperate about not going immediately because of family concerns, pay Morii hundreds of dollars and get placed conveniently on a committee. There are nearly two hundred on that "committee" now. Some people say he's distributing the money to needy families, but who knows?

There's a three-way split in the community—three general camps: the Morii gang, us—the Council group —and all the rest, who don't know what to do. The Council group is just a handful. It's grueling uphill work for us. Some people want to fight. Others say our only chance is to cooperate with the government. Whichever way we decide there's a terrible feeling of underlying treachery.

March 22, 1942.
Dear Diary,

I don't know if Nesan will ever see any of this. I don't know anything anymore. Things are swiftly getting worse here. Vancouver—the water, the weather, the beauty, this paradise—is filled up and overflowing with hatred now. If we stick around too long we'll all be chucked into Hastings Park. Fumi and Eiko are helping the women there and they say the crowding, the noise, the confusion is chaos. Mothers are prostrate in nervous exhaustion—the babies crying endlessly—the fathers torn from them without farewell— everyone crammed into two buildings like so many pigs—children taken out of school with no provision for future education—more and more people pouring into the Park—forbidden to step outside the barbed-wire gates and fence—the men can't even leave the building—police guards around them—some of them fight their way out to come to town to see what they can do about their families. Babies and motherless children totally stranded—their fathers taken to camp. It isn't as if this place had been bombed and *everyone* was suffering. *Then* our morale would be high because we'd be *together*.

Eiko says the women are going to be mental cases.

Rev. Kabayama and family got thrown in too. It's going to be an ugly fight to survive among us. They're making (they say) accommodation for 1,200–1,300 women and children in that little Park! Bureaucrats find it so simple on paper and it's translated willy-nilly into action—and the pure hell that results is kept "hush-hush" from the public, who are already kicking about the "luxury" given to Japs.

I'm consulting with Dad and Mark and Aya about going to Toronto. We could all stay together if we could find someone in Toronto to sponsor us. People are stranded here and there all over the B.C. interior. I want to leave this poisoned province. But Aya wants to stay in B.C. to be closer to Sam. I'm going to write to a doctor in Toronto that Dad knows.

March 27.

Dan's been arrested. The boys refused to go to Ontario. Both trainloads. So they're all arrested. Dan had a road map friends drew for him, so they suspected him of being a "spy" and now he's in the Pool.

Nisei are called "enemy aliens." Minister of War, or Defense, or something flying here to take drastic steps.

April 2, 1942.
Dearest Nesan,

If only you and Mother could come home! Dad's sick in bed. The long months of steady work. Since the evacuation started he's had no letup at all. Two nights ago, one of his patients was dying. He tried to arrange to have the daughter go to the old man's bedside but couldn't. Dad stayed up all night with the man, and now he's sick himself.

I'm afraid that those kept in Hastings Park will be held as hostages or something. Perhaps to ensure the good behavior of the men in the work camps. Dan was cleared of that idiotic spying charge and is helping at the Pool. The cop who arrested him was drunk and took a few jabs at him but Dan didn't retaliate, thank heavens. I'm applying for a pass so I can get to see him.

Dan has a lawyer working for him and his parents about their desire to stay together, especially since Dan's father is blind and his mother speaks no English at all. The lawyer went to the Security Commission's lawyers and reported back that he was told to let the matter drift because they were going to make sure the Japs suffered as much as possible. The Commission is responsible to the Federal Government through the Minister of Justice, St. Laurent. It works in conjunction with the RCMP. The Commission has three members—Austin C. Taylor, to represent the Minister of Justice, Commissioner Mead of the RCMP, John Shirras of the Provincial Police.

Only Tommy and Kunio, as active members of the Council, know what's going on and they're too busy to talk to me. The *New Canadian* comes out so seldom we have no way of knowing much and I've been so busy helping Dad I can't get to Council meetings very often. There's so much veiling and soft-pedaling because everything is censored by the RCMP. We can only get information verbally. The bulletins posted on Powell Street aren't available to most people. Besides, nobody can keep up with all the things that are happening. There's a terrible distrust of federal authorities and fear of the RCMP, but mostly there's a helpless panic. Not the hysterical kind, but the kind that churns round and round going nowhere.

My twenty-sixth birthday is coming up soon and I feel fifty. I've got lines under my eyes and my back is getting stooped, I noticed in a shopwindow today.

Mina Sugimoto heard from her husband. Why haven't we heard from Sam? Stephen asked me the other day "Where's Uncle?" What could I say?

April 8, 1942

Ye gods! The newspapers are saying that there are actually Japanese naval officers living on the coast. It must be a mistake. Maybe they're old retired men. I heard someone say it was just that they took courses when they were kids in school and that's the way schools are in Japan. I'd hate to think we couldn't tell a fisherman from a sailor. Maybe the articles are true. I wonder if there's a cover-up. Surely we'd know if there were any spies. But gosh—who can we trust? At times like this, all we have is our trust in one another. What happens when that breaks down?

A few days ago the newspaper reported Ian Mackenzie as saying, "The intention of the government is that every single Japanese—man, woman, and child—shall be removed from Vancouver as speedily as possible." He said we were all going to be out in three or four weeks and added it was his "personal intention," as long as he was in public life, "that these Japanese shall not come back here."

It's all so frightening. Rumors are that we're going to be kept as prisoners and war hostages—but that's so ridiculous since we're Canadians. There was a headline in the paper yesterday that said half of our boats "of many different kinds and sizes" have been released to the army, navy, air force, and to "bona fide white fishermen." I wonder who has Sam's beautiful little boat. It was such an ingenious design. They said they were hopeful about all the boats because one plywood boat passed all the tests. The reporter found someone he called a "real fisherman," a man from Norway who had fished all his life and used to have a 110-foot steam fishing boat when he fished off Norway and Iceland "close to home." That's one man who's profiting by our misery. He's quoted as saying, "We can do without the Japanese," but he's not loath to take our boats. Obviously white Canadians feel more loyalty toward white foreigners than they do toward us Canadians.

All this worrying is very bad for Dad. He's feeling numbness on the left side. I'm trying to keep him still but he's a terrible patient. He's very worried about

Stephen—the limp is not improving. Dad is so intense about that boy. He's also worried about Mark, says his coughing is a bad sign and he's losing weight too fast. A lot of his patients, especially the old ones, are in a state of collapse.

I haven't been to meetings of the Council lately. Too occupied with the sick ones around me. But I'm trying to keep an eye on what's happening. The Nisei who were scheduled to leave last night balked. I don't know the details. We haven't heard whether they're in the jug or the Pool or on the train. It's horrible not being able to know.

April 9.

It seems that all the people who are conscientious enough to report when they have to, law-abiding enough not to kick about their treatment—these are the ones who go first. The ones on the loose, bucking the authorities, are single men, so the married ones have to go to fill the quota. A lot of the fellows are claiming they need more time to clear up family affairs for their parents who don't understand English well enough to cope with all the problems and regulations.

I had a talk with Tommy on the phone. He said they can't do much more than they're doing without injuring a lot more people. "All we've got on our side," he said, "is time and the good faith of the Nisei." At times I get fighting mad and think that the RCMP in using Morii are trusting the wrong man— the way he collects money for favors—but in the end, I can see how complaining would just work even more against us. What can we do? No witnesses will speak up against him anymore. I'm told our letters aren't censored yet, but may be at any time.

April 11.
Dear Nesan,

Dad had a letter the other day from his friend Kawaguchi at Camp 406 in Princeton. It's cheered him up a lot. You remember Kawaguchi? His wife died a few years back. He left his kids with friends and he's asking us to see what we can do to keep Jack's education from being disrupted. He says, "I think we should always keep hope. Hope is life. Hopeless is lifeless. . . ."

This morning Dad got out of bed and went to the Pool bunkhouse for men (the former Women's Building). He was nauseated by the smell, the clouds of dust, the pitiful attempts at privacy. The Livestock Building (where the women and kids are) is worse. Plus manure smells. The straw ticks are damp and moldy. There are no fresh fruits or vegetables. He ate there to see what it was like. Supper was two slices of bologna, bread, and tea. That's all. Those who have extra money manage to get lettuce and tomatoes and fruit from outside. Nothing for babies. He's asking for improvement and so is the Council.

Dad saw Dan. He earns about two dollars a day at the Pool helping out—minus board, of course. There are a handful of others working there as well, getting from ten to twenty-five cents an hour for running errands and handling passes, etc. Dad, being a doctor, has a pass to come and go freely. The fact that he retired a few years ago because of his heart means the

Commission is not pressing him into service in the ghost towns.

We'll have to rent our houses furnished. Have to leave the chesterfield suite, stove, refrig, rugs, etc. We aren't allowed to sell our furniture. Hits the dealers somehow. I don't understand it, but so they say.

It's an awfully unwieldy business, this evacuation. There's a wanted list of over a hundred Nisei who refuse to entrain. They're being chased all over town.

April 20.

I have gone numb today. Is all this real? Where do I begin? First I got my pass and saw Dan at last. He's going to Schreiber in two days. I didn't feel a thing when he told me. It didn't register at all. Maybe I'm crazy. When I left, I didn't say goodbye either. Now that I'm home I still can't feel. He was working in the Baggage—old Horse Show Building. Showed me his pay check as something he couldn't believe—$11.75. He's been there an awfully long time.

After I saw Dan, and delivered some medicine for Dad, I saw Eiko and Fumi. Eiko is working as a steno in the Commission office there, typing all the routine forms. She sleeps in a partitioned stall—being on the staff, so to speak. The stall was the former home of a pair of stallions and boy oh boy did they leave their odor behind! The whole place is impregnated with the smell of ancient manure. Every other day it's swept with chloride of lime or something but you can't disguise horse smells, cow, sheep, pig, rabbit, and goat smells. And is it dusty! The toilets are just a sheet-metal trough and up till now they didn't have partitions or seats. The women complained, so they put in partitions and a terribly makeshift seat. Twelve-year-old boys stay with the women too. The auto show building, where the Indian exhibits were, houses the new dining room and kitchens. Seats 3,000. Looks awfully permanent. Brick stoves—eight of them—shiny new mugs—very very barracky. As for the bunks, they were the most tragic things I saw there. Steel and wooden frames at three-foot intervals with thin lumpy straw ticks, bolsters, and three army blankets of army quality—no sheets unless you brought your own. These are the "homes" of the women I saw. They wouldn't let me or any "Jap females" into the men's building. There are constables at the doors—"to prevent further propagation of the species," it said in the newspaper. The bunks were hung with sheets and blankets and clothes of every color—a regular gypsy caravan—all in a pathetic attempt at privacy—here and there I saw a child's doll or teddy bear—I saw two babies lying beside a mother who was too weary to get up—she had just thrown herself across the bed. I felt my throat thicken. I couldn't bear to look on their faces daring me to be curious or superior because I still lived outside. They're stripped of all privacy.

Some of the women were making the best of things, housecleaning around their stalls. One was scrubbing and scrubbing trying to get rid of the smell, but that wasn't possible. And then, Nesan, and then, I found Grandma Nakane there sitting like a little troll in all that crowd, with her chin on her chest. At first I couldn't believe it. She didn't recognize me. She just stared and stared. Then when I knelt down in front of her, she broke down and clung to me and cried and cried and said she'd rather have died than have come to such a place. Aya and Mark were sick when I told them. We all thought they were safe with friends in Saltspring. She has no idea of what's going on and I think she may not survive. I presumed Grandpa Nakane was in the men's area, but then I learned he was in the Sick Bay. I brought Eiko to meet Grandma but Grandma wouldn't look up. You know how yasashi Grandma is. This is too great a shock for her. She whispered to me that I should leave right away before they caught me too—then she wouldn't say any more. Nesan, maybe it's better where you are, even if they think you're an enemy.

Eiko has taken the woes of the confinees on her thin shoulders and she takes so much punishment. Fumi is worried sick about her. The place has got them both down. There are ten showers for 1,500 women. Hot and cold water. The men looked so terribly at loose ends, wandering around the grounds—sticking their noses through the fence watching the golfers. I felt so heavy I almost couldn't keep going. They are going to move the Vancouver women now and shove them into the Pool before sending them to the camps in the ghost towns.

The other day at the Pool, a visitor dropped his key before a stall in the Livestock Building, and he fished for it with a wire and brought to light manure and maggots. He called the nurse and then they moved all the bunks from the stalls and pried up the wooden floors, and it was the most stomach-turning nauseating thing. So they got fumigators and hoses and tried to wash it all away and got most of it into the drains. But maggots are still breeding and turning up here and there, so one woman with more guts than the others told the nurse (white) about it and protested. She replied, "Well, there are worms in the garden, aren't there?" This particular nurse was a Jap-hater of the most virulent sort. She called them "filthy Japs" to their faces and Fumi gave her what for and had a terrible scrap with her, saying, "What do you think we are? Are we cattle? Are we pigs?" You know how Fumi gets.

The night the first bunch of Nisei refused to go to Schreiber the women and children at the Pool milled around in front of their cage, and one very handsome Mountie came with his truncheon and started to hit them and yelled at them to "get the hell back in there." Eiko's blood boiled over. She strode over to him and shouted, "You put that stick down. What do you think you're doing? Do you think these women and children are cows, that you can beat them back?" Eiko was shaking. She's taken it on herself to fight and now she's on the blacklist and reputed to be a trouble-maker. It's people like us, Nesan—Eiko and Tommy and Dan and Fumi and the rest of us who have had faith in Canada, who have been more politically minded than the others—who are the most hurt. At one time, remember how I almost worshipped the Mounties? Remember the Curwood tales of the Northwest, and the Royal Canadian Mounted Police and how I'd go around saying their motto—*Maintiens le droit*—Maintain the right?

The other day there were a lot of people lined up on Heather Street to register at RCMP headquarters and so frightened by what was going on and afraid of the uniforms. You could feel their terror. I was going around telling them not to worry—the RCMP were our protectors and upholders of the law, etc. And there was this one officer tramping up and down that perfectly quiet line of people, holding his riding crop like a switch in his hand, smacking the palm of his other hand regularly—whack whack—as if he would just have loved to hit someone with it if they even so much as spoke or moved out of line. The glory of the Redcoats.

April 25.
Dearest Nesan,

Mark has gone.

The last night I spent with him and Aya and kids, he played the piano all night. He's terribly thin. Dad has been too ill to see him but he says Mark should not be going to the camps.

Is it true, Nesan, that you were pregnant just before you left? Mark said he wasn't sure. Oh, is there no way we can hear from you? I'm worried about the children. Nomi almost never talks or smiles. She is always carrying the doll you gave her and sleeps with it every night. I think, even though she doesn't talk, that she's quite bright. When I read to her from the picture books, I swear she's following the words with her eyes. Stephen spends his time reading war comics that he gets from the neighborhood boys. All the Japs have mustard-colored faces and buck teeth.

.   .   .

April 28.

We had our third letter from Sam—rather Aya did. All cards and letters are censored—even to the Nisei camps. Not a word from the camps makes the papers. Everything is hushed up. I haven't been to meetings for so long now that I don't know what's going on. Sam's camp is eight miles from the station, up in the hills. Men at the first camps all crowd down to the station every time a train passes with a new batch of men. They hang from the windows and ask about their families. Sam said he wept.

The men are luckier than the women. It's true they are forced to work on the roads, but at least they're fed, and they have no children to look after. Of course, the fathers are worried but it's the women who are burdened with all the responsibility of keeping what's left of the family together.

Mina Sugimoto is so hysterical. She heard about a place in Revelstoke, got word to her husband, and he came to see her on a two-day pass. She wanted them to go to Revelstoke together but of course that wasn't possible. He wasn't able to make it back to road camp in the time limit, so now they're threatening to intern him. In the meantime, Mina has gone off to Revelstoke, bag, baggage, and boys. I'll try to find out what happens to them for you, Nesan.

Eiko has heard that the town of Greenwood is worse than the Pool. They're propping up old shacks near the mine shaft. On top of that, local people are complaining and the United Church parson there says to "kick all the Japs out."

Eiko, Fumi, and I have gotten to be so profane

that Tom and the rest have given up being surprised. Eiko says, "What the hell," and Fumi is even worse.

What a mess everything is. Some Nisei are out to save their own skins, others won't fight for any rights at all. The RCMP are happy to let us argue among ourselves. Those of us who are really conscientious and loyal—how will we ever get a chance to prove ourselves to this country? All we are fighting for inch by inch just goes down the drain. There are over 140 Nisei loose and many Japanese nationals (citizens of Japan). The Commission thinks the nationals are cleared out of Vancouver, but oh boy, there are a lot of them who have greased enough palms and are let alone.

April 30.

We got another extension and are trying to get a place here in B.C. somewhere—somewhere on a farm with some fruit trees. We may have to go to some town in Alberta or Saskatchewan or Manitoba. I have to do some fast work, contacting all the people I think could help in some way. Dad doesn't want to leave B.C. If we go too far, we may not be able to come back. With you in Japan and Mark in Camp, Dad feels we should stay with the kids—but everybody has the same worry about their kids.

Stephen's leg was put in a cast. Dad thinks that rest will heal it. He says Grandma Nakane's mind is failing fast. She didn't speak to him when he was there today. He thought she'd be all right if she could see Grandpa Nakane but he wasn't able to arrange it.

Dad's worried about both of them. I'm trying to get them out of there but the red tape is so fierce.

May 1.

I have to work fast. The Commission put out a notice—everyone has to be ready for 24-hour notice. No more extensions. Everything piled on at once. We're trying to get into a farm or house around Salmon Arm or Chase or some other decent town in the interior—anywhere that is livable and will still let us in. Need a place with a reasonable climate. Some place where we can have a garden to grow enough vegetables for a year. Somewhere there's a school if possible. If there's nothing in B.C., I think we should go east and take our chances in Toronto. Fumi and Eiko and I want to stick together.

Monday, May 4.

Got to get out in the next couple of weeks. Dad's had a relapse. The numbness is spreading. He doesn't think it's his heart.

There's another prospect. McGillivray Falls, twenty miles from Lillooet. Going there would eat up our savings since that's all we'd have to live on but at least it's close to Vancouver and just a few hours to get back. There's no school. I'd have to teach the children.

It's because so many towns have barred their doors that we are having such a heck of a time. The Commission made it clear to us that they would not permit us to go anywhere the City Councils didn't want us. Individuals who offer to help have to write letters saying they undertake to see that we won't be a burden on the public. Who among us wants to be a burden on anyone? It'd be better if, instead of writing letters to help one or two of us, they'd try to persuade their City Councils to let us in. After all, we're Canadians.

Eiko and her mother might go to a ghost town to be closer to her father. Also most likely she'll have to teach grade school. The pay is two dollars a day, out of which she'd have to feed and clothe the four younger kids and try to keep them in a semblance of health. Honest, Nesan, I wonder if the whites think we are a special kind of low animal able to live on next to nothing—able to survive without clothing, shoes, medicine, decent food.

Aya just phoned that there's no electricity at McGillivray. What does one do without electricity? There are so many complex angles in this business my head aches.

Another thing that's bothering Aya is the cost of transportation and freight. We can take only our clothes, bedding, pots and pans, and dishes. We've sold our dining-room suite and piano. Mark didn't sell anything. Aya's house was looted. I haven't told her. It's in such an out-of-the-way place. When I took the interurban on Friday to see if the dog might have shown up, I was shocked. Almost all the hand-carved furnishings were gone—all the ornaments—just the dead plants left and some broken china on the floor. I saw one of the soup bowls from the set I gave them. The looting was thorough. The collection of old instruments Mark talked about was gone too and the scrolls. No one will understand the value of these things. I don't have the heart to tell Aya.

We're all walking around in a daze. It's really too late to do anything. If we go to the ghost towns, it's going to be one hell of a life. Waiting in line to wash, cook, bathe . . .

I've got to go to sleep. And I've got to pack. If we go to McGillivray, Fumi, Eiko, and family are coming with us. We have to go in a week or two. The Commission won't wait.

May 5.
Dearest Nesan,

We've heard from Mark. Crazy man. All he thinks about are Stephen's music lessons. He sent two pages of exercises and a melody which he thought up. He wrote about some flowers he found which he stuck on the end of his pick and says he thinks about you as he works. I read the letter three times to Dad. Dad says Stephen's health is more important than his music right now. Nomi is fine. She's so silent, though. I've never seen such a serious child before.

I got a letter from Dan as well. His address is Mileage 101, Camp SW 5-3, Jackfish, Ontario.

We've had three different offers since yesterday. Mickey Maikawa wants us to go to his wife's brother's farm in Sicamous. We're considering it. Everything is confusion and bewilderment.

Eiko has heard awful things about the crowding and lack of sanitation in the ghost towns. People have been freezing in tents. She's dead set against them now. She and Fumi and I are still trying to stick together. But you never know when we'll have to go, or which way our luck's going to jump. Every day's a different story, from nowhere to go to several choices. I want to go east. Rent at McG. Falls was reduced to $80 per year.

May 14.
Dear Nesan,

Aya, kids, Dad, and I have decided to go to Slocan. We hear that's one of the best of the ghost towns. It used to have a silver mine, or maybe a gold mine—I'm not sure. There are just abandoned old hotels there now and a few stores. I don't know the size of the white population but it's not very large.

The family—or what's left of it—intends to stick together one way or another, and after days and nights of discussion, chasing this elusive hope or that, worrying, figuring, going bats with indecision, with one door after another closing, then opening again—we finally realize the only thing to do is give in and stay together wherever we go, and moving to Slocan is the easiest.

Rev. Nakayama, who's already in Slocan, wrote and told me about a small house that Dad and I can have to ourselves, close to the mountains and away from the crowding. It makes all the difference. I'm so glad I thought to ask him for help. We'll be able to manage something for the kids—build an addition if we have to.

Now that the decision is taken, I don't want to be upset all over again. I don't want to go through all the hopes and the uncertainty of trying to find a loophole to escape from. I'm resigned to Slocan—and anyway, Rev. Nakayama says it's a nice place. It even has a soda fountain. So I'll settle for that until they say it's okay for us to join Mark and Sam and Dan again somewhere. Grandma and Grandpa Nakane have orders to go to New Denver. We've tried everything, I've cried my cry, I've said goodbye to this home. All fluttering for escape has died down. Just wish us luck, Nesan. We'll wait until that happy day when we can all be together again.

Now I must get to serious packing and selling and giving away and the same thing at your house.

I asked too much of God.

May 15, Friday.
There's too much to do. Dad's unable to help though he tries. After we get to Slocan things should calm down. The furor will die down when there are none of us left on the coast. Then we can discuss moving to Ontario. It's time that defeated us for the present but we won't give up yet. Not by a long shot.

Dan's new address—Dalton Mills, c/o Austin Lumber Co., Dalton, Ontario.

We got a letter today from the doctor in Toronto offering us the top floor of his house. That would be wonderful, but heck! how I'd hate to impose on anyone. Imagine being dependent like that. I think it was fated for me to taste the dregs of this humiliation that I might know just what it is that all the women and children are enduring through no fault of their own.

Once we're in Slocan, chances of going east are

better than here. The officials are terribly harassed
with the whole thing and exasperated with individual
demands for attention. So, Slocan City, here we come.

Goodness, I think I'll keep my golf clubs.

May 18, 1942.

Dear Nesan,

It's flabbergasting. I can't believe any of it. Here's
what happened.

I was all packed for Slocan and Dad was reason-
ably okay. In the middle of helping Aya, I thought—
just as a last gesture and more for my own assurance
than out of any hope—that I'd write to Grant Mac-
Neil, secretary of the Commission. So I wrote asking
for written assurance that I could continue negotia-
tions from Slocan about going to Toronto. That's all.
Just the word that there was hope for us all to get to
Ontario. No further aspirations. I was too tired to
start all over again anyway. Mailed the letter around
noon from the main post office on Friday. A little after
three o'clock, Mrs. Booth, who works there, phoned to
say that they'd got the letter and I was to come right
away. I couldn't believe it. I dropped everything and
ran. Mrs. Booth, speaking for Mr. MacNeil, said they
were not giving any special permits but they'd make
this one exception and told me to return next day with
bank accounts, references, etc. I was so excited and
happy, I assumed that included Dad and Aya and the
kids. Next day, Mrs. Booth said the permit was only
for the Kato family. One family only. I told her Stephen and Nomi are my sister's kids but she said some-

thing about Commission rulings and their name is Nakane and then she asked about the Nakane family and I had to say they were nationals and I think that settled it. But she said she would look into the business of the kids. I was so frustrated not having Mark or Dad or Aya to confer with. It seemed to me at that point that I should opt for Toronto with Dad and then negotiate having everyone else come to join us.

Do you think I did the right thing, Nesan? Eiko says I did and that we should try to keep as many out of the ghost towns as possible. So I went back and told Dad and he didn't say anything one way or the other. Just kept nodding his head.

When I discussed it with Aya, she was adamant about the kids. She says you entrusted them to her and they're her kids now until you return and she won't part with them. It's true they're more used to her than to either me or Dad. And as for being so far away, Aya says ten miles or ten thousand miles makes no difference to a child.

The whole point of all our extensions was to find a way to keep together, but now at the last minute everything has exploded. Aya is being very calm and she doesn't want any discussion in front of the kids. All she's told them is that they're going for a train ride.

Fumi is resigned to not coming with us. Eiko's mother wants to go to Slocan, but I can tell Eiko wants out. I don't know what Fumi is going to do now. I think she's going to Kaslo with Rev. Shimizu's group.

I'm going to the Custodian tomorrow and then to the Commission again. Maybe the permit won't be given at the last minute. What if I transfer the Slocan papers to someone else and then don't get the Toronto permit? There could be trouble with all these forms and deferments.

Well, I'm going to go ahead, repack everything and hope. The mover, Crone, is sending our boxed goods, beds, and Japanese food supplies—shoyu, rice, canned mirinzuke, green tea. I'm taking the Japanese dishes, trays, and bowls. Can't get any more miso now.

I'll just have to live on hope that Aya and the kids will be all right till we can get them to Toronto. I tell myself that at least they'll have their own place till then.

What will it be like, I wonder, in the doctor's house? I'll wire them as soon as I get the permit and we'll head their way for the time being. Do we eat with the family? First thing I'll do when I get to Toronto is go out *at night*.

In Petawawa there are 130 Nisei interned for rioting and crying "Banzai," shaving their heads and carrying "hino-maru" flags. Damn fools.

May 21.

Dearest Nesan,

Aya and kids are leaving with others bound for Slocan tomorrow. RCMP came in person to order Kunio off to camp. Rev. Shimizu and Rev. Akagawa had to leave immediately.

Yesterday I worked so hard—tied, labeled, ran to Commission, ran to bank, to Crone movers, to CPR, washed and cooked and scrubbed. Dad is saying goodbye to the kids now. They're spending the night in the church hall at Kitsilano. I'm going over there too as soon as I pack this last item.

Merry Christmas, Nesan.

This is the last word in the journal. The following day, May 22, 1942, Stephen, Aya Obasan, and I are on a train for Slocan. It is twelve years before we see Aunt Emily again.

15

I am sometimes not certain whether it is a cluttered attic in which I sit, a waiting room, a tunnel, a train. There is no beginning and no end to the forest, or the dust storm, no edge from which to know where the clearing begins. Here, in this familiar density, beneath this cloak, within this carapace, is the longing within the darkness.

1942.

We are leaving the B.C. coast—rain, cloud, mist—an air overladen with weeping. Behind us lies a salty sea within which swim our drowning specks of memory—our small waterlogged eulogies. We are going down to the middle of the earth with pickax eyes, tunneling by train to the interior, carried along by the momentum of the expulsion into the waiting wilderness.

We are hammers and chisels in the hands of would-be sculptors, battering the spirit of the sleeping mountain. We are the chips and sand, the fragments of fragments that fly like arrows from the heart of the rock. We are the silences that speak from stone. We are the despised rendered voiceless, stripped of car, radio, camera, and every means of communication, a trainload of eyes covered with mud and spittle. We are the man in the Gospel of John, born into the world for the sake of the light. We are sent to Siloam, the pool called "Sent." We are sent to the sending, that we may bring sight. We are the scholarly and the illiterate, the envied and the ugly, the fierce and the docile. We are those pioneers who cleared the bush and the forest with our hands, the gardeners tending and attending the soil with our tenderness, the fishermen who are flung from the sea to flounder in the dust of the prairies.

We are the Issei and the Nisei and the Sansei, the Japanese Canadians. We disappear into the future undemanding as dew.

The memories are dream images. A pile of luggage in a large hall. Missionaries at the railway station handing out packages of toys. Stephen being carried on board the train, a white cast up to his thigh.

It is three decades ago and I am a small child resting my head in Obasan's lap. I am wearing a wine-colored dirndl skirt with straps that crisscross at the back. My white silk blouse has a Peter Pan collar dotted with tiny red flowers. I have a wine-colored sweater with ivory duck buttons.

Stephen sits sideways on a seat by himself opposite us, his huge white leg like a cocoon.

The train is full of strangers. But even strangers are addressed as "Ojisan" or "Obasan," meaning Uncle or Aunt. Not one uncle or aunt, grandfather or grandmother, brother or sister, not one of us on this journey returns home again.

The train smells of oil and soot and orange peels and lurches groggily as we rock our way inland. Along the window ledge, the black soot leaps and settles like insects. Underfoot and in the aisles and beside us on the seats we are surrounded by odd bits of luggage—bags, lunch baskets, blankets, pillows. My red umbrella with its knobby clear red handle sticks out of a box like the head of an exotic bird. In the seat behind us is a boy in short gray pants and jacket carrying a wooden slatted box with a tabby kitten inside. He is trying to distract the kitten with his finger but the kitten mews and mews, its mouth opening and closing. I can barely hear its high steady cry in the clackity-clack and steamy hiss of the train.

A few seats in front, one young woman is sitting with her narrow shoulders hunched over a tiny red-faced baby. Her short black hair falls into her birdlike face. She is so young, I would call her "o-nesan," older sister.

The woman in the aisle seat opposite us leans over and whispers to Obasan with a solemn nodding of her head and a flicker of her eyes indicating the young woman.

Obasan moves her head slowly and gravely in a nod as she listens. "Kawaiso," she says under her breath. The word is used whenever there is hurt and a need for tenderness.

The young mother, Kuniko-san, came from Saltspring Island, the woman says. Kuniko-san was rushed onto the train from Hastings Park, a few days after giving birth prematurely to her baby.

"She has nothing," the woman whispers. "Not even diapers."

Aya Obasan does not respond as she looks steadily at the dirt-covered floor. I lean out into the aisle and I can see the baby's tiny fist curled tight against its wrinkled face. Its eyes are closed and its mouth is squinched small as a button. Kuniko-san does not lift her eyes at all.

"Kawai," I whisper to Obasan, meaning that the baby is cute.

Obasan hands me an orange from a wicker basket and gestures toward Kuniko-san, indicating that I should take her the gift. But I pull back.

"For the baby," Obasan says, urging me.

I withdraw farther into my seat. She shakes open a furoshiki—a square cloth that is used to carry things by tying the corners together—and places a towel and some apples and oranges in it. I watch her lurching from side to side as she walks toward Kuniko-san.

Clutching the top of Kuniko-san's seat with one hand, Obasan bows and holds the furoshiki out to her. Kuniko-san clutches the baby against her breast and bows forward twice while accepting Obasan's gift without looking up.

As Obasan returns toward us, the old woman in the seat diagonal to ours beckons to me, nodding her head, urging me to come to her, her hand gesturing downward in a digging waving motion. I lean toward her.

"A baby was born," the old woman says. "Is this not so?"
I nod.

The old woman bumps herself forward and off the seat. Her back is round as a church bell. She is so short that when she is standing she is lower than when she was sitting. She braces herself against the seat and bends forward.

"There is nothing to offer," she says as Obasan reaches

her. She lifts her skirt and begins to remove a white flannel underskirt, her hand gathering the undergarment in pleats.

"Ah, no no, Grandmother," Obasan says.

"Last night it was washed. It is nothing, but it is clean."

Obasan supports her in the rock rock of the train and they sway together back and forth. The old woman steps out of the garment, being careful not to let it touch the floor.

"Please—if it is acceptable. For a diaper. There is nothing to offer," the old woman says as she hoists herself onto the seat again. She folds the undergarment into a neat square, the fingers of her hand stiff and curled as driftwood. Obasan bows, accepting the cloth, and returns to Kuniko-san and her baby, placing the piece of flannel on Kuniko-san's lap. Both their heads are bobbing like birds as they talk. Sometimes Kuniko-san bows so deeply, her baby touches her lap.

Leaning out into the aisle I can see better, and the old grandmother nods, urging me to go to them. Kuniko-san is wiping her eyes in the baby's blanket, revealing the baby's damp black hair.

The baby doll I have brought has a hard lumpy brown wave for hair on the top of its hard head. I hold it on the train's window ledge on its buttocks and short bow legs in its pajamas and blue wool hat.

Another doll I have brought is a Japanese child doll my mother gave me before she went to Japan. It was meant to be mostly ornamental and has an ageless elegant face—tiny red bow lips open slightly in a two-toothed smile, clear exact eyes with black pupils in the center of the dark brown irises, tiny pinprick nostrils. Its hair, like mine, is a stiff black frame, the bangs a straight brush across the forehead. The right hand is a round fist with a hole in the middle. She carries a stick with a colorful box at the end and two threads with beads. Sometimes I replace the stick with a curved green wire branch on which are clustered tiny hard red lacquered dots for cherries and delicate five-petaled paper flowers. The red flowered ki-mono, which is not for removal, has been removed and the doll is no longer pristine and decorative. The legs, though wired in place, are dislocated and she cannot stand on her own. The fingers of her left hand are broken. Obasan sug-gested I take another but she is my favorite doll. She wears an oversized orange print dress from one of the other dolls in the kitchen bin, plus a coat. I stand her up to look out of the window at the passing scenery. Her feet clack against the pane.

"See," I whisper to her.

The doll does not respond. If she understands, she nods or she bows full tilt, but if she is unsure, her feet clack irrita-bly.

Stephen is scowling as Obasan returns and offers him a rice ball. "Not that kind of food," he says. Stephen, half in and half out of his shell, is Humpty Dumpty—cracked and surly and unable to move.

I have seen Obasan at home sometimes take a single grain of cooked rice and squash it on paper, using it for paste to seal parcels or envelopes. If I could take all the cooked rice in all the rice pots in the world, dump them into a heap, and tromp all the bits to glue with my feet, there would be enough to stick anything, even Humpty Dumpty, together again.

Unlike Stephen, the doll is quite happy and secretly ex-cited about the train trip.

"Want that?" she asks Stephen, looking at him with her bright almond eyes and pointing to a sandwich.

Stephen ignores her and stares at the treetops zipping past the window.

"Humpty Dumpty sat on a wall," she says to herself. "Humpty Dumpty had a great fall. . . ."

Getting no response from Stephen, I turn to my other toys—the red, white, and blue ball, the Mickey Mouse with movable legs which can rock and walk by itself down an incline, the two chicks from the sewing-machine cabinet, a metal cicada which can be squeezed to make a "click click" sound.

Stephen ignores everything and stares out the window at the changing shapes of sky. In a fit of generosity I take my ball and give it to Stephen. "You can keep it," I say solemnly. "It's yours." I put it in his jacket pocket, where it forms a fist-size lump.

The train moves in and out of tunnels, along narrow ridges that edge the canyon walls, through a toothpick forest of trees. Eventually the doll grows sleepy and falls asleep in the blanket that Obasan has arranged on her lap. Obasan's hand taps my back rhythmically and her smooth oval face is calm.

16

Twenty years later, in 1962, Aunt Emily wanted to take a trip through the interior of British Columbia. Off we went—Uncle, Aunt Emily, Obasan, and I—through Banff, down the Rogers Pass, through Golden, and Revelstoke, Uncle pointing out a small side road which he said was the place his work camp had been. I drove through what was left of some of the ghost towns, filled and emptied once by prospectors, filled and emptied a second time by the Japanese Canadians. The first ghosts were still there, the miners, people of the woods, their white bones deep beneath the pine-needle floor, their flesh turned to earth, turned to air. Their buildings—hotels, abandoned mines, log cabins—still stood marking their stay. But what of the second wave? What remains of our time there?

We looked for the evidence of our having been in Bayfarm, in Lemon Creek, in Popoff. Bayfarm and Popoff were farmlands in Slocan before the tar-paper huts sprang up. Lemon Creek was a camp seven miles away carved out of the wilderness. Tashme—formed from the names of Taylor, Shirras, and Mead, men on the B.C. Security Commission—also rose overnight, fourteen miles from Hope, and as quickly disappeared. Where on the map or on the road was there any sign? Not a mark was left. All our huts had been removed long before and the forest had returned to take over the clearings. What remained the same was the smell of pine and cedar. The mountains too were unchanged except for the evidence of new roads and a larger logging industry. While we stood there in Slocan, we could hear the wavering hoot of a train whistle as we used to years before. But the Slocan that we knew in the forties was no longer there, except for the small white community which had existed before we arrived and which watched us come with a mixture of curiosity and fear. Now, down on the shore of Slocan Lake, on the most beautiful part of the sandy beach, where we used to swim, there was a large new sawmill owned by someone who lived in New York.

We left Slocan and drove toward Sandon. The steep one-vehicle road dropped at such a perilous and tortuous slope, I turned around the first chance I could get. What a hole!

"It was an evacuation all right," Aunt Emily said. "Just plopped here in the wilderness. Flushed out of Vancouver. Like dung drops. Maggot bait."

None of us, she said, escaped the naming. We were defined and identified by the way we were seen. A newspaper in B.C. headlined: "They are a stench in the nostrils of the people of Canada." We were therefore relegated to the cesspools. In Sandon, Tashme, Kaslo, Greenwood, Slocan, Bayfarm, Pop-off, Lemon Creek, New Denver, we lived in tents, in bunks, in skating rinks, in abandoned hotels. Most of us lived in row upon row of two-family, three-room huts, controlled and orderly as wooden blocks. There was a tidy mind somewhere.

Some families who had gone ahead or independently had been able to find empty farmhouses to rent. In Slocan, several families lived in an abandoned bunkhouse at an old silver mine. Our own house was just a two-room log hut at the base of the mountain. It was shabby and sagging and overgrown with weeds when we first saw it on that spring day in 1942.

"Thank you, thank you," Obasan says to a man, an ojisan in a gray cap who reaches up and puts an arm around Stephen hesitating at the top of the train steps. I pick up Stephen's crutches and follow him as he is carried through the slow crowd of boxes and bodies. People are bustling about on the wooden platform in groups, carrying luggage here and there. Even in all this crowd, there is a stillness here. The sudden fresh air, touched with the familiar smell of sawdust, is crisp and private. Yet there is a feeling of open space. Through a break in the crowd, I can see a lake with a sandy beach and drift logs. All around its edge are mountains covered in trees, climbing skyward. The highest, farthest mountains are blue and purple and topped with white snow.

I am holding Obasan's hand and looking around when I hear Stephen say, "Hello, Sensei." Sensei is the word for teacher. I look up and recognize Nakayama-sensei, the round-faced minister with round eyes and round glasses from the Anglican church in Vancouver. He is talking to Obasan and to the man who helped Stephen. The boy carrying the kitten is holding the hand of a woman in a blue dress who is waiting to speak to Nakayama-sensei.

"It is not so far," Sensei says to Obasan. "I will show you the way." He turns to the woman in blue and nods gravely, says a few words to the ojisan and to a missionary, then disappears into the crowd.

Except for Stephen on his crutches, we all carry bags, furoshiki, suitcases, boxes and follow Ojisan down the middle of the road, past the gaunt hotels swarming with people, like ants in an overturned anthill. Ojisan puts down his heavy box and we wait till he returns with a homemade wheelbarrow.

"Ah, joto, joto," Nakayama-sensei says, rejoining us, "excellent, excellent."

We arrange our luggage and follow Nakayama-sensei and Ojisan down the street again, turning to the left past a building with the sign "Graham's General Store," and we walk up the flat gravel road through the valley to the mountain's foot. There are no streetcars here, no sidewalks or large buildings. On either side of the road are a few houses, smaller than the ones in Vancouver.

As we pass a wooden bridge over a creek, I think of the curved bridge over the goldfish pond at Obasan's house, and the bridges Stephen and I made in the sand to the desolate sound of the sea, and the huge Lions' Gate Bridge in Stanley Park, and the terrifying Capilano swinging bridge that trembled as we crossed it high up in the dangerous air.

Perhaps it is because I first missed my doll while standing on this bridge that often in the evenings, when I cross it, I feel a certain sadness.

Obasan, carrying a large furoshiki, waits for me as I linger looking down at the water burbling over the stones and a crow hopping on the bank.

"Where is my doll?" I ask, calling to her. I am not carrying anything since putting the bag of food and the furoshiki I was given onto Ojisan's pile.

Obasan looks startled and utters that short sharp word of alarm.

"Ara!"

She puts down her furoshiki and opens it, then calls to Ojisan.

He and Obasan examine the boxes on the wheelbarrow, lifting them off one by one.

"Ojisan will find your doll," he says heartily as I reach them. He squats down and faces me.

"The others are in the bin in the kitchen," I tell him.

His round face, crinkly with laugh lines, bounces like a ball. I do not doubt that he will bring them all. He slaps his knees as if the deed is already accomplished.

Stephen, on his crutches, has disappeared ahead of the rest of us. The mountain, immediate and immense as night, swallows us as we turn onto a path into a clump of trees.

"Stephen! Wait!" I call, running to catch up with him.

I find him and Sensei peering into the woods. There is nothing to be seen except trees, trees, and trees. The ground under our feet is soft and bumpy with needles, moss, pinecones, and small acorn hats. On either side of the path, green fronds of ferns are everywhere, open and extravagant as peacocks.

"See that, Nomi?" Stephen says, pointing. I can see nothing and everything, a forest of shadows and green shapes. "Over there," he says impatiently.

We walk a few steps farther down the path, and there, almost hidden from sight off the path, is a small gray hut with a broken porch camouflaged by shrubbery and trees. The color of the house is that of sand and earth. It seems more like a giant toadstool than a building. The mortar between the logs is crumbling and the porch roof dives down in the middle. A "V" for victory. From the road, the house is invisible, and the path to it is overgrown with weeds.

"That's our house," Stephen says. "Sensei told me."

We wade through the weeds to the few gray fence posts still standing beside a gate flat on the ground, anchored to the earth by a web of vines. Behind the house, the mountain lurches skyward above a vertical rock wall. When I look up the side of the mountain, above the gray rock, to the left, there is a thin stream of water falling straight down a gray rock wall.

Stephen clumps up the porch steps and pushes his way in the front door. It scrapes along the floor. I stand at the broken gate waiting, then follow him, crossing the rickety porch step. The pine-green outside air changes suddenly to the odor of attic gray. Everything is gray—the newspapered walls, the raw gray planks on the floors, the two windows meshed by twigs and stems and stalks of tall grasses seeking a way in. A rough plank bed is in the middle of the room. Grayness seeps through the walls and surrounds us. "See that?" Stephen says, pointing to the ceiling, which is an uneven matted mass of fibers. "That's grass and manure up there."

"What?"

"Sure. Cow manure."

"Says who?"

He shrugs his shoulders.

The ceiling is so low it reminds me of the house of the seven dwarfs. The newspapers lining the walls bend and curl, showing rough wood beneath. Rusted nails protrude from the walls. A hornet crawls along the ledge of a window. Although it is not dark or cool, it feels underground.

There is no expression on Obasan's face as she comes in following Nakayama-sensei and Ojisan. The room is crowded with the three adults, the suitcases, boxes, Stephen, and me.

Obasan takes a handkerchief from her sleeve and offers it to Ojisan. "Such heavy things," she says. "You must be weary."

"Ah," Ojisan says, "when one is almost fifty."

"Chairs just to fit," Sensei says, pulling up the wooden boxes. "A small house for small people."

Ojisan reaches up to touch the ceiling. "Short people lived here, the same as we are."

"So it seems." Sensei sighs.

Obasan sits beside me on the edge of the bed.

"Together," Sensei says, "by helping each other . . ." It sounds half like a rallying call, half like an apology as if he is somehow responsible.

"As long as we have life and breath," Ojisan says.

"That is indeed so," Sensei repeats, "while we breathe, we have gratitude." It is comforting to hear them talking calmly.

"For our life and that we are together again, thank you. For protection thus far, thank you. . . ." Nakayama-sensei is praying with his eyes open.

I follow Stephen into the other room. A rusty wood stove is against one wall. Stephen is poking at a bolt on the back door and pushes it back finally with the edge of his crutch. The rusty screen door opens with a scrape and shuts with a dusty clap as Stephen and I go outside.

Ah! The green air once more.

As we stand here looking over an overgrown tangle of weeds and vines, the air is suddenly swarming with butterflies. Up and down like drunken dancers, the gold-and-brown-winged things come down the side of the mountain fluttering awkwardly. There are dozens of them. Some park like tiny helicopters on grass stalks, flexing their wings as if for takeoff. Others hover near the ground before spilling back up into the air, ungainly as baby ballerinas. They are all dressed in the same velvet brown.

Stephen whacks his crutch into the grasses, scattering the butterflies. Each wing bears two round circles of gold, and when the pairs are spread, they are infant eyes, staring up at us bodiless and unblinking. I stare back as Stephen tramples and slashes, hopping deeper and deeper into the tall grasses, swinging his crutch like a scythe. Within moments, the ground and grasses are quivering with maimed and dismembered butterflies. The ones that are safe are airborne and a few have reached the heights of trees.

"They're bad," Stephen says as he wades through the weeds. "They eat holes in your clothes."

His crutch clears a wide path through the middle of the backyard as he continues his crusade. When he reaches the end of the yard, he turns around. Some brambles and vines are clinging to his pant leg and one butterfly he cannot see is hovering above his head.

17

Morning arrives and the next and the next and we are still here in the house in the woods. The grayness has rapidly become less gray. On a kitchen table is an oilcloth with a bold orange design and tiny daisies and blue flowers. Around it are wooden benches with box shelves beneath. The windows are covered with bright flowered curtains.

Stephen and I sleep on small bunk beds in the pantry. Aya Obasan shares the other room with Nomura-obasan, an elderly invalid with a long hollow face. Her mouth, when she talks, makes small munching sounds and is far down on her chin. She looks, it seems to me, like a camel. Several times a day, Nomura-obasan uses a bedpan, which Obasan empties in the outhouse.

One afternoon, when Obasan has donned her white brimmed hat and gone through the woods to Slocan for groceries, Nomura-obasan calls me urgently, her hand beckoning.

"Chotto chotto, Naomi-chan."

It is clear she needs the bedpan.

"Where is it, Stephen?" I ask. Stephen is sitting on the kitchen floor sorting the records for the cameraphone—the portable antique record player Father bought for us just before he left.

"Don't know," Stephen says crossly. With his cast stuck out in front of him, he is not about to hop up and help me find it. I search under the bed, under the kitchen stove, outside the back door, on the wooden stool that has a round washtub on it, outside by the wood pile and around the block used for chopping kindling. The bedpan is nowhere.

When I come back in the house, Nomura-obasan is standing holding the kitchen table with both hands, her stick legs strange and naked under her loose nemaki. Somehow, when lying down, she seemed to be an enormous person with a large blanket-and-bed body, like one of my ornamental dolls in Vancouver—a bodiless head glued onto a cotton-filled quilt. Upright, she is like a plucked bird.

She beckons to me and leans heavily as I help her outside and onto the path to the outhouse that stands between two trees beside the compost pile. She lets go of my shoulders as she reaches the wooden bench with the round hole in the middle.

The first time I saw the outhouse, I didn't know the bench was for sitting on and clambered up to squat the way one does on the ground. Nomura-obasan shuffles into place and makes short gasping groans.

"Ah," she says as she pushes her camel mouth even lower into her chin. I would like to wait outside but one hand grips my shoulder.

Why, I wonder, does she take so long, her chest jumping as she breathes in short jerky gasps? I visit this place as little as possible, with its horrid smell of lye and dung and its spiders around the vent and the hornets that sometimes get trapped in here. There is a small hand broom in the corner that Obasan uses to kill the insects and clean the floor.

At last Nomura-obasan reaches for the toilet paper and, leaning on my arm again, she stands up. I don't turn back to secure the door shut with the wooden bolt, but leave it swung open.

Obasan, carrying her black knit bag full of groceries, sees us inching our way to the house.

"Ara," Obasan calls in alarm, and hurries over to assist.

Nomura-obasan sinks onto Obasan's shoulders and sighs deeply. I go ahead and open the back door. The song from the record player is speeding up. Stephen must be cranking it with the miniature handle. He stares briefly as we come in, then turns back to the cameraphone, a rectangular wooden box about half the size of a loaf of bread. When it is open as it is now, the lid hinges back. In the lid is a metal slot for a steel leg assembly with an ostrich-egg-size celluloid loudspeaker on one end and, on the other end, a flat round head with a needle, like a beak on a strange metal bird.

Stephen hunches forward as if to shield his treasure from our presence.

"Such posture," Obasan says in a chiding voice to Stephen. "Tiredness is the cause," she apologizes to Nomura-obasan.

"Muri mo nai," Nomura-obasan replies. "It's no wonder. Without even a school . . ."

"Yes. Someday perhaps . . ," Obasan says.

Stephen cranks the machine again and puts on the same record he's been playing for days. "Silver Threads Among the Gold." All the records are Mother's favorites: "Believe Me If All Those Endearing Young Charms," "Lead, Kindly Light," "Humoresque," "Barcarole." On each label, Stephen has printed "Property of Mrs. K. Nakane. Handle with Care."

Obasan draws the covers over Nomura-obasan's shoulders. "It was a great strain, was it not?" she says. "Please rest."

Nomura-obasan sighs contentedly and listens to the nasal-voiced man on the record singing *"Darling, I am growing old, silver threads among the gold. . . ."*

It does not occur to me to wonder why Mother would have liked this song. We do not have silver threads among the gold.

In one of Stephen's books, there is a story of a child with long golden ringlets called Goldilocks who one day comes to a quaint house in the woods lived in by a family of bears. Clearly, we are that bear family in this strange house in the middle of the woods. I am Baby Bear, whose chair Goldilocks breaks, whose porridge Goldilocks eats, whose bed Goldilocks sleeps in. Or perhaps this is not true and I am really Goldilocks after all. In the morning, will I not find my way out of the forest and back to my room where the picture bird sings above my bed and the real bird sings in the real peach tree by my open bedroom window in Marpole?

No matter how I wish it, we do not go home. Ojisan does not bring my doll and I no longer ask for her.

18

It is twilight, and Obasan and I are standing on the bridge watching a large school of tiny fish shimmering upstream like a wriggling gray cloud. We are on our way to the wake in the Odd Fellows Hall. It is all so strange. Grandma Nakane, Obasan tells me, is in heaven.

"Dead?" I asked Stephen. "Grandma Nakane?"

Heaven, I am told, is where old people go and is a place of happiness. Why then the solemnness?

I stare straight down into the water past my new wine-colored loafers Obasan bought for me at Graham's General Store. Obasan is wearing her white summer shoes with a hole at the toe. Can Grandma Nakane see us from heaven? I wonder. Could her spirit be in the little gray fishes?

The last time we saw Grandma and Grandpa Nakane was a few weeks ago when they arrived by train. I know they wanted to stay with us. But an ambulance took them away. Stephen says it takes a whole hour to drive the twisting twenty miles from Slocan to New Denver, where they are.

Obasan held Grandma Nakane's hand tightly until the driver came to close the ambulance door. Grandpa Nakane strained to sit up and tried to smile as he waved goodbye to Stephen and me, the ends of his mustache rising and falling. None of us spoke.

It is always so. We must always honor the wishes of others before our own. We will make the way smooth by restraining emotion. Though we might wish Grandma and Grandpa to stay, we must watch them go. To try to meet one's own needs in spite of the wishes of others is to be "wagamama"—selfish and inconsiderate. Obasan teaches me not to be wagamama by always heeding everyone's needs. That is why she is waiting patiently beside me at this bridge. That is why, when I am offered gifts, I must first refuse politely. It is such a tangle trying to decipher the needs and intents of others.

This little bridge is where sad thoughts come. Memories of my doll. Memories of home. And thoughts now of Grandma Nakane. I remember the time she wore her kimono and knelt on the floor playing a slow sad tune on the koto, her graceful fingers plucking the strings.

I take Obasan's hand and we walk down the pebbly road to the Odd Fellows Hall, a building by itself at the side of the road in a field without any trees. On Saturday nights the building is filled with children, white and Japanese, who come and watch war movies and newsreels and Batman. The hall is long and heavy with darkness. Two light bulbs dangle from the ceiling. In front of the stage, far away at the end of the hall, there is the wooden coffin. Several people I do not know sit on folding chairs with their heads bowed. It is a long walk from the entrance to the front, our shoes echoing loudly on the wooden floor.

Obasan bows to the people as they come, thanking them quietly. The ojisan who first helped us when we got off the train is accepting envelopes of money, which he will later give to Obasan. Eiko's mother, her round face smiling wanly, takes both my hands as I stand near her. She presses an envelope firmly between the palms of my hands.

There are about twenty people who have come to the wake. From our family only Obasan and I are here. Grandpa Nakane is too sick to attend and Stephen didn't want to come. We sit on the chairs and wait till the ojisan goes to the front. He stands beside the coffin and begins to say a long prayer full of words I do not understand.

The next day, for the funeral, the prayers are just as long. The hall is so full that men and women stand along the back wall. Some people are holding handkerchiefs to their faces and whisper quietly to Obasan. The words that are spoken by the minister, Nakayama-sensei, are not understandable. Obasan's head is bowed the whole time. Because the service is so long, she gives me a pencil and a small notebook in which to draw. I make a house with a triangle roof and triangle windows in the roof. I fill the sky with seagulls. I have just learned to make birds like the letter "v." While I am drawing, I listen to Nakayama-sensei's voice rising and falling in the formal chant that comes from deep in his body, then up to the top of his head and down again. I feel that he could make the walls of the building fall down were he to let out all his breath. The words seem to come from somewhere inside his belly and stop before coming out of his mouth, so that the sound is swallowed up and remains loud and powerful but barely to be heard. Occasionally a word is surrounded or followed by a long sigh.

Obasan's eyes are closed as she listens. Stephen is sitting on the other side of her and kicks his good leg back and forth. His fingers are digging at a black piece of gum stuck on the bottom of his folding chair. When he gets it off, he leans over Obasan and sticks it on one of my seagulls.

" 'Nother mosquito for ya," he mutters.

Obasan opens her eyes and rummages through her purse for a pen to give to Stephen but he folds his arms and shakes his head, refusing it. I am about to take his gummy mosquito off my bird when everyone kneels and there is a rapid murmuring as the whole hall fills with voices joined in prayer.

After the service, Obasan, Stephen, and I walk behind some men who are carrying the coffin to a half-ton truck.

Stephen whispers to me that the man who is going to take Grandma's body up the mountain is called Mr. Draper. He owns a grocery store in New Denver, and when people die he uses his truck for funerals. He drove Grandma's body all the way down from the hospital at New Denver to Slocan.

Later in the evening, Obasan, Stephen, and I walk down the highway and up the steep road to the old silver mine. Obasan tells us that though she and Uncle are Christians, like Mother and Father and the Katos, Grandpa Nakane is Buddhist. It was Grandpa Nakane's wish that Grandma Nakane's body be sent for cremation and her bones and ashes returned to him. At first it was arranged to send the body to Spokane, but some carpenters told Obasan they would build a pyre and take turns keeping the fire going throughout the night at the old silver mine. Obasan is carrying a furoshiki full of delicious rice osushis and several of the new pound cakes for the men to eat.

The sun has been long gone behind the mountain ranges and the first stars are in view by the time we come to the end of the trail to the mine. There is a bunkhouse hidden in the trees where several families live. Farther up behind the rubble, where part of the mine used to be, is a clearing where the men are. The summer night sounds of insects have begun and there is a cool twirl of wind as we begin the last part of the climb. From off in the distance we can hear the low muffled sound of water from a waterfall.

We come in sight of a half dozen men and a rectangular pile of logs in the middle of the clearing. The logs remind me of a game Stephen and I play with matchsticks, when we try to make a square base and lay one match on top of another till we get a high tower. The one who makes the pile fall down is the loser. The difference here is that the sticks are huge tree trunks, logs so wide I could not put my arms around them. They are built in a crisscross up to the height of a table. In the hollow space in the center of the log pile there are dry twigs and smaller pieces of wood. Grandma's coffin rests on top.

The first ojisan who sees us comes to help Stephen up the last part of the climb, and when we arrive we sit down on a log to rest. A little distance from the pyre, there are two stacks of wood. One man is pouring gasoline from a rectangular tin carefully onto all the logs of the pyre and another is binding a cloth onto the end of a stick. Obasan puts her gift of food discreetly behind the second wood pile, where it will be seen after we leave, then returns to sit beside me and wait.

The ojisan who is binding the cloth on the stick pours some gasoline onto the cloth from another container and, setting a light to it, he holds the flaming torch high up in front of him. I am sitting on the log wondering what Grandma is thinking of all of us here in the cool night.

"Sa," the ojisan says as he comes toward us, holding the torch, "shall we begin?"

He beckons to Stephen. "Your grandmother and grandfather are my old friends," he says. He hands the torch to Stephen and helps him hop to the gasoline-soaked pyre.

Swift as the crack of a whip the flames shoot along the edge of the log, and before Stephen can reach another corner to spread the fire, the entire platform is a dancing bright-dark rage of crackling in the night. The heat is as intense and roaring as the sawdust furnace in the basement in Vancouver when its door is open. Who, I used to wonder, could survive such heat? The angel in the Old Testament story kept three men safe in the middle of a place like that.

"It's in the heat of fire where the angel is found," Obasan once told Stephen. She also told him that the best samurai swords are tempered over and over again in the hottest flames and people too are made strong and excellent when they go through life's difficulties. Stephen always scowls when Obasan says these things.

From where I am sitting I can feel the fire, hot and dry on my face. Obasan has been using a handkerchief to chase the mosquitoes diving around us, but now she puts the handkerchief in front of my face and we move farther back where it is not so hot.

It is strange to think that the coffin will soon be touched by the yellowish red-streaked light. And what of Grandma Nakane? She will turn to ashes, Stephen told me, on this mountain tonight.

19

As soon as the coffin begins to burn, one ojisan says quietly to

Obasan, "There is no need to stay longer."

She bows and thanks each of the men in turn and we

walk back down the mountain with one ojisan holding a flash-

light to show us the way.

In the morning, before I waken, Obasan returns to the

silver mine with chopsticks and a tin to gather the bones and

ashes. She sends them to Grandpa Nakane, who says he will

bury them when we all return home again.

The days of mourning gradually end and the yellow-red

leaf days of autumn also pass.

One afternoon, soon after the first snowfall, I come in after a sleigh ride down the road and hear Obasan chatting to Nomura-obasan.

"When good things happen they come in a cluster, do they not?" she is saying cheerily.

Nomura-obasan nods and her strings of gray hair flap into her long cheeks.

Nakayama-sensei, the Anglican minister, has just left, Obasan says, with the news that Uncle will be arriving this afternoon. The doctor also said this morning that Stephen's cast will be removed this week.

"Such good news," Obasan repeats.

The snow outside is falling like tufts of cotton and the fence post wears a white puff hat. The whole mountainside is muffled and soft, with blobs of snow perched on the trees like a popcorn extravaganza. By late afternoon, the shadows have deepened to a purple-gray and the coal-oil lamps are lit.

The furniture in the two rooms has been shuffled all day. Nomura-obasan's cot is now in the kitchen, wedged against a wall beneath the shelves of food. The kitchen table is in the front room and we set it with a place for Uncle. A blue-and-white tablecloth covers the oilcloth and the blue rectangular plates and small round ones are placed in a triangle with the rice bowls. The miso shiru, smelling of brine and the sea, is on the stove and the black lacquered bowls with the black lids wait on a tray on the warmer above the stove beside the King George/Queen Elizabeth mugs Mother bought to commemorate the royal visit. The dried fiddleheads with their slightly tough asparagus texture have been soaked and are cooking in a soy sauce sugar base with thin slivers of meat and mushroom. Salty, half-dried cucumber and crisp yellow radish pickles are in a glass dish.

Obasan is showing no signs of impatience as she brings in

an armload of logs and fills the box beside the stove. Stephen, hopping with the help of one crutch, pokes a log into place in the stove.

"When is he coming?" Stephen asks for the third time.

"The snow is too much perhaps," Obasan says as she looks at the clock on the windowsill.

I have been making paper baskets out of folding paper and filling them with jelly beans, one basket for each of us.

"Ah," Nomura-obasan says as I bring her one. She holds the basket in the palm of her hand and raises it above her head with mock gravity. "Thank you. This is for after supper, is it not?" She puts it on the stool at the head of her bed, beside her basket full of medicine and her knitting.

"If there is hunger," Obasan says, handing me the chopsticks, "let us eat."

I am matching the chopstick pairs—the red ones, black ones, two ivory sets—when Stephen, peering through the window, calls out. Obasan wipes her hands on her apron and looks up as Stephen heaves himself to the door and opens it wide, letting in a flurry of snow. Uncle's voice is hearty as he stamps his feet outside.

"Ha-ro Stee-bu!" Uncle places a wooden box, a flashlight, and a sack on the floor before he steps in halfway, shaking the snow off his black coat and pant legs, a bear-shaped man stomping in the doorway. "Ha-ro ha-ro, Naomi-chan!" His arms are wide open and he lifts Stephen up in his arms. "What this what this?" he asks, poking Stephen's cast.

Stephen is grinning widely, the dimples on his cheeks wide parentheses. "I don't need it anymore," Stephen says.

Obasan stands at the doorway to the kitchen and removes her apron.

"Okairi nasai," she says briskly. Her voice is almost crisp

and military and sounds like a salute. Her hands are in front
of her, folded, holding her apron.

"Okairi nasai," Nomura-obasan calls from the other
room. It is the most familiar greeting I know. "Welcome
home." Every day, Mother would say this to Stephen as he
came home from school. Or to Father whenever he came in.
Stephen and Father would reply immediately, "Tada-ima—I
have just now returned."

"Ah," Uncle says, seeing the table. He puts Stephen down
to remove his shoes and puts on the slippers waiting for him.
Obasan fills the black lacquered bowls with the miso soup.

"Just the right time," Obasan says, handing me the bowls.

Some snow from Uncle's head falls on the black stove
surface with a spit and a hiss as he comes into the kitchen to
greet Nomura-obasan. She sits up and bows formally, greeting
Uncle, who bows in return.

"A difficult time, is it not?" Uncle says.

"The kindness of everyone," Nomura-obasan replies formally. "My presence is a nuisance. . . ."

"Not so," Obasan replies, handing me the miso soup to
give Nomura-obasan.

"And your brother Tadashi-san," Nomura-obasan asks
Uncle. "How is his health?"

I hold the soup and wait to hear what Uncle will say
about my father. Stephen, his mouth open as if ready with
another question, is also waiting to hear.

"Eh"—Uncle nods briefly—"thank you for your concern."

"There is only prayer," Obasan says. "Nothing else will
help."

"Will it be a long time, one wonders, before he can come
to us?" Nomura-obasan asks.

"Sa," Uncle says thoughtfully, "there is no telling."

Is Uncle saying he does not know where Father is?

"Why is it not known?" I ask. "Where is Father? When will he come?"

Uncle smiles at me as I hand the soup to Nomura-obasan. "And this o-jo-chan, this little girl—who can she be?"

He is joking, of course, but I wonder if I have changed since he last saw me. He is still the same, his open face round like Grandma Nakane's, his black hair a cap straight back from his forehead.

This is the way it is whenever I ask questions. The answers are not answers at all.

"Don't you know where Dad is?" Stephen says scornfully to me.

One time Stephen was reading a letter Father sent but I did not know where Father was. The handwriting in the letter was as even as waves along the beach, row on row of neat curls and dots, perfect pebbles and shells on an ordered shore. I could only stare at the waves as Stephen deciphered their code. Father was telling us to be like Ninomiya Kinjiro, to help Obasan, and to study hard.

Uncle goes to his sack and brings out two wooden instruments each about a foot long.

With a whoop, Stephen throws his crutch to the floor and lunges for them. "The flutes!" The room fills with music as Stephen plays and Uncle nods his head encouragingly.

Nomura-obasan claps her hands. "Oh, when the cast is removed there will be dancing," she says.

Stephen is playing a song he learned at school.

The mountain and the squirrel had a quarrel
And the former called the latter "little prig" . . .

"Music all the time, just like your father," Uncle says, shaking his head.

Obasan, who has been smiling and putting the food on the table, calls us to sit down.

"Sa," Obasan says, filling the last of the rice bowls. "Let us eat." She folds her hands, signaling the saying of grace, and waits until we are quiet. The light from the coal-oil lamp is lowered slightly and her voice is almost a whisper as she gives thanks for Uncle's return. "Father in heaven—that until now there has been protection, arigato, thank you. Tonight, for the safe return, thank you. For the food, thank you . . ."

"Amen," Uncle says in a loud voice.

Nomura-obasan from the other room also adds, "Aaah-men," drawing the "A" sound out from deep within her like a groan.

Within days, everything changes. Bright wallpaper covers the newspapered walls. Above my bunk, a shelf is made for my clothes. The kitchen table returns to the kitchen and a folding screen gives Nomura-obasan privacy.

On the Friday following Uncle's return, Stephen must go to the hospital to have his cast removed. In the morning he is out in the back shed, pounding the ice off the runners of his homemade sled with a split log. Humpty Dumpty, I am thinking, will fall out of his shell, and what will he be then?

"Without doubt, the young heal easily," Nomura-obasan says.

"That is so," Obasan agrees. "It is an easy matter for the young."

We watch them going through the deep fresh snow, Uncle floundering as he pulls Stephen behind him. The track they leave shows not just the thin metal runners but the whole underside of the sled as well. What strange giant winter slug must this be that leaves such a mark as it slithers down the snowy slope? I have often seen small animal tracks in the path and under the trees, though I have not seen any creatures around the house. The road is mostly downhill all the way to the hospital.

By early afternoon they return. Stephen sits on a bench in front of the open oven door. Obasan bathes his feet in a basin of water. Hesitant as a spring robin, Stephen stands and hops, hops to the kitchen table, where Uncle is sipping a mug of tea and watching him solemnly. Stephen's whole body tilts slightly as he rests briefly on his bad leg.

"It will improve," Uncle says softly.

More boldly, Stephen limps around the room. Even when he moves slowly he looks as if he is in a hurry. Back and forth he goes, like Long John Silver with a peg leg, like a sailor on a rolling ship. Step hop, step hop.

"Together, with strength, with energy, let us walk," Nomura-obasan says.

20

Until May 1943, when we first attend school, Stephen and I have no formal studies except for Sunday-school and handicraft classes held in the missionaries' big house. At home, Obasan keeps me busy making a scrapbook of the Royal Family.

Some of the children attend Japanese-language classes but I hear Obasan and Uncle whispering that it is unwise to have us go. The RCMP, they are saying, are always looking for signs of disloyalty to Canada. Stephen and I are unconcerned with such worries and life for us is a quiet and pleasant holiday.

Stephen's limp has almost disappeared by late spring. When he runs he sometimes looks like a galloping horse. Once the earth is firm underfoot, the whole mountain is for galloping in, for climbing and for exploring.

Slocan greening in spring is vulnerable as birth, the bright yellow-green turning steadily deeper into shades of blue. Uncle makes a rock garden in the front yard with a tiny stream and waterfall winding around the base to a small pool. At the top of the garden, Stephen digs a hole and plants a flagpole with an oversized Union Jack. He and Uncle work together and the fallen fence is mended. A vegetable garden, flowers, a lawn, and a chicken coop with several chickens appear. Sweet peas climb the wire-covered walls of the chicken coop. More and more, the yard is a miniature of Uncle and Obasan's place on the island.

Beyond the natural stone steps at the back of our yard is the path Uncle makes by which we enter the moist forest and the glade that is speared alive with fiddlehead stems. "Warabi," Uncle calls them. He shows us which ones we are to pick. We carry metal syrup tins, Uncle, Obasan, Stephen, and I, as we forage through the woods in the green mountain light. Beyond a certain point of unfurling the ferns are stringy and inedible, but the crooked asparagus-like stems, not yet ornate with curls, are just right. The green flesh snaps apart with the slightest bend.

Through the seasons, we trace and retrace the woodland mazes, harvesting the wilderness. Dog-eared mushrooms are here and there like hidden treasures, scattered over the spongy earth. Under the canopy, Uncle says, if the mushrooms are white, they are not good. The ones that grow on trees, floppy and dark, are fine. At home they are tested by boiling them with a dime in the pot. The weeds that look like carrots are poisonous and Uncle brings the news from town that several families are ill from eating them. But there are the safe berries —wild strawberries the size of shirt buttons, piercingly sweet, and gooseberries large as marbles.

Underfoot, the mountain floor is a soft covering of pine needles, plant leaves, green growths. We breathe and are stabbed alive by the air, the sap from the trees, the slight metallic smell of cedar and pine. The rain, the warmth bring to bloom the wildflowers that hide beneath the foliage. Everywhere is the mountain's presence. Our bones are made porous.

It's a warm blue day in June 1943, a month after we first attend school in Slocan. Unlike at Stephen's school in Vancouver, all the teachers and children in our school are Japanese. The white children in Slocan go to a different school. Two of the children from my class have come to visit. There's Kenji, a boy with thick glasses stuck together with a knob of adhesive tape, and Miyuki, the shy girl who always wears a pretty dress and has shiny black shoes. Her hair is in ringlets that bob up and down like springs. Kenji, in a sweater that comes almost up to his elbows and in pants so tight they hug his legs, looks like a scarecrow leading the way. We start climbing the road toward the old mine and come to the bridge of logs over a stream. A short distance along the stream is a stone ledge beside a tuft of orange water lilies.

Miyuki squeals as she dangles one toe into the creek and jumps away from the shock of cold, her dancing ringlets quivering.

Kenji stabs the moss with a stick and prods at a frayed husk of a pinecone emptied of seeds. A long multilegged bright red insect moves across the rubble he has made, like a derailed train in search of its tracks. It crawls onto the end of Kenji's stick and mounts steadily in a straight line toward his hands.

"Get off," Kenji shouts. He turns the stick around and the insect crawls back to the other end, leaning out into the air and waving its feelers, as it looks for a toehold.

"Get off!" He flicks the stick like a whip, then whacks it against the stone ledge.

"Don't kill it," Miyuki says in her high tiny voice.

Kenji weighs the matter, then tosses the stick, with the insect still clinging tenaciously, into the stream. It bobs once, then rushes headlong downstream, and we run down following it till we come back to the log bridge.

The insect is still on the stick, twirling in an eddy at the end of the bridge. We abandon it there, a tiny red dot, bobbing and dancing in its whirlpool.

"C'mon," Kenji says, and we follow the road again till we come to the oval stone that marks the beginning of a path. We enter a thick army of trees, then a glen and a lookout point called Pluto's Bluff. From here we can see directly down on top of our house. Kenji stands on the edge and tosses a stone high up and over the trees. "See, it'll hit the chicken coop," he says. It's a few seconds before we hear the faint crack of rock hitting rock.

Miyuki, halfway up the path to Minnie's Bluff, is calling us to hurry up. This lookout is so full of trees and bushes we can hardly see the town at all. Then we are on our way again to the last stretch of the two-mile trek and the highest lookout point, Mickey's Bluff.

The entrance to this bluff is a sheer edge of rock with toeholds and an overhanging tree branch, which we grab one at a time, pushing and hauling one another till the three of us stand on the rounded mound of rock as large as a rooftop.

Up and over the mossy rock surface we run to the mountain edge and here we are, suddenly looking down on Lilliput from the top of the world. A dizzying kingdom. Far below us and for miles around are the tiny houses with thin streams of real smoke rising out of toothpick chimneys. The river is a silvery black snake that winds in and out of the woods to the lake. In the distance beyond the lake are the mountain peaks, purple and blue and jagged with snow. The world is as immense as sky and tiny as the pin-dot flowers in the moss.

On this day we stay, playing, arranging stones, watching chipmunks, gathering pinecones and wildflowers. We are lying on our backs, watching the sky in silence, when suddenly Miyuki gasps. "Look!" Her startled voice is like the sudden sharp sound of a twig snapping.

She is pointing excitedly at a sleek gray shadow plummeting to earth like a falling kite, straight down in front of us and below to the trees. We inch as close as we dare to the edge of the bluff and stare down the rocky hillside.

"Must be the King bird," Kenji says in awe. He lies flat on his stomach and leans out over the edge. "It was big, eh?" With his head hanging over the lip of stone and his arms and legs spread apart, he looks like some sky creature that has fallen to earth and landed here in a splat. "That's the one Rough Lock Bill saw, I bet," he says.

Kenji has been bragging for days that he sat in Rough Lock Bill's cabin. I don't believe Kenji. Stephen told me Rough Lock Bill yells at kids if they come too close. His cabin is right near the beach where Stephen and I play and I have never seen him close up.

Although we keep staring into the trees, the shape does not reemerge. On the way back down the mountain, Kenji tells us that Rough Lock Bill saw the King bird one day near an old gold mine.

"If you tell lies," Kenji says, "the King bird cuts your

tongue in half and you can't talk. That's what it did to the birds. All they can say now is 'twit twit.' Betcha that was the King bird, eh, Nomi? Gonna come after you if you tell lies."

"Sh," I whisper to Kenji. I am listening to the sound of a bird in the trees that is fluttering and darting ahead of us down the road. The small chirp is like part of a trill that was cut off too soon. Somehow it reminds me of musicians tuning up at the outdoor theater in the dusk at Stanley Park. Perhaps, I am thinking, the King bird was a conductor that called all the birds together to some auditorium in the woods where people couldn't go. Perhaps they sang together, a great bird choir, each bird adding its part to the melody, till some catastrophe happened and the songs disappeared into chirps and tweets.

By the time we get home, it's late afternoon. The long shadow is like a giant wing, a mountainous King bird hovering over us, listening to our whispers and stories, alert for lies. Is it at midnight the King bird will descend to cut off our tongues? Which lies, I wonder as I fall asleep, has the King bird overheard today? In the night, I dream of a red red bird, tiny as an insect, trapped in a whirling well.

21

The following week Kenji is with me again. We have come

through the woods to the lake. The pathway here is well worn,

like Rough Lock Bill's porch floor where the rocking chair has

worn a smooth groove—well worn like his socks, through

which his big toe protrudes dark as a walnut.

This, of course, cannot be seen from where we are playing

in a corner of the beach. Beside us is the rocky cliff and the

tortuous single-lane road which snakes its way to the New

Denver hospital. Stephen told me Father and Grandpa

Nakane are there. But the way is too far, far too far, for our

walking.

It's a calm summer day. The lap lap of the waves against the shore is Obasan's slippers slapping against the soles of her feet. Sluff whoosh. Sluff whoosh.

Kenji is paddling around on a log raft he found grounded half in and half out of the water. I would like to go with him but Uncle says I must not go on rafts. When he jumps off, his wobbly glasses bounce diagonally so that one eye is suddenly naked and surprisingly small. He straightens the elastic band on the back of his head that keeps his glasses snug, and the band breaks, making his glasses fall across his cheeks.

I am wearing my green-and-white cotton-knit bathing suit with a string net bib. At my feet is a moist sand village, the slanting roofed houses packed firm and peaked by two flat pieces of wood. Feathery tops of bromegrass gone to seed are drooping trees lining the white pebble sidewalks. There are twig chimneys, twig bridges, twig people, one plump twig dog with three legs and no head.

The sun is a warmth against the coolness of the water's tickle along the quiet sand. We are absorbed in our play and do not see the man standing behind us watching.

I am startled when Kenji suddenly leaps up and calls, "Hi, Rough Lock."

The first things I see are his feet in a pair of sand slippers. One big toe sticks out through a hole in his sock. He is a thin man, skinny as a tree, his face grooved like tree bark. His arm is a knobbly branch darker than mine. His hair is scraggly and covers his head like the seaweed on Vancouver beaches draped on the rocks. I have never seen him close up before.

"Whatcher name?" he asks me.

I stare up at him, then down at the village.

"Can't talk, eh? King bird got your tongue?" He lifts his eyebrows and nods knowingly. His Adam's apple is a lump in his dark wrinkled neck. I feel an urge to reach out and touch it—pluck it from his throat.

"Well, Ken, what's your friend's name?"

"Naomi," Kenji says.

"Can't hear you. Speak up." The man's tone of voice is neither angry nor kind.

"Naomi," Kenji blurts.

"Here," the man says, handing me a stick. "Print me your name. Can you print?"

I brush the wet sand off my hands and take the stick. NAOMI, I print in large letters in the sand.

He kneels beside me, reading. "Aha, Na-o-mi. That right? Can you read?" He prints BILL with his forefinger. "Rough Lock," he says, "my name's Rough Lock Bill. And what's this?" He smooths the sand with one brown hand and prints a large SLOCAN.

I can read but I don't answer.

"How old are you?"

"She's seven," Kenji says.

"Can't read. Can't talk. What's the good of you, eh? Look. SLOCAN." He sits down on the sand in his dungarees and stares out over the water, tapping his stick in the sand. "You from Vancouver?"

I nod.

"Big city." He shakes his head. "All that cement ["see-ment," he says] addles the brain."

He jabs his finger in the sand. "This here's the best place there is."

He scoops a handful of sand and lets it trickle into a pointed mound. Then another and another. Three sand hills. Three small pyramids. "What have I got here, eh, Ken?" In front of the three hills he has dug a well, the walls of damp sand patted firmly into a bowl shape. "Them's mountains," he says, indicating his mounds. "Lake here, and three mountains."

He picks up several twig people from our sand village and puts them in a cluster at the base of one mountain. "These," he says, "are people. And this"—he points to the hole again —"lake. Wanna hear a story?"

"Sure," Kenji says, flopping on his stomach in the sand and resting his chin on his elbows.

Rough Lock cleans off a bromegrass tree and shoves it in between two teeth at the side of his mouth. As he talks, the grass moves back and forth like a flag. "Never met a kid didn't like stories. Red skin, yellow skin, white skin, any skin." He puts his brown leathery arm beside Kenji's pale one. "Don't make sense, do it, all this fuss about skin?"

"Nope," he says when we don't answer. "It sure don't, Rough Lock."

He picks up one of the sticks and begins. "Well, this here is an Indian brave." He marches it slowly around the base of the sand mountain and in between where the mounds meet, as he talks. "Long time ago these people were dying. All these people here. Don't know what it was. Smallpox maybe. Tribe wars. Starvation. Maybe it was a hex, who knows? But there's always a few left when something like that happens. And this brave, he set out to find a place. A good place with lots of good food—deer, fish, berries. Know where that was?"

"Where?" Kenji asks.

"Well, I tell ya, it took him a long time to get here. But he knew it when he saw it. This right here. Right here." He waves his arm, indicating the lake and the beach. "So he goes all the way back to where his people are, back past these mountains, and he says to them, 'If you go slow, you can go.'

So off we go, these few here, some so weak they have to be carried. Took all of them together—how long? Months? A year? 'If you go slow,' he says, 'you can go. Slow can go. Slow can go.' Like a train chugging across the mountains."

Kenji is helping him march the stick people around and around the mountains till they come to the edge of the sand-hole lake. "We call it Slocan now. Real name is Slow-can-go. When my Granddad came, there was a whole tribe here." He points a stick at his cabin. "Right there was the chief's tepee. But last I saw—one old guy up past the mine—be dead now probably."

He spits out the bromegrass and grins at me.

"Don't talk much, do ya?" he says as he flattens his mountains. "Like that old fella up past the mine. Never said a word. Almost like a mute, he was. But I heard him chirping one time just like a bird. Don't you never talk?"

I scuff the sand with the heels of my feet. "I can talk."

Rough Lock grunts. "I tell ya, the old man there could talk to the birds as if he was one of them. One time he had the whole forest singing so loud you'd think there was a hoo-tenanny up there."

"We saw the King bird," Kenji says.

"Say, you don't say," Rough Lock says, scratching his head. He shades his eyes with his hands and looks up at the mountains. "See how quiet it is? A whole mountain full of birds and not a peep out of 'em. Used to be a time there'd be music in the morning—enough to drive you deaf ["deef," he says] just sitting here."

Rough Lock Bill shakes his head slowly, pushing his lips down at the corners. "Birds could all talk once. Bird language. Now all they can say is their own names. That's all. Can't say any more than their names. Just like some people. Specially in the city, eh? Me, me, me." He jabs his chest with his thumb and grunts. "But smart people don't talk too much. Redskins know that. The King bird warned them a long time ago."

He sits back on his haunches, shaking his head. "Rough Lock, ya talks too much." He mutters something I don't understand, then stands up slowly and walks back toward his cabin.

Kenji and I watch him till he disappears briefly, then reappears on his porch. We can see him rocking in his rocking chair, his head bobbing steadily as driftwood on the waves.

"I told ya," Kenji says. He jumps up and runs back into the water, pushing his log raft out till the water reaches the level of his short tight pant legs.

"Come on, Nomi," he calls, prodding a pole into the sandy lake bottom to steady the raft.

My toes curl against the foamy fringe of spittle and the cool shock of the water's lip.

"Come on. I won't go far."

I have never gone in past my buttocks.

"Like this," Kenji says, standing astride in the middle and pushing the raft close to shore. It sinks and touches bottom, wobbling unsteadily, as I climb on. I kneel behind him.

"Okay," he says as he leans into the pole and the raft lurches out over the surface. The water is clear and the sand at the bottom is ribbed in smooth rills. Briefly there is the cool gray darting of a fish beneath us and countless tiny fish glide past like one shadow. I stretch out, resting my chin in my hands, watching the water shadows and the patterns of cloud and sky reflected in the lake. I dangle my hand in the water, making a wake within the wake of the raft. As we push deeper, there is a sudden change in the temperature of the water. When I look up, the shoreline is farther away than I have ever seen. I cannot locate the sand village at all.

"It's too far here, Kenji. Let's go back."

"Okay, just one more shove," Kenji says. His pole is about five feet long and easily reaches the sandy bottom. His hands are about two-thirds up the pole and he leans back like a man with a harpoon, then forward, plunging the pole deep. One lunge, and—splash!—the pole torpedoes out of his hands as Kenji tumbles sideways, one leg raised high. He falls with a splat into the water. A cold spray spatters my back and the raft jerks and tilts, angling up like a seesaw. I clutch the edges of the bobbing raft, my whole body suddenly tense as a cat ready to spring. Several feet away, the pole springs to the surface. In the splutter of waves, Kenji's head reemerges, his bent glasses dangling from one ear.

I rise slowly on my hands and knees. Kenji grabs his glasses and clamps them between his teeth like a dog. The water around us is sharply dark and the bottom is no longer visible. A drop-off. He jerks the water off his head and paddles with kicks and splashes to the beach. Closer to shore, he stands up in the water, turning to face me.

"Jump!" he shouts.

"I can't! I can't swim!"

He holds his hands up to the sides of his head as if he cannot see. Then slowly he steps backward till he is out of the water.

I stare down into the black hole and back to where Kenji is standing, his glasses in his fist. His hands are clenched and his arms are out to the side stiff as poles.

I am engulfed by knowing. He will not help. He does not know how to help. He turns suddenly and flees down the beach, disappearing into the woods. I know he will not return. He will tell no one.

The raft drifts, barely moving in the stillness. I must decide quickly quickly what I am to do. Last month a boy drowned in the lake. Farther out the lake goes on forever. I will be utterly lost. Perhaps I can swim. I have watched the others. I must leap now, without hesitating, before I drift farther.

There is a cold sickening impulse and then I jump.

The water is a shock spurting into the cavities of my head. I fight the panic and urge my legs to churn against the enclosing weight. My toes scrape a sharp edge. With all my gathered strength, I push and claw and with a gasp my head is above water. I choke with air and water and a heavy salt blood mucus taste. I am overcome with dizziness. I cannot tell which direction the beach is, where the raft is, where the nearest point of safety is. Sky and lake swirl as I gasp and swallow. From somewhere in my body, a sound comes out intended as a cry—but deep and guttural like the growl of an animal. Again and again I am plunged and twirled in the frantic dizziness.

Then, as through a wavering tunnel, there is something pulling me along, through the water, slow as a courtly dance. I am hanging in a whiteness, limp as laundry on a line. Eventually there is the sound of a steady slap somewhere in the distance beyond the numbness that surrounds me.

Suddenly my ears clear and I am aware that I am dangling in half and the sound of pounding is a steady whack on my back. With the pounding is a dull unlocatable weight and a roaring sound.

"Okay, okay, I gotcha," a man's voice is saying.

Between gasps, I am breathing, I am breathing and I know I am safe. Phlegm and water gush from my mouth and nose.

Eventually I am placed on my stomach on the sand, my head turned sideways on a cloth surface.

"Okay now, hey?"

I lie, exhausted and cold with spasms of shivering, the

blood a taste in my nostrils. When I open my eyes at last, it is to a red-and-blue-checkered flannel shirt. Rough Lock Bill is kneeling beside me. There is a smooth groove beside his rocking chair. I attempt to move but my arms are weak. My chest heaves and I hear whimpering and a hacking sob that seems to be coming from within. I curl my knees up to my chest. In the effort, more water and phlegm gush from my nostrils and mouth, covering the shirt.

"'At's it," Rough Lock says. He is peering at me, his face close to mine. My cheek is pressed into some granular chunks of sand in the shirt. I wipe my nose on the sleeve and close my eyes again.

22

I am in a hospital. Father is in a hospital. A chicken is in a hospital. Father is a chicken is a dream that I am in a hospital where my neck and chin are covered with a thick red stubble of hair and I am reading the careful table of contents of a book that has no contents.

When I waken fully at last, I am in the Slocan hospital and a nurse is standing beside me smiling. I have been asleep, it seems, forever. Vaguely I remember Rough Lock carrying me here. I also remember Obasan's hand rubbing my back. The nurse starts to comb my tangled hair, pulling so that the roots clinging to the scalp strain the surface of the skin.

"Does it hurt?" she asks me.

"No," I reply. The weeds in the garden do not moan when they are plucked from the skin of the earth. Nor do the trees cry out at their fierce combing as they lie uprooted by the roadside. Rapunzel's long ladder of hair could bear the weight of prince or witch. I can endure this nurse's hands yanking at the knots in the thick black tangles.

The beds are as close together as the desks in the schoolroom where we are jammed two to a seat. If I lean out, I can almost touch the bed of the woman beside me, who sits up washing her face in a basin, cupping the water in her hands and rubbing her face up and down, her eyes squeezed shut. The heads of the beds are against a windowed wall and the feet point to the door and the hospital corridor.

Obasan has brought me my blue *Highroads to Reading, Book Two,* with the bright orange lettering and the happiness inside.

> *Minnie and Winnie slept in a shell;*
> *Sleep, little ladies! And they slept well.*

The fairies, white-gowned with white-veined wings, sleep wispy as smoke in a blue shell, and the woman in the next bed sleeps, her mouth open, and all the others in the room also sleep and sleep, and Father, I was told, is in a hospital too with Grandpa Nakane in New Denver and are they also sleeping in a room full of people like this?

I am in a grade-two reader full of fairies, sitting in the forest very still and waiting for one fairy tiny as an insect to come flying through the tall grasses and lead me down to the moss-covered door on the forest floor that opens to the tunnel leading to the place where my mother and father are hiding.

What does it mean? What can it mean? Why do they not come?

"Daddy is sick, Nomi," Stephen said.

"When will he come home?"

"I don't know. Maybe never."

"Never? Is he going to die?"

The kids in school said that when old Honma-san died in Bayfarm, there was a ball of fire that came out of the house and then moved off up the mountain. The kids know about the place by the mine road where Grandma Nakane was cremated.

The nurse is never going to be finished with my hair. I am quite capable of combing it myself. Why is this spectacle being made of me? If I cry now while I sit on this bed, all the people will turn and look.

"It's old people who die, isn't it, Stephen?"

"Yes."

"Daddy won't die."

"Of course not."

"And Mommy?"

Obasan has also brought me a thin book with a picture of animals in it called *Little Tales for Little Folk*. There is an oversized baby chick called "Chicken Little" standing on the front cover.

What is this thing about chickens? When they are babies, they are yellow. Yellow like daffodils. Like Goldilocks' yellow hair. Like the yellow Easter chicks I lost somewhere. Yellow like the yellow pawns in the Yellow Peril game.

The Yellow Peril is a Somerville Game, Made in Canada. It was given to Stephen at Christmas. On the red-and-blue box cover is a picture of soldiers with bayonets and fists raised high looking out over a sea full of burning ships and a sky full of planes. A game about war. Over a map of Japan are the words:

> *The game that shows how*
> *a few brave defenders*
> *can withstand a very*
> *great number of enemies.*

There are fifty small yellow pawns inside and three big blue checker kings. To be yellow in the Yellow Peril game is to be weak and small. Yellow is to be chicken. I am not yellow. I will not cry however much this nurse yanks my hair.

When the yellow chicks grow up they turn white. Chicken Little is a large Yellow Peril puff. One time Uncle stepped on a baby chick. One time, I remember, a white hen pecked yellow chicks to death, to death in our backyard.

There it is. Death again. Death means stop.

All the chickens in the chicken coop, dim-witted pinbrains though they are, know about it. Every day, the plump white lumps are in the chicken yard, scratching with their stick legs and clucking and barkling together. If anything goes overhead —a cloud, an airplane, the King bird—they all seem to be connected to one another like a string of Christmas-tree lights. Their orange eyes are in unison, and each head is crooked at an angle watching the overshadowing death. They stop for a moment, then carry on as death passes by. A little passover several times a day. Sensei said in church, the Death angel passes over at Passover.

Hospitals are places where Death visits. But Death comes to the world in many unexpected places.

There is that day on the way to school. When was it? Just a week ago?

The long walk from Slocan to school in Bayfarm is by way of a path through a heavily wooded forest, past some houses and the white house where the missionaries live, and onto the highway to Lemon Creek. The road curves up in a long slow slope near Bayfarm.

Stephen and I are walking to school that death day, my schoolbag slung over my shoulder, his strapped to his back. In my bag are two new scribblers, one with a picture of a dog and one with two little girls. I have pencils, wax crayons, scissors, a cube eraser, all new in a new pencil case, and my lunch is in a rectangular metal lunch box with a diagonal slot in the lid for a small pair of ivory chopsticks. My lunch that Obasan made is two moist and sticky rice balls with a salty red plum in the center of each, a boiled egg to the side with a tight square of lightly boiled greens. Stephen has peanut-butter sandwiches, an apple, and a thermos of soup. My schoolbag thumps against my hips as we walk.

We have just come out of the patch of woods near the missionaries' place when I see two big boys, Percy Bower and another boy, running down the road. Stephen sees them too and freezes briefly.

"Don't notice," he whispers, barely moving his mouth.

Percy has a handful of stones and throws them down the road. When he sees us, he calls out, "Hey, Gimpy, where ya goin'?"

"Takin' yer girlfriend to school?" the other boy shouts.

They catch up to us and begin dancing in front of Stephen, jabbing him on the shoulder. "Fight, Jap. Fight!"

Stephen stands still as a stone. One of his hands is on the strap of his backpack ready to take it off.

"C'mon, ya gimpy Jap!"

Stephen hands me his lunch box. I step backward, wanting to run away, wanting to stay with Stephen. He is taking his schoolbag off when we hear one of the missionaries shouting at us. She is a thin woman with light brown hair. I see her at Sunday school.

"Here here!" The voice is sharp, like an ax chopping logs into kindling. She is standing at the side of the house, her hands on her hips, her feet apart.

The boys flee, sprinting down the road. Stephen, with his schoolbag dangling from one shoulder, begins walking rapidly in the opposite direction toward Bayfarm. I catch up to him and hand him his lunch box.

We walk together rapidly and in silence, past the Doukhobor store and across the road to the open field. In the middle of the field stands the school and, behind the school, the rows and rows of small wood huts, each with its stack of wood—round logs, logs chopped in quarters, neat stacks of kindling wood. Miyuki's place is hidden from view by the school. All the houses are the same—fourteen feet wide and twenty-eight feet long. Two families live in each house. Laundry hangs from lines strung on poles. Wooden sidewalks extend out short distances from doorways to outhouses, and around gardens.

"Miyuki's sister likes you," I say to Stephen.

"Hah!" Stephen snorts.

Sometimes, instead of staying at school to eat lunch, I go to Miyuki's house. We sit on a bench by a table that takes up almost all the room. On the other side of a partition is a family with three children. We can all hear each other talking. Miyuki's mother gives me some pickles and a plate of lightly fried vegetable okazu to eat with my rice balls. After the meal she usually hands me a wet cloth to wipe the sticky film of rice off my fingertips.

I am telling Stephen about Miyuki's sister when I turn and see that Stephen is no longer walking beside me. We are about halfway into the open field. I turn around and Stephen is standing still and staring past me.

Not far from school, and directly in the line of our walk, is a cluster of boys. It is something about the way they stand there—not moving. Not making a sound.

"C'mon, Steef," I say, feeling curious.

Stephen is shifting back and forth uncomfortably, then turns abruptly and walks away from me.

There are six boys altogether. I glance down as I approach them. The circle is tight and their heads are bent, the bodies tense. I peer through a space between two of the boys. At first all that I can see are the hands and the white feathers fluttering on the ground. One boy suddenly breaks and runs from the circle.

"Hey, Jiro," the boy closest to me shouts after him. None of the others move. I am unable either to move or to avert my eyes.

I recognize two of the boys standing. Tak and Seigo are big boys in grade five. Danny, a small boy in Stephen's class, is kneeling on the ground. Danny is tough. His clothes are always shabbier than everyone else's. His socks hang over his boots or sometimes he has no socks at all.

The boy who is doing the killing is Sho, a shiny-faced boy in grade five, with slippery smooth skin and sharp round eyes.

A hole about the size of both my fists is scooped out of the ground. The hen's neck is held over the hole. Danny grips the white body. Sho holds the head, pulling it taut. Blood drips like a slow nosebleed into the hole. The chicken's body quivers and jerks, its feet clutching and trembling.

"Got to make it suffer," Sho says. He is sitting on his

haunches and his hand squeezes the chicken's tiny head. Its beak is open, but there is no sound. The pocketknife is on the ground beside him, the blade smeared red. Sho's eyes are like the pocketknife, straight, bright, sharp.

"Is it dead yet?" I ask. My question is a prayer. I am paralyzed.

The boys ignore me. I wait, attending the chicken's quivering, the plump body pulsing and beating like a disembodied heart. As long as the moving continues, I wait. Sho picks up the knife and cuts into the neck wound. The chicken jerks and Danny loses his grip. It lurches away and flaps drunkenly over the field. Sho jumps up and runs after the chicken as it leaps and flutters high in the air, then comes crashing down to the ground, one wing slapping and dragging on the earth. He grabs the chicken by the wing, clutching its body against his shirt. Its feet stick straight out. The wings flap wildly as Sho grabs the feet. His arm jerks high up over his head and the air stirs even where I stand. The chicken's neck gyrates and it splatters the ground and Sho's face and shirt with its dripping blood. There is no sound from the chicken except a strange squeaking noise from the wings as if they are metal hinges.

"Kill it, Sho."

Although the air is raining with feathers and sudden red splatterings, there is a terrible stillness and soundlessness as if the whole earth cannot contain the chicken's dying. Over and over, like a kite caught in a sudden gust, it plunges.

"Kill it, Sho."

Danny kneels on the ground, his fist clutching the knife. From across the field, I can hear the sound of the school bell and the shouts of the children as they run to their places. Sho begins to run, swinging the bleeding struggling chicken as he goes. I run too, following the boys across the field to the schoolyard, where a loudspeaker is summoning us.

We are late. The singing is already beginning.

> *O Canada, our home and native land*
> *True patriot love in all thy sons command*
> *With glowing hearts we see thee rise*
> *The true north, strong and free. . . .*

We scuttle into place like insects under the floorboards. I am the last child in the single file of children in my class, standing to the left of the main wooden sidewalk in front of the wide stairs. The stairs lead to the center of the long covered platform like a hall connecting the two buildings of Pine Crescent School.

> *O Canada, glorious and free*
> *O Canada, we stand on guard for thee!*

Kenji is in the row ahead of me, behind a girl called Hatsumi, and Miyuki is in front of her. When the principal, Mr. Tsuji, starts to talk, we stand with our hands straight down our sides.

"Good morning, boys and girls," he says.

"Good morning, Mr. Tsuji," we reply in unison. I am barely listening to what Mr. Tsuji is saying. From behind the school, I can see Sho running, then slowing to a walk as we start our school song.

> *Slocan, get on your toes*
> *We are as everyone knows*
> *The school with spirit high!*
> *We all do our best*

And never never rest
Till we with triumph cry . . .

I am wondering where he left the chicken and if it is dead at last. The teacher in front is waving her arms vigorously and urging us to sing. All her gestures are as intense and jerky as a hen's and she flutters and broods and clucks over us.

Work with all your might
Come on, rise up, and fight
And never give up hope
The banner we will hold with pride
As to victory we stride.

Sho is at the end of his line and his smooth face is streaked. His shirt sleeve has a red blotch on it and a small pocketknife dangles from a string tied to a belt loop. He is not singing. I don't sing either.

"Once more," Mr. Tsuji says, "Slocan, get on your toes . . ."

I hate school. I hate running the gauntlet of white kids in the woods close to home. I hate, now, walking through the field where the chicken was killed. And I hate walking past the outhouse where the kitten died. At least it should be dead now.

That other death place by the skating rink is close to where the girl with white hair lives. Her hair is so white and fine that it flies around her like a cloud. Her eyebrows are white too. Whenever she sees me, her eyes grow narrow, one shoulder rises slightly, her nostrils widen, and she turns her head away, as if she has suddenly smelled something bad.

One Thursday after school, I am walking down the path close to the skating rink and can hear a kitten mewing. The girl with white hair is standing by the outhouse at the edge of the rink.

"You threw my kitten down there," she says.

I stand still listening. The voice is weak—a faint steady mewing.

"Go in there and get her for me," she orders.

"I didn't do it," I say.

"You did too."

"I didn't."

"Did."

"Didn't."

Her eyes grow small and beady. Two bullets. She thrusts her chin out and lunges with her foot as if she is about to rush at me. I run home.

The next morning on the way to school, there is no sound from the outhouse, but on the way home, the kitten is mewing again. No one is nearby. I stand and wait. I wait till long after the sun goes behind the mountain. No one comes to help. Even the white-haired girl does not come by.

It all becomes part of my hospital dream. The kitten cries day after day, not quite dead, unable to climb out and trapped in the outhouse. The maggots are crawling in its eyes and mouth. Its fur is covered in slime and feces. Chickens with their heads half off flap and swing upside down in midair. The baby in the dream has fried-egg eyes and his excrement is soft and yellow as corn mush. His head is covered with an oatmeal scab, under which his scalp is a wet wound. The doctor in the dream is angry and British. His three uncomely children all take aspirins to fight their headaches. The nurse combs and combs my hair, the sharp teeth scraping the top of my head.

23

When I come home from the hospital, Nomura-obasan is no longer there. The quilt of blue and white squares on her cot is strangely straight and orderly, as if a hill had suddenly been flattened into a farmer's field. She's moved, Obasan tells me, back to her daughter's family in town. For a few days, I sleep in Nomura-obasan's bed, resting and reading and rereading two books so often I almost memorize them. One is about a little girl called Heidi who lives in the mountains with her grandfather and another is a book called *Little Men*. I keep them at the head of the bed on the stool where Nomura-obasan used to have her knitting and her pills.

The rest of that summer in Slocan, the fall and winter of 1943, and all the following year are a crowded collage of memories—Sunday-school outings, Christmas concerts, sports days, hikes, report cards, letters from Aunt Emily and Father, the arrival of a piano in the crowded room where Uncle and Obasan sleep.

On Saturdays, Stephen and I often stand in the long long line of children at the Green Light Café near the Orange Hall for an ice-cream cone each. Or we walk down the main street, peering in at the women trying the new cold permanent wave at Ikeda's Beauty Salon, beside the bathhouse the carpenters made. In the evenings we read at the kitchen table by the light of the gas lamp, poring over every word in the mimeographed school paper, the *Pine Crescent Breeze*. There's also the regular appearance of the *Vancouver Daily Province* with war stories that Stephen reads. When Germany surrenders he tacks the headline page over his bed. I am more interested in the lives of Little Orphan Annie, Mandrake the Magician, Moon Mullins, the Gumps, the Katzenjammer Kids, Myrtle with her black pigtails sticking out the sides of her wide-brimmed hat. My days and weeks are peopled with creatures of flesh and storybook and comic strip.

In Bayfarm, in Slocan, the community flourishes with stores, crafts, gardens, and homegrown enterprise: Sakamoto Tailors, Gardiner General Merchant, Nose Shoe Hospital, Slocan Barber T. Kuwahara Prop., Tahara's Barber Shop, Slocan Dress Shop, T. Shorthouse Meat Market, Tokyo Sobaya for Chinese noodles, Tak Toyota's photo studio, Shigeta watch repair, Kasubuchi dressmaker, Ed Clough groceries. The ghost town is alive and kicking like Ezekiel's resurrected valley of bones, the foot bones connected to the ankle bones, the ankle bones connected to the leg bones, and all them bones, them bones, jitterbugging in the Odd Fellows Hall, skating in the

rinks, hiking and running up and down the mountainsides
and the streets and paths of Slocan. There are craftsmen carv-
ing ornaments and utensils from tree stumps, roots, and driftwood, making basins, bins, spoons, flower stands, bowls;
building wooden flumes, bathhouses, meeting halls. There are
times for resourceful hands to be busy with survival tasks—
pickling, preserving, gardening, drying and smoking food.
There are times to relax and talk, to visit, to worship, to com-
mune.

One place that we meet regularly is the public bathhouse.
Every few evenings or late afternoons we walk the half mile to
town with our basins and bars of soap and washcloths. Sometimes we go just before supper, when the place is not too
crowded, but more often we go in the early evening. Those
who arrive late are likely to find the bath less hot and less
clean.

The bath is a place of deep bone warmth and rest. It is
always filled with a slow steamy chatter from women and girls
and babies. It smells of wet cloth and wet wood and wet skin.
We are one flesh, one family, washing each other or submerged in the hot water, half awake, half asleep. The bath
times are like a hazy happy dream except for the one occasion
that remains in my memory like an unsightly billboard on an
otherwise pleasant scene.

One evening in the late spring of 1945, Obasan and I are
much later than usual for the bath. After supper, she and I
are removing the tiny round black dots, hard as BB shot, that
are found in the sack of white rice we have recently bought.
She dips a cup into the sack and pours the rice onto our trays,
the sound like a sudden spattering of hail against the window.
She is much faster than I am, spreading the pile to a thin
layer, then placing her index finger on a black dot or an occasional stone and pushing it swiftly off the tray. When our

trays only contain the white grains, we pour them into a square tin between us. We are still at work when Uncle and Stephen return from their bath.

"Mada?" Uncle asks in surprise. "Are you still at work? Late, is it not?"

Obasan murmurs agreement, but she continues doing a few more trays.

When we are finished, we finally set off for the bathhouse. It is the latest that we have ever gone. We arrive and push open the swinging door as some older girls are leaving, their skin still glowing and hair damp. It is so late there are hardly any people left in the bath. The shelves above the long bench, along the back wall, usually piled high with neat bundles of clothes, are surprisingly bare. In front of the bench area is the slatted floor with its square wooden basins piled up in the corner. The bath is about as large as two double beds.

I go to the bench and begin to remove my clothes beside a thin old woman whose back is to me. I am slipping out of my shoes and socks when the woman turns around. Her breasts are loose flaps of skin that hang flat and long like deflated balloons.

"Kon-ban-wa, good evening," says Nomura-obasan's familiar voice. She holds her washcloth over her abdomen with one hand and her other hand covers her mouth. Her false teeth are in her basin beside her. She bows to Obasan, who has put our basins onto the washing area.

"Tonight, such lateness," Nomura-obasan says. "The bath will be lukewarm." When she talks without her teeth, she sounds as if she is chewing her words.

Obasan is removing her clothes as she chats with Nomura-obasan, and I am already in the washing area, dipping my basin into the tub and pouring water over my shoulders. A woman with a face like a monkey, and her hair piled high in a bun, is squatting on her haunches against the wall of the tub, beside a puffy-faced woman. The water covers their shoulders and necks right up to their chins. In a corner opposite them are Reiko and Yuki, two sisters I know from school, one older and one younger than I am. The woman with the monkey face has a squashed-down nose that almost meets her protruding lower lip. I have seen her before in stores, scuttling along with her eyes darting. The two women are glancing in the direction of Obasan and Nomura-obasan.

I dip my basin in again and again and rinse myself thoroughly before Obasan is even undressed. Beside me are scattered a few of the square wooden basins, the corners slippery with soap.

"So fast," Nomura-obasan says as she joins me on the slatted floor. She is almost bent over double as she walks on the slippery slats. Tonight the water is not as boiling hot as it usually is and I do not hesitate to step right in for the soaking. I move toward the corner of the tub where Reiko and Yuki are. As I draw nearer, I see that the monkey-faced woman is beckoning to them. Is she their mother? When I look back, she acknowledges me with a crooked unfriendly smile but keeps nodding to the girls. For some reason she is disapproving of me. I search her face, then look away, puzzling.

"Let's swim," Yuki says in greeting to me, and she and Reiko dog-paddle through the hot water to the other side. I stay in the corner alone, watching the two women whispering with their eyes lowered, the monkey woman occasionally glancing at Nomura-obasan.

Obasan rinses off Nomura-obasan and as they step into the water together the two other women do not look up. Apart from Reiko and Yuki splashing, and the steady hissing stream of cold water from the cold-water tap in the washing area, the bathhouse is strangely silent. I have never found it so empty of banter. I have never felt the edges that I find here tonight.

The two women are whispering to Reiko and Yuki and avoiding all contact with us, greeting us neither formally nor informally. Obasan and Nomura-obasan also have their heads down. Yuki, who has been swimming around and calling to me, stops and looks at me oddly. What, I wonder, can it be?

The two women step out, beckoning to the girls to follow them. Reiko leaves at once, but Yuki lingers in the water, paddling back and forth along the width of the tub.

"Hurry," the monkey woman says in a sharp voice to Yuki. She beckons with her hand in the waving slapping motion and the quick nodding of the head that means "Come at once." On the bench, Reiko is drying herself and making hissing noises, pointing to an insect.

Obasan is talking to Nomura-obasan in a quiet voice. "Much strength has come to you," she says.

"Thanks to your prayers," Nomura-obasan murmurs through her toothless mouth.

"A matter of great thankfulness," Obasan says, smiling. When Obasan smiles, sometimes her eyes grow soft and moist as if she is about to cry.

I feel reassured to hear them talking and push out toward Yuki, who is still swimming back and forth. Yuki stops swimming and backs away from me. She steps out of the tub and goes to join her sister and the two women as they dress.

"Come," Nomura-obasan calls to me. "Baa-chan will wash your back tonight."

We climb out to the washing area as Reiko and Yuki and the two women dress and leave. There are still no words, even as they go, although I wave to Yuki and Reiko.

"Bye," Yuki calls, and the monkey woman seems annoyed with her.

"Why was there no speaking?" I ask when the door swings shut. Nomura-obasan is making her washcloth into a fist to rub the aka off my back.

"There was nothing to speak of perhaps," Obasan says lightly.

"A shameful matter," Nomura-obasan says quietly.

"It is nothing," Obasan says as she washes herself.

I kneel with my head bent forward as Nomura-obasan rubs vigorously, then it is my turn to wash her. I am pouring a wooden basin full of water over her shoulders when the door opens and Sachiko Saito peers in. I have often taken a few eggs from our chickens to the Saito house. Obasan says I must always say hello to old Mr. Saito, whose limbs are always trembling. Once when I handed him the eggs, he dropped them and looked as if he would weep.

"Kon-ban-wa," Nomura-obasan calls. "Good evening. The water is still fine."

"Gomen-nasai," Sachiko apologizes. "I'm sorry to disturb you. I will come later."

"No no," Nomura-obasan says. "Come. No worry."

"Yes, come," Obasan says, nodding. "It is so late tonight, we are the last."

Sachiko hesitates, then pushes open the door. Her old grandfather follows her, one hand on a cane and the other gripping her arm. Old Saito-ojisan coming to the girls' bath?

"Gomen-nasai," he says. His voice shakes like autumn leaves. "Later, we will return."

"It is fine, it is fine," Nomura-obasan says. "The same as our own family. Come. Ira-shai."

"Do you mind if my grandfather comes in?" Sachiko says, asking me.

"It's okay," I say, not looking up.

Sachiko is a pretty high school girl with large eyes. She is apologizing that she must bring her grandfather to the girls' side because her brother is ill.

"Dozo. Please feel free. We are finished," Obasan says as we reenter the bath for the final soaking. We are careful not to watch as Sachiko helps her grandfather to undress, but Nomura-obasan chats easily with them.

"It is peaceful, is it not, when the crowd is gone?"

Sachiko's grandfather sits on one of the small wooden stools as Sachiko dips the basin in the tub. His face, neck, and hands are dark, but below his neck his body is pale as ivory. He seems to be trembling less as the hot water pours over him. All across his back, around to the side, and down one leg, there is a red scar. Sachiko scrubs his back and chats with Nomura-obasan, as Obasan and I get out to dry ourselves and dress.

Most afternoons, the room is thick with the steam from the bath and the water rolls down in little streams from the walls, but this late at night, the water has cooled and there is only a little mist with water drops on the ceiling and walls.

I am not hot enough tonight to douse myself with a basin full of cold water before dressing.

Outside the bathhouse, the air is clear and cool as fresh running water, and full of the damp wood and sap smell from the sawmill. The green air whisks away the wetness from the bath.

Just as we come to the crossing where the road to the Green Light Café meets the road to our place, I see Yuki and Reiko and two other girls. Yuki waves to me. Obasan continues walking up the road, but I stay behind, waving back to Yuki and waiting for them to reach me. When they are almost beside me, Reiko stops.

"My mom says we can't play with you," she says.

Yuki and the others stop when Reiko says this.

"Why not?"

"You're sick. You've all got TB. You and the Nomuras and your dad." Her words are spraying out in a rush and she points her finger at me. "That's why Stephen is limping."

"It is not!"

"It is too!" Her voice is rising and she keeps pointing her finger at me. "Nobody will marry you," she says, in a taunting singsong voice.

"What!"

"You sleep on the floor!"

"I do not!"

"Yes, you do. That's how you get it."

"I haven't got it."

"Yes, you have. Your dad is in the hospital, so there. My mom told me."

I flee. I run along the shortcut toward home and burst in through the kitchen door, slamming the screen door behind me. Stephen and Uncle are at the table.

"What is TB?" I ask.

Stephen ignores my question. When I continue asking, Uncle says quietly, "For some people it is a shameful matter to be ill. But it is a matter of misfortune, not shame."

24

The bantam rooster's early-morning crow is more a choked

chirp than the full-throated call of the regular rooster.

It is early autumn in 1945, several months after the eve-

ning of the late-night bath. I waken suddenly, before the reg-

ular summons of the rooster, to the soft steady steam of rain

and fog and a grayness thicker than sleep. Something has

touched me but I do not know what it is. Something not

human, not animal, that masquerades the way a tree in the

night takes on the contours of hair and fingers and arms.

Only my eyes move, searching the shelf ceiling above my

bunk. Stephen in the bunk below is asleep, his mouth squashed open on his pillow.

She is here. She is not here. She is reaching out to me with a touch deceptive as down, with hands and fingers that wave like grass around my feet, and her hair falls and falls and falls from her head like streamers of paper rain. She is a maypole woman to whose apron-string streamers I cling and around whose skirts I dance. She is a ship leaving the harbor, tied to me by colored paper streamers that break and fall into a swirling wake. The wake is a thin black pencil line that deepens and widens and fills with a grayness that reaches out with tentacles to embrace me. I leap and wake.

Something is happening but I do not know what it is. I listen intently, all my senses alert.

Yesterday Stephen came running back from town shouting that the war was over and we had won. "We won, we won, we won!" he cried, running through the yard with both hands raised and his fingers in the V-for-Victory sign. The bantam rooster that roams freely in the yard squawked and flew away to a branch in the apple tree, from which it stared down fluffing its brown-and-red feathers till it looked twice its size.

After Stephen calmed down, he climbed the woodshed and hopped to the roof of the house, carrying a hammer and nails and a flagpole with a well-worn Union Jack.

This morning there is no shouting, only the familiar soft thudding of a log dropping into the wood stove and the clank of the stove grate being pushed back into place. Obasan is up and there is the plip noise of the dipper entering the bucket of water and—splash—the kettle filling, once, twice, three times, then the lid of the kettle, clink, the shuffle to the stove, the slide of the kettle, and the hiss of the water turning to steam where it spills on the hot surface.

The grayness moves aside, then returns, separates, but returns confident as breath.

Obasan's feet are treading a faster rhythm than normal.

I turn my head and peer down into the kitchen. The coal-oil lamp on the table is lit, the wick turned just high enough that there is no smoke going up the glass chimney. On the window ledge by the cactus plants is the bowl of water with the three black hairs that Stephen has been watching for days. Miss Pye, Stephen's music teacher in Vancouver, wrote him that black hairs turn into water snakes.

"How long does it take?" I asked Stephen a few days ago.

Stephen shrugged as he stared into the bowl and pushed the hairs with his forefinger. However long the hair stays hair, Stephen swears Miss Pye never tells lies. Somewhere between her words and his watching is a world of water snakes he cannot find.

Uncle is up and sitting at the table, stretching his arms.

"Sa!" he says, punctuating his stretch as if he has come to the end of his thoughts. Obasan turns the toast on the wire grill and pours tea into one of the large flat-bottomed mugs.

I curl up under my covers again and close my eyes. The weight of the nightmare is as persistent as rain, a shape that falls and evaporates, rises up from the earth and disappears again.

"Stephen," I whisper, leaning over the side of the bunk and blowing at his face. I push aside the heavy futon with my foot and feel for the ladder rung with my toes. "Wake up," I say as I step onto his bed.

The bantam rooster has started a gurgle of croaks as if he is trying to outdo the proper rooster.

"So early?" Uncle asks as I appear.

"Sleep some more," Obasan whispers.

They are both still in their nemaki and Obasan's long braid of hair dangles down her back.

I stumble out to the outhouse. The sharp air of the mountain morning cuts through my fog. When I come back Obasan hands me a square of toast.

I glance at the water-snake bowl to see if the hairs have changed, but nothing has happened. And then, as I finish my toast, I see through the doorway that Uncle and Obasan's room is different. The cupboard bookshelf Uncle made which stood along the wall is no longer there and instead I can see the end of Nomura-obasan's cot. I stand up to see better and Obasan gestures me to silence.

"Quietly," she whispers.

"Who's here?" I ask, tiptoeing into the room. Has Nomura-obasan come back?

On the side of the room in front of the narrow bed and the piano, and all over the rest of the room, there are piles of empty boxes. Someone is in the bed, an arm crooked above the pillow. The sleeves of the nemaki cover the head.

The arms move then, and I see the familiar head, the smooth face, the high cheekbones, the black hair straight back over his head as if it had just been combed. Without moving from the spot, my body leaps. My hands, palms open, fall to my thighs.

Without turning his head to look at me, he beckons, and I see the same hand, the long thin fingers that I have watched moving with confidence over the keyboard.

"Good morning, Naomi-chan." He is talking to me. How does he know it is me? He has not moved. His back is toward me.

He turns then and smiles and I scrape my knees on the cupboard as I fling myself onto the bed. He sits up and gathers me into his serious smile. His forehead is wrinkled with new puzzle lines as if he has been asking questions all the time.

We do not talk. His hands cup my face. I wrap my arms around his neck. The button of his pajama top presses into my cheek. I can feel his heart's steady thump thump thump. I am Minnie and Winnie in a seashell, resting on a calm seashore. I am Goldilocks, I am Momotaro returning. I am leaf in the wind restored to its branch, child of my father come home. The world is safe once more and Chicken Little is wrong. The sky is not falling down after all.

There is no sound in the house except the satisfied "Aah" that Uncle makes after he has swallowed a hot drink, and the scrape scrape of Obasan's knife buttering the toast. In the chicken house outside the rooster is still crowing and the neighbor's dog barks three short excited blasts.

The laughter in my arms is quiet as the moon, quiet as snow falling, quiet as the white light from the stars. Into this I fall and fall and fall, swaying safe as a feather through all my waiting hours and silent night watchings, past the everyday walk through the woods and the noisy school grounds, down past the Slocan City stores and the sawmill whine and Rough Lock Bill's cabin, back along the train journey and the mountain ridges and the train station in Vancouver with all the people and the luggage and missionaries and women trotting here and there, carrying babies and boxes. Back up the long bus ride to Marpole and our house and the hedge around the yard and the peach tree outside my window and the goldfish bowl in the music room and I am in my father's arms again my father's arms.

When I move my head finally, the words rush around stumbling to form questions, but there are no questions and I do not understand how he has found us or when we will return home. But he is here now and his hand strokes my sleep-tangled hair.

Then suddenly Stephen is in the room, barefoot, with his nemaki open to his belly and the sash half undone. He has his flutes in his hand as he usually does.

Father nods as Stephen stands there staring, wiping the sleep from his eyes. "Good morning," Father says.

"Dad!" Stephen is upon us with a howl.

Father releases me and takes a flute, his wide-set eyes delighted. For a moment, the lines disappear from his brow and he is exactly as he used to be. "These?" Father turns the instrument around, fondling it with his fingertips.

Uncle grins and squeezes into the room. He sits on the edge of the cot, pushing the wooden boxes aside.

Deftly, Father places the pads of his fingertips on the holes and, holding the mouthpiece flat against his lower lip, he plays arpeggios rapidly. Then, with a light legato, he opens with the first few notes of "The White Cliffs of Dover." Stephen picks up the tune immediately and Father's flute dips and trills birdlike notes in and around the tune. Without a break, Father leads into "Waltzing Matilda," and Stephen improvises harmonies. Their heads nod in time to the music and their elbows sway like airborne birds as the clear notes bounce off the walls and the cow-dung ceiling. Stephen's head is angled up like the rooster when it crows and flaps its wings sending out its call.

The music goes on and on from song to song. Uncle taps with spoons on his knees. "Whoo," Father says finally, and shakes his head approvingly. "Not bad," he says, and Stephen is on center stage, beaming.

"Not bad," Uncle says.

Obasan turns down the coal-oil lamp and, cupping her hand behind the chimney, she blows out the night's light. She hands us all pieces of toast.

25

After music, after breakfast, Uncle and Father sit at the kitchen table and I can see it in Father's eyes. It's happening again, it's happening again—the same stare, the eyes searching elsewhere.

I do not understand the words.

"What are they saying, Stephen? What are the boxes for?"

"We're moving."

"We're going home?"

"No."

"Why not?"

"We can't."

"But why?"

Everyone, Stephen tells me, is going away again, and again we do not know where. Every day or so since spring, a few families at a time have been leaving on a passenger car attached to the local freight train. Obasan and I go quite often to the station to wave goodbye. Last week Uncle was called to the office of the Security Commission, a small hut on the main street with a long table and an oval-shaped tin stove.

"Why can't we go home, Stephen?"

"Because. That's why," Stephen says crossly, and tells me no more. His eyes are like Father's, searching.

The orders, given to Uncle and Father in 1945, reach me via Aunt Emily's package in 1972, twenty-seven years later. The delivery service is slow these days. Understanding is even slower. I still do not see the Canadian face of the author of those words.

The letters, from the Department of Labour, British Columbia Security Commission, are in purple mimeograph ink —form letters with Father's and Uncle's names typed in the left-hand corner.

Tadashi Nakane

As you have no doubt already heard, the Government has ordered that people of Japanese origin are to be segregated into different camps according to the category under which they come.

As you have expressed your desire to remain in Canada and for various reasons you are not considered suitable for Eastern Placement, you will be required to remain in New Denver.

This order is imperative and must be obeyed.

B.C. Security Commission

The letter that Uncle received is different.

Isamu Nakane

In accordance with the segregation programme which is now being carried out by the Government, you will be required to move to Kaslo where you will await Eastern Placement; as Slocan project has been selected as a Repatriation Camp and will house only those who have elected at the present time, or who may elect in the near future, to return to Japan.

Transportation arrangements will be made for you and for shipment of your effects and you will be notified as to the exact time that you will leave for Rosebery to entrain for Kaslo.

Beds, tables, stoves, stools, and all fixtures must be left in house or rooms you are now occupying.

No extension of this order can be granted.

Obasan is wrapping the pretty blue-and-white shoyu bottle shaped like a tiny teapot in a piece of the *Vancouver Daily Province*.

"Where are we going?"

No one answers me and I know it is not a time for talking. The page that Obasan is using is the one with the Tillicum Club news. Stephen and I are both members and I keep my badge—a totem-pole pin—in a round ivory box. I always read the pet market and the list of pen pals on the Tillicum Club page. Once my name was in the Happy Birthday column and I never knew how it got there. The Tillicum slogan is "Kla-How-Ya, we're all friends together."

"Shall I pack too?"

"In here," Obasan replies. She is wrapping the Mickey Mouse plates and the rice bowls in layers of comics, crumpling them all together—the Katzenjammer Kids with naughty Rollo and Lena Dollink, Prince Valiant and Aleta, white-eyed Little Orphan Annie with her dog Sandy and her Daddy Warbucks, who always rescues her, and Jiggs and Maggie with their pin-thin dog.

"Kla-How-Ya," I say, as I push my box into the colorful crumples.

Night falls and we are all working except Uncle, who has gone to town. Father is hammering boxes shut and Stephen is helping to secure them with ropes. We stop when we hear footsteps on the porch.

"Kon-ban-wa," a familiar voice calls. "Good evening."

Obasan opens the door and Nomura-obasan comes in, bowing deeply. "Iso-gashi toki ni—in a time when you are busy . . ." She is even thinner than before and holding a cane. Behind her is old Saito-ojisan, dressed in a suit, with Sachiko leading him.

"Kon-ban-wa," he says, his voice rasping as he enters the room. Sachiko is out of breath as she bows lightly and sits on a box.

"Tadashi-san, you have come well," Nomura-obasan says when she sees Father. She wipes tears from her eyes. "Such a long time."

"A long time," Saito-ojisan repeats, nodding his head and resting a trembling hand on Father's shoulder.

Obasan pushes the boxes aside as the minister, Nakayama-sensei, arrives carrying a black bag. The room is full of bowing and boxes are arranged in a semicircle.

Nakayama-sensei opens his black bag and takes out a long black gown with black cloth buttons and a black cord which he ties around his waist. Over this he dons a shorter white gown.

Obasan, Father, Uncle, Sachiko, Stephen, Nomura-
obasan, and I kneel on the floor but Saito-ojisan remains
standing, leaning on his stick as Sensei says loudly, "Let us
pray." He begins the service, speaking rapidly, sometimes in
Japanese, sometimes in English.

"Almighty God, unto whom all hearts be open, all desires
known and from whom no secrets are hid . . ."

My head is down and I can see Sachiko's shiny shoes beside me and the soles of Sensei's boots, as he rocks up and
down. When I glance up quickly for a moment, I see that
everyone's eyes are closed except Sensei's. His head is tilted
up as if he is addressing the ceiling.

"Zenno no Kami yo subete no hito no kokoro wa Shu ni
araware . . ."

"Amen," everyone says at the end of the prayer, and Sensei addresses them. "Hear what our Lord Jesus Christ saith.
Thou shalt love the Lord thy God with all thy heart, and with
all thy soul, and with all thy mind. This is the first and great
commandment, and the second is like unto it: Thou shalt
love thy neighbor as thyself . . ."

Nomura-obasan has trouble balancing and Obasan puts
her arms around her to steady her and help her to her feet for
the reading of the gospel and the recitation of the creed.

"I believe," Sensei says in a loud voice.

And everyone repeats in a mixture of Japanese and English. "I believe in one God, the Father Almighty, Maker of
heaven and earth—miyuru mono to miezaru mono no
tsukurinushi o shinzu . . ."

Saito-ojisan's false teeth clack as he says the words, his
voice wheezing as he stumbles to keep up to the others.

Nakayama-sensei plunges on as if there is no time to
spare. "Almighty and ever-living God, who by Thy holy Apos-

tle has taught us to make prayers and supplications, and to give thanks for all men. We humbly beseech Thee most mercifully to receive these our prayers which we offer unto Thy Divine Majesty; beseeching Thee to inspire continually the universal church with the spirit of truth, unity, and concord: And grant, that all they that do confess Thy holy Name may agree in the truth of Thy holy word, and live in unity and godly love. We beseech Thee also to save and defend all Christian Kings, Princes, and Governors; and specially Thy servant George, our King: that under him we may be godly and quietly governed. . . ."

Stephen has been kneeling but shifts and sits on the edge of an open box. There is a muffled crack like the noise of a twig breaking under a pile of pine needles. Stephen leaps off the box and kneels beside it. Father glances over at him.

Sensei keeps praying. ". . . And to all Thy people give Thy heavenly grace and specially to this congregation here present . . ."

Stephen reaches into the box, removing fistfuls of crumpled newspapers. He lifts out the cameraphone carefully and sets it beside him.

"What broke?" I whisper as he stares into the box.

He looks up at Father as he brings out Mother's "Silver Threads Among the Gold" record. One small piece is broken off like a bite off a giant cookie.

Father holds out his hand and Stephen passes the broken piece to him.

"Lift up your hearts," Sensei says.

"We lift them up unto the Lord," Sachiko and Father reply in English.

"Let us give thanks unto our Lord God."

"It is meet and right so to do."

"It is very meet, right, and our bounden duty, that we should at all times and in all places, give thanks unto Thee, O Lord . . ."

Father places the broken record down beside him and beckons Stephen over. He holds Stephen close as the prayers continue.

"Hear us, O merciful Father, we most humbly beseech Thee . . ." The words, rushing by in a whirl, sound as familiar as the wind rushing through the pines behind the house. But the meaning of the words is unknown.

Sensei carries a small silver box in one hand and lifts out a tiny paper-thin white square which he snaps in half. He raises the broken wafer as he says ". . . in the same night that He was betrayed He took Bread; and when He had given thanks, He brake it, and gave it to His disciples, saying, 'Take, eat . . .'"

Father, Obasan, and Uncle are kneeling but the others stand, their hands formed into cups in which Sensei places the paper bread. One by one the hands rise to the mouths, taking first the wafers, then the wine from the silver chalice, tiny as an egg cup.

"Drink this in remembrance that Christ's blood was shed for thee and be thankful."

Nomura-obasan is trembling so much that Obasan stands beside her and holds her.

". . . And here we offer and present unto Thee, O Lord, ourselves, our souls and bodies to be a reasonable, holy, and living sacrifice. . . ."

Obasan and Sensei help Nomura-obasan to sit down as Sensei ends the prayers and begins to sing, his voice strong and deep. He flings his head back.

Till we meet
Till we meet
God be with us. . . .

Father's eyes are closed. He joins in the singing but his rich baritone voice is weak and thin as if his throat is in pain. Saito-ojisan takes breaths between the syllables, sitting down finally on a wooden box as the others stand to sing.

Ma-ta o-o-o
Hi-ma de
Ma-ta o-o
Hi-ma de
Kami no-o-o
Ma-mo-ri
Nagami o
Hanare za-re

It is as if Saito-ojisan is singing alone to his own rhythm. As we come to the end he is still singing, his voice straining.

"Once more," Sensei says. "Utai masho. Let us sing again."

The voices fill the tiny room and I take in the sound as if the music could shut out the night terrors.

When the song ends for the third time, Obasan takes Saito-ojisan's bony hands in her own. "Mata itsuka. Again someday. Let us meet."

Nomura-obasan draws a handkerchief from her sleeve and holds it over her trembling face. Nakayama-sensei puts his hand on her back and says, "In a time like this, let us trust in God even more. To trust when life is easy is no trust."

"There is a time for crying," Saito-ojisan whispers, his voice quavering. "Someday the time for laughter will come."

"Assuredly, that must be so," Sensei says. He gathers his silver box and chalice and flasks of water and wine and puts them into a small case and into his bag. "Wherever you go, God willing, I will visit you. We will not abandon one another. We will meet again," he says as he removes his gowns.

He puts a hand on Stephen's head. "Be a great musician like your father," he says. He turns to me. "Shikkari—be sturdy." He bows to everyone and is gone, trotting rapidly down the path to the next waiting group.

26

Bowing deeply one by one, Sachiko and her grandfather leave, Nomura-obasan leaves, disappearing forever into the night and the dispersal.

From time to time over the days and weeks of our departures I hear the wavering sound of music from a loudspeaker in town, reaching us in wails and echoes, as Guy Lombardo sings over Slocan.

Should auld acquaintance be forgot

And never brought to mind . . .

Then one day suddenly Father is not here again and I do not know what is happening.

On certain days when I go to town I see the trucks. They are full of children, mothers, fathers, boxes, old people, suitcases, furoshiki—all the people standing because there is no room to sit. The day we leave, the train station is a forest of legs and bodies waiting as the train jerks and inches back and forth, its black hulk hissing with steam and smelling of black oil drops that drip onto the cinders.

We are all standing still, as thick and full of rushing as trees in a forest storm, waiting for the giant woodsman with his mighty ax. He is in my grade-two reader, that giant woodcutter, standing leaning on his giant ax after felling the giant tree.

> *If all the seas were one sea,*
> *What a great sea that would be!*
> *And if all the trees were one tree*
> *What a great tree that would be!*
> *And if all the axes were one ax,*
> *What a great ax that would be! . . .*
> *And if all the men were one man . . .*

What would it be like if all the people at the station could be rolled up into one huge person? The trees would be as tiny as toothpicks. He could cross the mountain in one leap. He could wade through Slocan Lake and it would be like stepping in a puddle.

The missionaries are moving through the crowd, saying goodbyes. One of them bends down, saying, "Goodbye, Naomi. Goodbye, Stephen."

"Goodbye."

"Will you miss us?"

"Nope," I say with a toss of my head.

"You won't miss us even a little bit?"

"Nope." I am uncomfortable with all this talking.

She puts her arms out to hug me and I stiffen and draw back, bumping into Kenji's big brother, Mas. Mas stares at me blankly as I jostle him. He is carrying a black cloth bag over one shoulder and swings it to the other side. Where's Kenji? I wonder.

There is a loud clanging of the train bell and like a long caterpillar those who are leaving move forward onto the train, step by step, no turning back, no stepping out of line, Stephen behind Mas, Uncle behind me. The crowd stands aside, waving steadily, bowing, touching arms here and there, and then they are out of view and I'm clambering up the train steps again as I did three years ago.

We sit in two seats facing each other once more, exactly like the last time. Where is Father? Why is Kenji not with Mas? Where are we going? Will it be to a city? Remember my doll? Remember Vancouver? The escalators? Electric lights? Streetcars? Will we go home again ever?

The train shudders out of the station. I press my face against the glass as we move away from Slocan Lake and Rough Lock Bill's cabin, past the sea of upturned faces and waving hands and along the edge of the town, then into the trees and up along the thin ridges into a tunnel and we are on our way again. Clackity clack, clackity clack, clackity clack, so long, Slocan.

27

In Aunt Emily's package, the papers are piled as neatly as the thin white wafers in Sensei's silver box—symbols of communion, the materials of communication, white paper bread for the mind's meal.

We were the unwilling communicants receiving and consuming a less than holy nourishment, our eyes, cups filling with the bitter wine of a loveless communion.

Along with the letters from the government, there are copies of telegrams and the copy of the memorandum for the House of Commons and Senate prepared by the Co-operative Committee on Japanese Canadians.

Do I really want to read these?

This is Thursday. It's almost four o'clock. Stephen and Aunt Emily will be here soon. Obasan is asleep. Nakayama-sensei should be coming by at some point today. I phoned him the news earlier and he said he would drive up from Coaldale. His voice sounded remote on the phone, the steady "nh nh" sound indicating he heard what I was saying, but he had no words of comfort to offer. After a pause, he said, "Such a good man," in a tired voice. That was all he said. Nakayama-sensei is old now too and sounded almost as weary as Obasan, who can, it seems, barely keep awake. One minute she is sitting in front of me paring an apple, and the next minute her head is back on the sofa and her mouth is open in sleep, like a newborn baby. She is tired today because of Uncle's death and because so many others are dying or have already died and the time is approaching for her.

And I am tired, I suppose, because I want to get away from all this. From the past and all these papers, from the present, from the memories, from the deaths, from Aunt Emily and her heap of words. I want to break loose from the heavy identity, the evidence of rejection, the unexpressed passion, the misunderstood politeness. I am tired of living between deaths and funerals, weighted with decorum, unable to shout or sing or dance, unable to scream or swear, unable to laugh, unable to breathe out loud.

(Keep your eyes down. When you are in the city, do not look into anyone's face. That way they may not see you. That way you offend less.)

I am tired, tired like Obasan, and what will she do now what will she do?

I can escape from the question into the papers, I can escape from the papers into the question, back and forth like a hamster in a tube in a cage that hasn't been cleaned for months.

What does it all matter in the end?

"It matters to get the facts straight," Aunt Emily said last May. It was late, but she was still so full of the California conference that she was unable to sleep. The tone of her voice had softened since earlier in the evening and she sounded neither bitter nor angry. "Reconciliation can't begin without mutual recognition of facts," she said.

"Facts?"

"Yes, facts. What's right is right. What's wrong is wrong. Health starts somewhere."

The fact is that, in 1945, the gardens in Slocan were spectacular. In the spring there had been new loads of manure and fertilizer and the plants were ripening for harvest when the orders came.

The fact is that families already fractured and separated were permanently destroyed. The choice to go east of the Rockies or to Japan was presented without time for consultation with separated parents and children. Failure to choose was labeled noncooperation. Throughout the country, the pressure was on.

The Under Secretary of State for External Affairs, Norman Robertson, said, "Canada has done rather a poor job with the whole matter of the Japanese ever since they have been in Canada, therefore it might be better for them in their own interest to go to Japan." The *Vancouver Daily Province* reported, "Everything is being done to give the Japanese an opportunity to return to their homeland." Everything was done, Aunt Emily said, officially, unofficially, at all levels, and the message to disappear worked its way deep into the Nisei heart and into the bone marrow.

She showed me a circular sent from T. B. Pickersgill of the Department of Labour to every Japanese-Canadian person over the age of sixteen, telling us of "various forms of assistance provided by the Government of Canada."

"Such a generous country," Aunt Emily said as she read from the form, " '. . . This assured assistance from the government as outlined . . . will mean, to many who desire repatriation, relief from unnecessary anxiety and it will allow them to plan for their future and that of their children, along economic, social, and cultural lines which they fear might be denied them were they to remain in Canada.'

"The truth of the matter is that this—this mess of pottage—was used to strip Canadian children of their birthright."

I opened the kitchen door to let in the late-night air. It was soothing and cool and gave me a comforting feeling of distance from all the things she was saying. She took off her reading glasses and rubbed her eyes wearily as she joined me at the screen door and handed me the last of the sheaf of papers. "I know you were too young to know what was going on," she said, "but it must have been hell in the ghost towns."

The light at the door was not very good but I could read the large print of the copy of a telegram sent to Mackenzie King from some concerned missionaries in Slocan. "Conditions worse than evacuation. Repatriation and dispersal policies the cruelest cut of all. Expensive, inhuman, and absolutely unnecessary. Not even a semblance of democracy or common sense in this latest racial persecution. Segregation being rushed. Loyal people being squeezed out. Elderly parents separated from families. Work offered to the Japan-bound but none for those who stay. . . ."

"Are you in touch with any of the friends you made in Slocan?" Aunt Emily asked.

"No," I said. "Not one."

Aunt Emily knew what had happened to quite a number of people, many of whom were now living in Toronto. Kenji's grandfather, she told me, was a veteran in the Princess Pats in World War I. He cooperated with the will of the country by taking all his family and grandchildren to hunger, poverty, and ostracism in Japan. Only Mas, Kenji's older brother, remained in Canada.

"And where's Kenji?"

She didn't know. I have never found out.

Distanced as I felt in time to the people of Slocan, I could not feel as remote as the report in the *Vancouver Daily Province* sounded.

" 'Indifferent' Jap Repats Start Homeward Trek" was the headline of a report dated June 1, 1946.

Six hundred and seventy solemn-faced Japanese . . . sailed out of Vancouver Friday night bound for the "land of the rising sun." They were the first of Canada's Japanese to follow soon under Canada's Japanese Repatriation plan. One thousand of them will sail for Japan about June 15.

There were few smiling faces among the boatload. Solemnness was written in their faces; only indifference they showed. The ship of the voluntary repatriates was SS *Marine Angel.* Friday the first group watched silently as their possessions were hoisted aboard. RCMP carefully scrutinized each bundle, each suitcase, each barrel. They were searching for liquor or firearms. . . .

"What it must have been like," Aunt Emily said. "Who knows how or why they decided to leave? Some Issei without their children around couldn't read and simply signed because they were urged to."

The breeze was making a soft whistling sound as it rushed past the screen door. That and Uncle's snoring were the only other sounds to be heard in the post-midnight hour.

"What do you think happened to Mother and Grandma in Japan?" I asked. "Did they starve, do you think?"

Aunt Emily's startle was so swift and subtle it barely registered. But I could feel that somewhere, beneath her eyes, a shutter had clicked open and shut at my mentioning Mother and Grandma. It was as if my unexpected question was a sudden beam of pain that had to be extinguished immediately.

She stared into the blackness. Sometimes when I stand in a prairie night the emptiness draws me irresistibly, like a dust speck into a vacuum cleaner, and I can imagine myself disappearing off into space like a rocket with my questions trailing behind me.

"Let's go for a walk," Aunt Emily whispered.

Our eyes took a few moments to adjust to the starlight. We walked slowly along the driveway and down the middle of the gravel road. All the town lights were out and there was no sign of life anywhere except for a neighbor's cat that sauntered out of the ditch beside the road and followed us.

The quietness and spaciousness of the night altered the concentration of our evening's conversation.

"Nomi, I've told you all I can about them," she said. We walked in silence a short distance, then she asked about Obasan's and Uncle's health. And about Nakayama-sensei and his visits to them. For a while she talked sadly about Nakayama-sensei's desperation to keep the community together. To a people for whom community was the essence of life, destruction of community was the destruction of life, she said. She described Nakayama-sensei as a deeply wounded shepherd trying to tend the flock in every way he could. But all the sheep were shorn and stampeded in the stockyards and slaughterhouses of prejudice.

"I remember one time Mr. Nakayama came out east to take pictures of as many young Nisei as he could find to prove to the parents back in the camps that their children were alive. How could they know whether the girls working as domestics were all right—whether the young people on the farms were eating adequately—whether the boys who had left the road camps were managing in the cities? The rumors were so bad."

Throughout the country, here and there, were a few people doing what they could. There were missionaries, sending telegrams, drafting petitions, meeting together in rooms to pray. There were a few politicians sitting up late into the night, weighing conscience against expedience. There were the young Nisei men and women, the idealists, the thinkers, the leaders, scattered across the country. In Toronto there were the Jews who opened their businesses to employ the Nisei. But for every one who sought to help, there were thousands who didn't. Cities in every province slammed their doors shut.

"Didn't any of us sneak back to Vancouver?" I asked.

Aunt Emily shrugged. "I heard of one fellow who changed his name to Wong and passed for Chinese."

"Masayuki Wong? Kenzaburo Yip?"

"There must have been a few who tried the trick."

"Did any of us try to get our property back?"

Aunt Emily shook her head. "Well, there's Uncle Dan," she said.

Uncle Dan has become a widower in recent years and I've often wondered whether more than a friendship might not yet spring up between them. Aunt Emily was obviously not thinking of romance. She started telling me instead of his dealings with the government when he was trying to get his farm back.

Uncle Dan, she told me, was one of the most fiercely loyal Canadians among the Nisei, and toward the end of the war he was among the handful of men picked to serve in intelligence work in the Far East. He was a sergeant stationed at H.Q. Malaya Command in Kuala Lumpur, and Aunt Emily said she wrote him letters about what was happening on the home front. The one thing that kept Uncle Dan going, according to Aunt Emily, was his gratitude for the legal assistance of Saskatchewan's politicians and lawyers.

Uncle Dan, I knew, had owned a strawberry farm in the Fraser Valley and his property was included in the land that the Veterans Land Administration bought at scandalously low prices in order to sell it to Canadian war veterans. Uncle Dan, himself a Canadian war veteran, fought his battle but never saw his farm again.

"It's all recorded," Aunt Emily said. "And you know about the Fraser Valley Relief Fund, of course?"

I didn't know. She told me that when the Fraser Valley flooded and the land that had once belonged to Japanese Canadians was under water, there was a public outpouring of help to the farmers and residents of the area. "We sent money," she said, "money to help the people who had taken our farms! I imagine we were hoping that it would show our good faith. Just like a bunch of unrequited lovers. We end up being despised twice as much and treated like cringing dogs."

We were walking up the gravel road again, having done our midnight sightseeing of the two blocks of the main street with its two garages, one Chinese restaurant, a grocery store, one general store, and another restaurant and poolroom where the bus stops. We walked east past the railway tracks and out along the highway a short distance before turning back.

It was after two o'clock by the time we got in. Aunt Emily wanted to show me a memorandum to the House and the Senate written by the Co-operative Committee on Japanese Canadians. I was ready for bed.

"I'll read it another time," I apologized, and Aunt Emily said she'd mail it to me with Uncle's documents. "For your education," she said.

I don't know what use Uncle's documents are to him now that he's dead. As for me, I suppose I do need to be educated. I've never understood how these things happen. There's something called an order-in-council that sails like a giant hawk across a chicken yard, and after the first shock there's a flapping squawking lunge for safety. One swoop and the first thousand are on ships sailing for disaster. I can remember the chickens in Slocan, their necks and tiny heads thrust low, diving for shelter, one time that a hawk came circling down.

Elsewhere, people like Aunt Emily clack away at their typewriters, spreading words like buckshot, aiming at the shadow in the sky. And the people on the Co-operative Committee on Japanese Canadians rally together, gathering their desperation into cool print.

"It is urgently submitted," they state in the memorandum, "that the Orders-in-Council are wrong and indefensible. . . ."

The paper battles rage through the mails onto the desks of busy politicians, while back in the chicken yard one hawk after another circles overhead till the chickens are unable to come out of hiding and their neck feathers molt from the permanent crick. The seasons pass and the leghorns no longer lay eggs. The nests are fouled and crawl with lice.

All of Aunt Emily's words, all her papers, the telegrams and petitions, are like scratchings in the barnyard, the evidence of much activity, scaly claws hard at work. But what good they do, I do not know—those little black typewritten words—rain words, cloud droppings. They do not touch us where we are planted here in Alberta, our roots clawing the sudden prairie air. The words are not made flesh. Trains do not carry us home. Ships do not return again. All my prayers disappear into space.

28

1945. Lethbridge, Alberta. A city. Ah. We have come to a city of wind with stores and streets and people angled against the gusts and behold we are sitting safely out of the blowing debris in a restaurant at a round table and there are flat oval-shaped dishes with vegetables and thick cup-shaped bowls containing strange, dry, rather hard rice.

In a corner by the window is a jukebox like the one in the Green Light Café in Slocan. Two unshaven men are sitting beside it. Throughout the meal, one keeps beckoning to me with his crooked finger and he winks and holds out a five-dollar bill. Whenever I glance around he is there staring, his stubbly red-blotched face hanging down, and as he breathes, his whole chest and shoulders heave. The man beside him grins and nods, pointing to the money. Beyond them, bits of dust and papers splat against the window and the pane sucks back and forth. The walls shudder.

I poke Obasan's arm and she shakes her head so slightly it is almost as if there is no movement. Her lips have barely changed but there is a tightness to them. She has the same wary expression as we leave the restaurant.

The truck in which all our luggage has been piled is pulled up outside and the wooden sides of the truck heave in the wind. I stand close beside Obasan, watching but not watching as Uncle, his eyes looking sideways to the ground, nods as a man talks to him. The man's cap is drawn down so far I cannot see his face. Uncle turns and I am lifted onto the back of the truck with Stephen and the boxes and bags. Uncle climbs into the back with us and we are off down across the city streets and out over a strange empty landscape. It is flat as the ocean for as far as I can see with a few farmhouses like ships on the horizon. Here and there are straight unnatural rows of fierce almost leafless trees pruned like the brooms of a chimney sweep.

I am standing balancing against the corner, and peer through my fingers into the wind. We have bumped off the pavement onto a washboard road and there is a whirling storm of dust that flumes behind us. In the shaking of the truck and the buffeting of dust and wind, I can only breathe in short shallow gasps. The sides of the truck and the floor shake and bounce and the chains at the back clank in a Raggedy Ann jig. I squeeze my eyes together against the wind and hold the corners of the truck, my arms outstretched. My dress flaps wildly. I am a flag fraying against the sky. Or a scarecrow or a skeleton in the wind.

"Where are we going?" I shout to Uncle.

He is sitting up straight like a sphinx on a box and staring at the land. We have come to the moon. We have come to the edge of the world, to a place of angry air. Was it just a breath ago that we felt the green watery fingers of the mountain air? Here, the air is a fist. I am leaning into the corner, a boxer cowering against the ropes. Uncle, his hands on his knees, is a statue beside me.

"Where are we going?" I shout again, moving along the edge of the truck, closer to Uncle.

He nods but doesn't reply. The wind howls and guffaws at my eardrums.

Running along beside the wind-tunnel road is a ditch of brown water bordered with grass and weeds fluttering like laundry. On the miles of barbed-wire fences, there are round skull-shaped weeds clinging or occasionally careening off into the brown air. We keep heading straight down the road and we are the only thing moving on the earth.

When we stop finally, it is at the side of a small hut, like a toolshed, smaller even than the one we lived in in Slocan. We are at the far end of a large yard that has a white house in the middle. Between the shed and the farmer's house are some skeletons of farm machinery with awkward metal jaws angled upward, like the remains of dinosaurs in a prehistoric battle-ground. There is a mound of earth beyond the machines which Uncle tells me later is a root cellar. The farmer's house is a real house with a driveway leading into a garage. It makes me think of our house in Vancouver, though this is not as large. Through the whipping brown dust, I can see its white lace curtains in the window and its border of determined orange flowers. Our hut is at the edge of a field that stretches as far as I can see and is filled with an army of spartan plants fighting in the wind. Every bit of plant growth here looks deliberate and fierce.

Uncle leaps off the truck and talks with the man, then they both begin unloading the boxes, the wind whipping Uncle's thick hair till it stands up like a rudder on his head. Obasan and Stephen and I carry a box into the one-room hut. The door slams open and soot and dust leap to the walls. We prop open the door against the buffeting wind and form a convoy, carrying and dragging boxes into the room. When we are done at last, and close the door, we are finally able to breathe.

A round stove stands in the middle of the room like a fat sentry on duty. There are a broom and some rags in a corner and a wooden stand against the wall by the door. Nothing else. One room, one door, two windows. One window faces the farm machines, one faces the field.

The farmer's truck is thrumming across the yard and we are alone in this wind-battered place. Uncle and Stephen are piling the boxes against the wall opposite the door, and Obasan squats, pressing the rags against the space under the door.

The first night we sleep on quilts on the floor, the four of us side by side, my legs held stiff and straight. In the morning I waken to the sound of Uncle coming through the door with a bucket of water. A thick brown dust has settled over everything, and as I sit up the blanket moves, leaving its imprint on the naked floor. I lie down again and close my eyes.

29

There is a folder in Aunt Emily's package containing only one newspaper clipping and an index card with the words "Facts about evacuees in Alberta." The newspaper clipping has a photograph of one family, all smiles, standing around a pile of beets. The caption reads: "Grinning and Happy."

Find Jap Evacuees Best Beet Workers

Lethbridge, Alberta, Jan. 22

Japanese evacuees from British Columbia supplied the labour for 65% of Alberta's sugar beet acreage last year, Phil Baker, of Lethbridge, president of the Alberta Sugar Beet Growers' Association, stated today.

"They played an important part in producing our all-time record crop of 363,000 tons of beets in 1945," he added.

Mr. Baker explained Japanese evacuees worked 19,500 acres of beets and German prisoners of war worked 5,000 acres. The labour for the remaining 5,500 acres of Alberta's 30,000 acres of sugar beets was provided by farmers and their families. Some of the heaviest beet yields last year came from farms employing Japanese evacuees.

Generally speaking, Japanese evacuees have developed into most efficient beet workers, many of them being better than the transient workers who cared for beets in southern Alberta before Pearl Harbor. . . .

Facts about evacuees in Alberta? The fact is I never got used to it and I cannot, I cannot bear the memory. There are some nightmares from which there is no waking, only deeper and deeper sleep.

There is a word for it. Hardship. The hardship is so pervasive, so inescapable, so thorough it's a noose around my chest and I cannot move anymore. All the oil in my joints has drained out and I have been invaded by dust and grit from the fields and mud is in my bone marrow. I can't move anymore. My fingernails are black from scratching the scorching day and there is no escape.

Aunt Emily, are you a surgeon cutting at my scalp with your folders and your filing cards and your insistence on knowing all? The memory drains down the sides of my face, but it isn't enough, is it? It's your hands in my abdomen, pulling the growth from the lining of my walls, but bring back the anesthetist turn on the ether clamp down the gas mask

bring on the chloroform when will this operation be over
Aunt Em?

Is it so bad?

Yes.

Do I really mind?

Yes, I mind. I mind everything. Even the flies. The flies
and flies and flies from the cows in the barn and the manure
pile—all the black flies that curtain the windows, and Obasan
with a wad of toilet paper, spish, then with her bare hands as
well, grabbing them and their shocking white eggs and the
mosquitoes mixed there with the other insect corpses around
the base of the gas lamp.

It's the chicken coop "house" we live in that I mind. The
uninsulated unbelievable thin-as-a-cotton-dress hovel never
before inhabited in winter by human beings. In summer it's a
heat trap, an incubator, a dry sauna from which there is no
relief. In winter the icicles drip down the inside of the windows and the ice is thicker than bricks at the ledge. The only
place that is warm is by the coal stove, where we rotate like
chickens on a spit, and the feet are so cold they stop register-
ing. We eat cloves of roasted garlic on winter nights to warm
up.

It's the bedbugs and my having to sleep on the table to
escape the nightly attack, and the welts over our bodies. And
all the swamp bugs and the dust. It's Obasan uselessly packing all the cracks with rags. And the muddy water from the
irrigation ditch which we strain and settle and boil, and the
tiny carcasses of water creatures at the bottom of the cup. It's
walking in winter to the reservoir and keeping the hole open
with the ax and dragging up the water in pails and lugging it
back and sometimes the water spills down your boots and
your feet are red and itchy for days. And it's everybody taking

a bath in the round galvanized tub, then Obasan washing clothes in the water after and standing outside hanging the clothes in the freezing weather where everything instantly stiffens on the line.

Or it's standing in the beet field under the maddening sun, standing with my black head a sun trap even though it's covered, and lying down in the ditch, faint, and the nausea in waves and the cold sweat, and getting up and tackling the next row. The whole field is an oven and there's not a tree within walking distance. We are tiny as insects crawling along the grill and there is no protection anywhere. The eyes are lidded against the dust and the air cracks the skin, the lips crack, Stephen's flutes crack and there is no energy to sing anymore anyway.

It's standing in the field and staring out at the heat waves that waver and shimmer like see-through curtains over the brown clods and over the tiny distant bodies of Stephen and Uncle and Obasan miles away across the field day after day and not even wondering how this has come about.

There she is, Obasan, wearing Uncle's shirt over a pair of dark baggy trousers, her head covered by a straw hat that is held on by a white cloth tied under her chin. She is moving like a tiny earth cloud over the hard clay clods. Her hoe moves rhythmically up down up down, tiny as a toothpick. And over there, Uncle pauses to straighten his back, his hands on his hips. And Stephen farther behind, so tiny I can barely see him.

It's hard, Aunt Emily, with my hoe, the blade getting dull and mud-caked as I slash out the Canada thistle, dandelions, crabgrass, and other nameless nonbeet plants, then on my knees, pulling out the extra beets from the cluster, leaving just one to mature, then three hand spans to the next plant, whack whack, and down on my knees again, pull, flick flick, and on to the end of the long long row and the next and the next and it will never be done thinning and weeding and weeding and weeding. It's so hard and so hot that my tear glands burn out.

And then it's cold. The lumps of clay mud stick on my gum boots and weight my legs and the skin under the boots beneath the knees at the level of the calves grows red and hard and itchy from the flap flap of the boots and the fine hairs on my legs grow coarse there and ugly.

I mind growing ugly.

I mind the harvesttime and the hands and the wrists bound in rags to keep the wrists from breaking open. I lift the heavy mud-clotted beets out of the ground with the hook like an eagle's beak, thick and heavy as a nail attached to the top of the sugar-beet knife. Thwack. Into the beet and yank from the shoulder till it's out of the ground dragging the surrounding mud with it. Then crack two beets together till most of the mud drops off and splat, the knife slices into the beet scalp and the green top is tossed into one pile, the beet heaved onto another, one more one more one more down the icy line. I cannot tell about this time, Aunt Emily. The body will not tell.

We are surrounded by a horizon of denim-blue sky with clouds clear as spilled milk that turn pink at sunset. Pink I hear is the color of llama's milk. I wouldn't know. The clouds are the shape of our new prison walls—untouchable, impersonal, random.

There are no other people in the entire world. We work together all day. At night we eat and sleep. We hardly talk anymore. The boxes we brought from Slocan are not unpacked. The King George/Queen Elizabeth mugs stay muffled in the *Vancouver Daily Province*. The cameraphone does not sing. Obasan wraps layers of cloth around her feet and her torn sweater hangs unmended over her sagging dress.

Down the miles we are obedient as machines in this odd ballet without accompaniment of flute or song.

"Grinning and happy" and all smiles standing around a pile of beets? That is one telling. It's not how it was.

I can't remember when Uncle stopped talking about going back. It may have been the first year after the ghost towns, or the next year, or the year after that.

In 1948, three years after our exile from our place of exile, I am twelve years old and Stephen is fifteen. We are still here in Granton, Alberta, still here on the Barker farm, attending school except in thinning season or harvesttime.

"Bar Japs for Another Year from Going Back to B.C." says a newspaper clipping from the *Toronto Star,* written by Borden Spears.

Tues. March 16, 1948

Nearly 20,000 Canadian citizens will be deprived for another year of one of the fundamental rights of citizenship, the House of Commons decreed last night. They are the Canadians of Japanese origin who were expelled from British Columbia in 1941 and are still debarred from returning to their homes.

Led by Angus MacInnis of Vancouver, CCF members made a vain but valiant effort to have the last restriction on the freedom of Japanese Canadians removed at once. The attempt was eloquently supported by David Croll (Lib. Toronto Spadina) and three Liberals declared themselves in opposition to the government.

They were branded, however, as theorists, visionary idealists, purists, talkers of academic nonsense, weepers of crocodile tears. By a standing vote, 73 to 23, the House decided that for another year no Japanese Canadian may enter British Columbia without an RCMP permit, and those now in the interior may not return to the coastal area.

Defenders of the restrictions denied they were motivated by racial considerations. But in nearly four hours of increasingly bitter debate, there was no direct answer to the blunt question posed by Mr. MacInnis: If the national security is no longer in danger, what is the reason for curtailing the freedom of Canadian citizens? There was even, from Tom Reid (Lib. New Westminster), this statement: "As long as I have breath in my body I will keep fighting in this House of Commons to see that the heritage which belongs to Canadians should be returned to the white people."

Maj. Gen. G. R. Pearkes (PC Nanaimo) suggested there would be "crimes of revenge" if the exiles were permitted to return home now. In war, he said, the innocent suffer with the guilty; there was still hatred among the white people of B.C., and he thought the government was wise in giving the old sores another year to heal.

Another year? Which year should we choose for our healing? Restrictions against us are removed on April Fools' Day 1949. But the "old sores" remain. In time the wounds will close and the scabs drop off the healing skin. Till then, I can read these newspaper clippings, I can tell myself the facts. I

can remember since Aunt Emily insists that I must and release the floodgates one by one. I can cry for the flutes that
have cracked in the dryness and cry for the people who no
longer sing. I can cry for Obasan, who has turned to stone.
But what then? Uncle does not rise up and return to his
boats. Dead bones do not take on flesh.

What is done, Aunt Emily, is done, is it not? And no
doubt it will all happen again, over and over with different
faces and names, variations on the same theme.

"Nothing but the lowest motives of greed, selfishness, and
hatred have been brought forward to defend these disgraceful
Orders," the *Globe and Mail* noted. Greed, selfishness, and
hatred remain as constant as the human condition, do they
not? Or are you thinking that through lobbying and legislation, speechmaking and storytelling, we can extricate ourselves from our foolish ways? Is there evidence for optimism?

30

Those years on the Barker farm, my late childhood growing-up days, are sleepwalk years, a time of half dream. There is no word from Mother. The first letter from Father tells us that Grandpa Nakane died of a heart attack the day before we left Slocan. The funeral was held before we reached Granton. Later, there is news of an operation from which Father has not been able to recover. The last letter we receive around Christmas 1949 tells something about a doctor he doesn't trust.

The sadness and the absence are like a long winter storm, the snow falling in an unrelieved colorlessness that settles and freezes, burying me beneath a growing monochromatic weight. Something dead is happening, like the weeds that are left to bleach and wither in the sun.

Sometimes in the summer, Stephen and I go to cool off in the main irrigation ditch, which is wider than the ditches along the side of the road. Thistles grow along the bank and we are careful where we walk. The water is always muddy, so brown that we cannot see the submerged parts of our bodies at all. Under the bridge, we are even cooler and we often sit there in the thick silt, hiding while the occasional farm truck rumbles overhead.

The only other place that is cool is the root cellar, which is an earth-covered mound over a cavelike excavation the length of a garage, angling underground in a slow slope. There are boxes and sacks and piles of potatoes and other vegetables lining the shelves. I cannot stand the odor of decaying potatoes in this damp tomb, but on certain days I am so dizzy from hoeing in the heat that Uncle carries me here, leaving the door open so that I can breathe.

One time, Uncle squats beside me as I lie on a potato sack, my body drenched in cold perspiration.

"Itsuka—mata itsuka," he says, rubbing my back. "Someday, someday we will go back."

On school-day mornings, Stephen and I wait at the end of the driveway for the yellow school bus to drive us the seven miles to the Granton school. Penny Barker, the farmer's daughter, also waits with us. Penny has a thin face and brown braids and her teeth have metal bands across them. She has pretty dresses that are bought from stores, unlike mine that are made from Obasan's old dresses. Penny never talks with me in school—only when we wait for the bus.

Sometimes I stand too close to the edge of the ditch and the thistles, even in winter, jab me in the calf. The thistles, it seems to me, are typical of life in the Granton school. From nowhere the sharp stabs come, attacking me for no reason at all. They come at unexpected times, in passing remarks, in glances, in jokes.

"How come you got such a flat face, Naomi? Steamroller run over ya?"

Sometimes I feel a prickly sensation at the back of my head and a tiny chill like a needle on my neck. Or the area around my eyes gets stinging hot and I wonder if it shows I'm about to cry, not that I ever do.

Once Penny, who is in Stephen's class, sidles up to Stephen on the school bus and says, "Come here, blackhead, and let me squeeze you." Stephen doesn't know whether to scowl or laugh.

"Hyuk hyuk," he says sourly.

None of the children in the Granton school are from Slocan. There is a boy from Kaslo in Stephen's class who is the home-run king on the ball team. And a few others from other ghost towns—the Takasakis, Sagas, Sonodas. One family, the Utsunomiyas, have been in the area from before the war. There are also several Okinawan families—the Kanashiros and the Tamashiros, who shortened their name to Tamagi. They have been here from the time of the coal mines and the construction of the railroad and the establishment of the North West Mounted Police in Fort McLeod.

Almost all of us have shortened names—Tak for Takao, Sue for Sumiko, Mary for Mariko. We all hide our long names as well as we can. My books are signed M. Naomi N., or Naomi M.N. If Megumi were the only name I had, I'd be called Meg. Meg Na Kane. Pity the Utsunomiya kids for their long, unspellable, unpronounceable surname. Oots gnome ya. Or the Iwabuchis. The Eye Bushys.

There is a black-haired Native Indian girl in my class

called Annie Black Bear. Once the teacher called her Annie Black by mistake. Annie looked so pleased—throwing a furtive happy swift glance at me.

One of the first things I notice at the Granton school is that arithmetic is easier and spelling is harder than in Slocan. There are certainly more books in Granton: *Anne of Green Gables, The Secret Garden, Girl of the Limberlost, The Prince and the Pauper*.

Stephen receives permission to play the piano in the auditorium and every noon hour and recess, and before school begins, he is there alone or with a few girls who stand in the hall outside giggling and listening. Skinny Miss Giesbrecht, who teaches music, lends him her music books and coaches him from time to time. Uncle takes her some vegetables or a loaf of his stone bread every time he comes to town. For two years in a row, 1948 and 1949, Stephen comes in second in the talent show on CJOC Lethbridge radio. All of Granton is proud of Stephen. Especially his teachers. In Miss Langston's grades seven and eight class, I have a hard time living up to his reputation. He was her favorite student. Sometimes I wonder if she is so disappointed in me that she marks me extra hard. Her red X's on my papers are like scratches and wounds.

"Not like your brother, are you?" she said once, returning a poor paper.

Thistles, as I say, are typical of my life in Granton and grow everywhere.

Occasionally, at Thanksgiving, Easter, or Christmas, we drive the seventy-odd miles in the old pickup truck Uncle has bought, across the coulee to the village of Coaldale on Highway 3, between Taber and Lethbridge. Nakayama-sensei was moved there. A number of other people from Slocan are scattered throughout southern Alberta, working on sugar-beet farms like us.

The kindergarten building in Bayfarm, near Pine Crescent School, was dismantled and shipped by rail to Coaldale in 1946. Uncle and another boatbuilder, Mr. Mototsune from Taber, who is also on a sugar-beet farm, erected the building. It's the only public building from Slocan that remains standing today. Everything else was destroyed.

Some days, we see Nakayama-sensei in his black suit, riding his bicycle, his short legs pumping along—a plump black dot on the empty road. If we are out in the field, he leans his bike against the side of the house, finds an extra hoe or beet knife, and comes to work beside us. Sometimes Uncle and Nakayama-sensei joke and talk, taking time out at the end of a row with a thermos of tea. At other times, the only sounds are the whacking of the hoes and the trill of a meadowlark.

31

On spring evenings I often go alone to the swamp. It's about a mile from the house, kitty-corner through the fields. To get there the shortest way, I hop across the rows of beets. The cows are always standing around in the weedy mud, their hoofprints filling with ooze. On the far side of the swamp, there's a clump of spindly bushes and bulrushes like chopsticks or candles with their furry brown tip flames. The only tree here is dead. Its skeleton is a roost for a black-and-white magpie that I often see angling across the sky.

I squat on the tree's dead roots in the whine of mosquitoes, watching the dragonflies skimming over the water.

The longer I sit, the more I see. It's like the puzzle in the comic section of the newspaper where you find faces among the leaves and tree trunks and fences.

All over the ground the cow-dung saucers bake in the sun like gray pancakes among the thistles and weeds. The clay earth is as cracked and scored as broken pottery.

The creatures reveal themselves in unexpected places. Water spiders and poppy-seed-size swimming creatures churn at the edges. Yellow-green jelly eggs cling to the tall grasses. Tadpoles wriggle clumsily through the water, their tails churning and undulating like the mosquito larvae that gyrate energetically up to the water's surface. One toad sitting in a cow's hoofprint suddenly claws its tongue to rid itself of a stinging insect it has mistakenly trapped. If I do not move at all the toads and frogs croak and breep rhythmically.

All along the western horizon the sky is a display of fuchsia flames, and I can see Stephen this evening, a silhouette riding on his bike down the road toward me. He looks like one of the Israelite children moving unharmed through the fiery furnace. I am sitting motionless as the dead tree. Near my foot is a tiny green frog the size of half my thumb. One of its back legs dangles to the side.

"Sh," I whisper to Stephen as he lays his bike down at the side of the road and hops the ditch. There is a swift plip plip of water as frogs and toads disappear to safety. At my foot, the green frog's chin neck palpitates rapidly and it crawl-hops under my leg. I cup my hands over it, lifting my thumb for Stephen to peer in.

"Leg's broken," I say to him.

"It'll give you warts."

"It will not."

The swamp is as still now as an orchestra poised waiting for a signal from the conductor. It listens to us.

Stephen squats beside me and seems about to say something several times but stops. He looks at me, then off in the distance, frowning.

"Don't move," I whisper as the swamp sounds begin again.

He grinds some ants to death under his heel and kicks at the tree root where the ant mound is.

"C'mon home," he says at last.

"What for?"

He swats at a mosquito. "Nakayama's here."

"So?"

"So c'mon home."

The frog slithers and pushes its way out of my hands and I catch it, almost crushing it.

"C'mon," Stephen repeats. He shakes his head at the mosquitoes diving around his ears.

Reluctantly, I get up and we walk, Stephen propelling his bike by one hand on the seat. The last of the sun's rays are focused on an overhang of frayed clouds.

"Do you think the frog'll live?" I ask.

All the way home Stephen has nothing to say.

"Tad" is what I think I'll call my frog—short for Tadpole or Tadashi, my father's name. There was a fairy tale I read in Slocan about a frog who became a prince. Hah! Well, what, after all, might not be possible? Tad is a frog prince. Prince Tadashi. He wears a dark green suit, not the rough green army garb, but a smooth suit, silky and cool as leaves. He is from the mountains. Certainly not from Granton. He was hidden under the tree roots waiting for me, a messenger from my father.

By the time we reach home, the gas lamp is on in the house, sending out its hissing white light. Nakayama-sensei is at the table reading from the Bible in Japanese. It is the first time he has been to see us in a long time. Obasan has her head bowed and her eyes are closed. Uncle is quietly scraping out ashes from the stove with the flat paddle-shaped scoop.

I am not sure, as I remember the scene, whether I am told after I come in, or later at night when I am in bed, or if I am even told at all. It's possible the words are never said outright. I know that for years I simply do not believe it. At some point I remember Uncle's hand on my head, stroking it. I remember the strange gentle smile on his face when he sees my two hands in a ball raised toward him.

"What you got?" he says in a soft voice.

My frog is a tiny green triangle in the large glass fruit bowl. Uncle has put his reading glasses on and is peering at it, nodding his head slowly. I take two of the tin cans from the pile in the corner and go out to look for mud and stones and ditch water.

The air is rapidly cooling outside and a few stars are visible in the shadowless twilight. The irrigation ditch by the roadside is close to the house. I dip the tin in and scoop a glop of water and mud. The feel of it is silkier than pancake batter. From the driveway I gather a handful of stones and one stone bigger than my fist that has a jagged wedge shape.

When I get back to the house, I remove my muddy shoes and set to work making and unmaking a home for the frog in the glass bowl. Eventually I settle on one arrangement—water in half the bowl, land in the other half. The rock forms the base of the land section and mud, grass, earth, and stones are piled on and around the rock. Near the top of the earth hill, I poke my thumb in to form a cave about the size of the frog. After the water settles, I plop the frog in. With its one good leg, it makes two glide-kicks and scrambles up the rock hill and heads straight into the cave headfirst. A quick turnabout and the frog's nose protrudes from the home, its tiny black needle-point nostrils facing the water. A good lookout place.

I do not know when Nakayama-sensei leaves. I only know there is a pervasive weight of gentleness, even from Stephen, that is strange and discomfiting. Only the frog remains unchanged.

The next day and all week long and every day after school or in the mornings, I feed the frog. The best and most eagerly eaten insect and the easiest to catch is the aphid, light and plump as a soap bubble. Flip, and it's gone with barely a blink of the frog's eyes. Smaller flies, with half a wing removed, are a challenge. With its one good leg angling it forward, it pursues the crippled insects. Larger flies are generally avoided, though on several occasions it downs large bluebottles, blinking and gulping fiercely. Ants it hates, spiders it generally shuns, worms are of no interest, beetles are too brittle. I sometimes put flies in the bowl and cover the top with a pie plate, which they whap loudly with their shiny black bodies as they buzz about.

I wonder what will happen in winter when the insect supply dies.

"Without moving there is not eating," Uncle says when I ask.

"Try meat," Stephen suggests.

I squeeze a dot of hamburger on the end of a thread and swing it back and forth in front of the frog. It pushes itself out of the cave, its eyes fixed on the moving meal. It lunges once, then again, and the meat is gone, its eyes rotating as it swallows.

One morning, the frog is on the rim of the bowl, sitting there ready to leap. Another time it is on the table. Once I find it in a corner of the room covered in fluff. And then it is nowhere. The bowl sits empty on the table.

My last letter to Father has received no answer.

When the snow falls and covers everything, I hardly know that it is snow. The sky is the underbelly of a fish.

32

Perhaps, in the end, it's Penny Barker who really convinces me that Father is dead. I say the words so casually. "My father's dead." It's as if I've known for years, yet when I actually hear myself talking I feel a strange shock as if I am telling a monstrous lie. It happens the first time Penny visits us in 1951, the year we move from her father's farm to our new house in town. In 1951, I'm in grade nine at Granton High School and Stephen is in his final year, completing grades twelve and thirteen in one year.

In all the time that we lived on the Barker farm, neither Penny nor her father and mother visited us in the hut at the back of their yard. It was just as well. There wasn't enough room for the four of us, let alone anyone else. Throughout high school, Stephen became increasingly angry about our cramped quarters on the farm. Finally we moved to a two-bedroom house about half a mile from the main street.

The new house is at least a house. The yard is treeless with an outhouse at the back. A few yards from the back door, there is a cistern for the irrigation water. It's a deep cement hole with a square wooden box and lid. For the first few months, we use a pail on the end of a rope to get the water out. After that a water and sewage system comes to Granton and Uncle builds a bathroom on the days that he is not working at a nearby potato farm.

In our house, we have a living room, kitchen, one large bedroom, and one small room that is about twice the size of the pantry we slept in in Slocan. Uncle and Obasan have a double bed in the bedroom and I sleep on a cot separated from them by a pink flowered curtain hung from a clothesline wire. Stephen is in the other room with all his musical instruments. There's an old violin that Miss Giesbrecht sold to him for five dollars and a trombone that belongs to the school band. He has a glass-bottle xylophone, which he is always adjusting and tuning with water and a crayon mark showing the level for the right note. There are also several sizes of wooden-box and rubber-band instruments he made while he was on the farm. I don't know where he keeps the cracked wooden flute. I'm sure he hasn't thrown it away. On his desk he has a tiny crystal radio—one of the first things he made on the farm. Once he managed to hear a police conversation on it.

Now that we are in town, Stephen is able to stay after school to practice on the piano. He and Miss Giesbrecht are working together on a cantata for the music festival. A num-

ber of the girls in grade twelve are trying out for solo parts—
even Penny Barker, who can't carry a tune, is auditioning.

I write a letter to Aunt Emily with a copy of the cantata
and circle the sections that Stephen has composed.

"It's so sad your dad isn't here, Nomi," she writes back.
"He'd be so happy and proud to know how well Stephen is
progressing."

The noon hour that Penny visits us is early in December
1951, following a warm chinook wind that has melted all the
snow. She catches up to me in the hall after my first-period
chemistry class and asks if she can drop by to see our new
place.

"Sure," I say uneasily. I have not invited anyone to visit
me before. I suspect she only wants to see Stephen and ask
him to pick her for one of the leading parts.

The first thing she notices in the cluttered living room is
the photograph taken when Stephen was born, showing both
sets of grandparents, Aunt Emily, Mother, Father, Obasan,
and Uncle.

"That's Stephen," I explain, pointing to his bun face, and
Penny squeals, hiding her teeth with her hands the way she
always does when she laughs. "And that's my father holding
him."

"He doesn't look like your father," Penny says.

The Barkers and everyone else have assumed that Uncle
and Obasan are our parents and we've never bothered to cor-
rect them.

"My father's dead," I reply as calmly as if I were offering
the time of day. But a few moments after I say it, I find
myself collapsed on the sofa with a sharp pain in my abdomen
and a cold perspiration forming on my forehead.

After this, when my eyes pass over the few framed photographs on the kitchen sideboard, I stop and examine the small black-and-white snapshot of a graveyard scene. There are half a dozen unknown men and a white clergyman standing beside a freshly covered grave. Father was buried by a few friends in the spring of 1950 following an extensive operation at the New Denver hospital. His plot is close to the spot where Grandpa Nakane is buried. Grandma Nakane's ashes, Stephen tells me, were buried with Father. In the snapshot one of the men is holding a pick with flowers tied to the handle.

"That's a friend of Dad's," Stephen says when I point him out. "He worked with Dad on the roads and always remembered how Dad stuck flowers on his pick to remind him of us and Mother."

About Mother and Grandma Kato, Stephen knows nothing. In 1949, he says, Nakayama-sensei went to Japan, the first Japanese Canadian to visit Japan after the war. Sensei promised to find out about Mother and Grandma Kato but the moment he stepped onto Japanese soil, his wallet, his address book containing all the names of our relatives, and his pocket watch were stolen by pickpockets. All he was able to learn was that the house in Tokyo where Grandma Kato's mother lived was gone.

"They must be dead," Stephen says. "If they weren't they'd write to us."

"But they don't know where we are."

"They'd write to the church. They'd write to somebody. They must," Stephen repeats, "be dead."

I write a stream of letters to Aunt Emily asking about Mother, but she too only echoes Stephen's bleak words. "They must be dead." She has written, she tells me, hundreds of letters, to friends of friends, distant relatives, to churches, hospitals, government officials, police, and Red Cross agencies, but there have been no clear clues to their whereabouts. One of Grandma Kato's nephews reported that he visited Mother in a Tokyo hospital a few times but then lost track of her. A Canadian missionary wrote that a young English-speaking Japanese woman arrived one night at their women's hostel begging for help for her mother. She was given the medication she sought, plus some food, and left, returning the next day to thank them. But whether that was Mother was uncertain. Sometime later that same missionary, Miss Best, reported that another English-speaking woman had shown up who might have been Mother. She was very ill and refused to give her name. Miss Best took her to the nearest hospital.

"If that woman was your mother," Aunt Emily writes, "she died that month. I have no other leads. I have come to the conclusion after all this time that Grandma and your mother are both dead."

Eventually I too stop hoping that they are alive but sometimes I find myself imagining that they are somewhere, surviving somehow. I think of them in a mountain village being cared for by strangers, or in a hospital suffering from memory loss. I never speak of my thoughts to anyone.

In Aunt Emily's file, there are two government letters about Mother and Grandma Kato that tell me clearly they survived the war and were in touch with her.

The first is a terse note about Grandma Kato, Mrs. K. Kato, written in 1950.

Dear Madam,

I have your letter of April 18 concerning your application for readmission to Canada from Japan of Mrs. K. Kato. I note that Mrs. Kato, who was born in Japan, returned to that country and it would seem evident that she has accordingly relinquished any claim to Canadian domicile which she might previously have acquired. As Japanese nationals are not admissible under existing regulations I regret to inform you that no encouragement can be offered with respect to her desire to return to Canada at the present time.

There's also another puzzling letter about Mother and a child who I assume is a cousin of mine on Grandma Kato's side.

Dear Miss Kato,

This refers to your letter of April 18 concerning your application for readmission to Canada of your sister, Mrs. Tadashi Nakane, Canadian-born, also for the admission of her four-year-old adopted daughter and niece.

The status of Mrs. Nakane has been carefully reviewed and it has been decided that she has retained her Canadian citizenship and therefore would be readmissible to Canada. However, the child is a national of Japan and as such is inadmissible under existing immigration regulations. It is regretted that the Department is unable to extend any facilities for admission of the child at the present time. It is assumed that Mrs. Nakane would not desire to come forward alone, leaving the child in Japan, and therefore it can only be suggested that the matter of her return be left in abeyance until such time in the future as there may be a change in the regulations respecting admission of Japanese nationals which would enable the Department to deal with the application of the child.

What I do not understand is Mother's total lack of communication with Stephen and me. Aunt Emily has said nothing more on the subject. I assume nothing more is known.

On the other hand, there was a puzzling incident one night during her first visit to us in 1954.

33

By 1954, Obasan, Uncle, and I have grown accustomed to the new quiet in the house. Stephen has been away for two school years, having left Granton for Toronto in the fall of 1952, after winning top marks at the music festival.

From the local and district festival in May that year, Stephen, Miss Giesbrecht, and the choir went on to win first place in the larger southern Alberta festival at Lethbridge. One of the adjudicators from Toronto praised Stephen profusely, both as a choir leader and as a pianist, and the newspaper reported, "Stephen Nakane—a young man with a future."

He was modest enough to leave the clipping behind, saying, "Don't need that." What he did need was the calendar from the Royal Conservatory of Music he had received. He also took a list of recommended names of teachers from the adjudicator with letters of reference to each. His new address book had only Aunt Emily's address in it.

"A good thing she is there," Uncle said. "A good thing there is enough room for you."

"Write to us, Stephen," I shouted as he watched us from the train window. I was feeling proud of him and thinking of Momotaro going off to conquer the world.

He scratched his chin, grinning awkwardly at us. When the train left, he waved a half-salute.

Obasan kept standing in the same spot after he was gone, her hands folded in front of her.

In the spring he returned.

"A grown man now," Uncle said. But at nineteen, he hardly seemed grown up to me.

The following Christmas he was in Europe as part of a young artists' tour. He also won first prize that winter for an original piano composition. It was Aunt Emily who sent us the news.

"No big deal," he wrote, when I sent a card of congratulations.

The *Granton District News* headlined "Local Musician Makes Good" with a review of his successes.

This spring, 1954, he is back again. When he stands around the yard, chewing on grass stems with his hands in the pockets of his old bomber jacket, he looks as if he never left Granton. It's hard to imagine him onstage somewhere in Europe. If he has changed at all, perhaps he is less surly—less easily angered. But he still seems irritable and is almost completely noncommunicative with Obasan.

She mends and re-mends his old socks and shirts which he never wears and sets the table with food, which he often does not eat. Sometimes he leaps up in the middle of nothing at all and goes off, inexplicably, no one knows where.

How, I wonder, does he get along with Aunt Emily?

"What is she like, Stephen?" I ask. Since I have not seen her in twelve years I can hardly remember her at all.

"She's not like them," Stephen says, jerking his thumb at Uncle and Obasan. He shows me a recent photograph of Aunt Emily standing behind a frail Grandpa Kato in a wheelchair. The picture was taken this year. They are strangers to me.

In June, a letter comes telling us that Aunt Emily will be coming for a visit, arriving on the 4:40 train of July 12.

It is so hot the afternoon of her arrival that even the train heaving into Lethbridge reeks of oily perspiration and gasps as it stops in front of us.

The only others waiting at the station besides Uncle, Stephen, and me are a small cluster of Hutterite people—three dark-gowned and kerchiefed women with a miniature dark-gowned and kerchiefed child and a bearded man in a collarless black suit. They all wear thick glasses and stand silently, not facing us.

A slightly chunky Japanese woman, wearing glasses and a gray cotton suit, steps off the train into a hot gust of cinders and dust. She shields her face from the spitting steam and walks toward us waving one hand wildly. Her black solid hair flames like a cape to her shoulders. I lift my hand hesitantly.

Uncle, with his bowlegged rolling gait, hurries up to greet her, but Stephen reaches her first and grips her suitcase.

When he carries it, he leans so heavily to one side that his limp becomes noticeable. I hang back.

"I can't believe it," Aunt Emily says, shaking her head in greeting as they approach me. She pushes her glasses back up the short nose of her round face with the back of her hand. When she smiles, her tadpole eyes almost disappear beneath the surface of her face.

We walk through the train station to the half-ton pickup angled in front. She is asking Uncle and me questions, one after the other, and shaking her head over and over as she looks at me.

Stephen puts her suitcase into the back and starts the old engine turning, slamming his foot down on the gas till the motor sputters and races to a roar. Uncle prompts her in beside Stephen. I lean heavily against Uncle to avoid squishing her. When she takes off her hat there is a fierce streak of white in front.

"Everyone gets older," Uncle says, noting her hair. "Emi-san is what age now?" He answers himself. "Nearing forty already. Is there to be no marriage?"

Aunt Emily dismisses the subject with a "knh" through her nose. "And you're how old now, Nomi? Seventeen? School finished yet?"

It is odd to hear someone besides Stephen calling me by my childhood name. "The finals are next week," I reply.

The pickup chugs the two blocks to Nakagama's, the Japanese store, where we pick up some salted kazunoko—herring roe on slabs of seaweed—fresh tofu, which they luckily have, and a can of mochi. The next stop is the Spudnut shop, where Stephen runs in to buy a dozen sticky doughnuts for fifty cents, then past McGavin's Bakery with its giant hand holding a giant loaf, and on down the highway beyond the stockyards. Both windows are down and we stop eating our doughnuts till we are past the strong manure smell. Uncle rolls his window up as he always does, saying in disgust, "Ah kusai—what a smell!"

Aunt Emily takes some Kleenex from her purse and holds it over her nose.

"That reminds me," Uncle chuckles, "chisai toki—when Stephen was small his favorite food was Ex-Lax." ("Exu raxu," Uncle says.)

Aunt Emily snuffles through the Kleenex and her eyes swim beneath the crinkles again as she laughs. "The time Stephen found the Ex-Lax in my purse." She pats Stephen on the back. "And my poor sweater."

"Not so bad smell as this," Uncle says, rolling the window back down again.

"Some not so good old days," Stephen grunts. He's heard this before.

"We had some good times," Aunt Emily says. "Do you remember at all, Nomi? You were so little."

"Fubuki hodo, chika yori soe ba, atataka shi," Uncle responds in mock formality.

"Whazzat?" Stephen asks.

It's a haiku, a seventeen-syllable word picture.

Stephen rubs the sticky sugar of the doughnut off his stubbly chin and keeps rubbing in his nervous way. He is always uncomfortable when anything is "too Japanese."

Aunt Emily works the translation, her voice rising above the rattle of the truck as we hit the gravel of road construction and a detour on Highway 3. "As the storm rages . . . our drawing closer . . . keeps us warm."

The dust plumes about us in a brown cloud. After a few yards we come to fresh tar, which splats against the side of the truck, then a stretch of gravel and washboard, our bones turning to jelly as we shake and clank along.

The traffic on the road is, in general, slow, but one empty truck passes us and lobs a rock against the windshield.

"Sakana fish," Stephen mutters as he steps on the brakes.

Aunt Emily looks startled. "What did you say?"

Some of the ripe pidgin English phrases we pick up are three-part inventions—part English, part Japanese, part Sasquatch. "Sonuva bitch" becomes "sakana fish," "sakana" meaning "fish" in Japanese. On occasion the phrase is "golden sakana fish."

"Is that how you talk out here?" Aunt Emily laughs. "What a place." She shakes her head as she stares out at the flat land.

"Toronto too far, Emi-san," Uncle says.

"Too far," Aunt Emily agrees.

The truck hiccups along over the potholes until the clank of the jack in the back marks our leap over the irrigation ditch bridge.

Obasan is standing in the doorway wiping her hands in her apron as we pull up. She is wearing her white-and-blue silk dress with a little fringe at the waist. I've never seen her wear it in all the time we've lived in Granton.

"Maa, Emiri-san, you have come well," she says as we climb down from the truck. "A long time. From so far."

Aunt Emily stands silent and unsmiling in front of her. She nods her head slowly as she looks at Obasan, then looks away.

"And Father's health," Obasan asks. "Is he well?"

Stephen and I disappear into the house with Aunt Emily's suitcase.

For the week that she stays with us, I am so absorbed in studies that I hardly speak to her. The senior matriculation exams obliterate everything. Even, it seems to me, if a war were on in Canada, I'd be found studying like deaf Beethoven playing his piano while Vienna burned.

Aunt Emily approves. "Don't let anything distract you," she says.

On the last night of Aunt Emily's stay, there is a barely audible whispering that keeps me awake wondering late into the night.

I've gone to sleep at 10:30 with an unresolved algebra equation and about 2 A.M. I'm awakened by a light in the kitchen. Uncle's voice is a low murmur. After a pause, he clears his throat.

"Kodomo no tame."

That phrase again. "For the sake of the children." Which children? Stephen and me? Stephen in particular, home for the summer after his time in Toronto, can hardly be called a child.

I strain to overhear what is being said. Did Aunt Emily whisper "Nesan" and "Japan"? Through the crack in the door, I can see Uncle folding a piece of blue paper and handing it to Aunt Emily. He takes his glasses off as he shakes his head once and speaks in a low voice.

"But they are not children. They should be told," Aunt Emily whispers.

Obasan is sitting on a stool and shelling beans. She neither looks up nor seems to be listening, but her lips are pursed in concentration as her fingertips unbead the black bean necklets from their crackling pods.

Aunt Emily leans toward Uncle and her head nods insistently as she whispers to him. She is patting some papers on the table as she speaks.

When Aunt Emily finishes speaking, Obasan stops shelling and leans forward, her hands flat on the table and her eyes closed. Her lips are moving slowly, deliberately. The expression on her face is as soft as a child's.

Aunt Emily leans back in her chair and breathes deeply. She covers her face with both hands and drops her head forward. Uncle, his hands clasped between his knees, nods his head rhythmically.

I know Obasan is praying. I've seen her before—the time Stephen leapt out of bed in the middle of the night yelling, "I've got to get out of here," and ran down the road away from the farm in the dark. Obasan sat at the table and prayed till he returned. He said when he came back he'd had a nightmare. Something about a metallic insect the size of a tractor, webbing a grid of iron bars over him. (Later, he told me he had the same nightmare again, but escaped the web by turning the bars into a xylophone.)

What is Obasan praying about this time?

Aunt Emily wipes her closed eyes with the back of her hand. She is crying. What can it be? When Obasan finishes, there is a long silence. The three sit without moving.

"Amen," Uncle says at last.

My bed squeaks as I strain closer to the crack. All three glance in the direction of the door.

The new stillness in the house is unrelieved by the sound of Uncle's chair scraping the floor.

"Well," he says in an audible voice. "What will be will be."

I can see Aunt Emily putting the papers into a gray cardboard folder. She twirls a red string around a red circle tab deftly three times, then places the folder in her briefcase.

34

The gray cardboard folder. It's here in Aunt Emily's package.

Early this afternoon Obasan opened the check-sized rice-paper envelopes that were inside it. I watched her smooth and read the slippery blue-lined papers, with the magnifying glass held over the pages. She followed each line down, then, lifting her head, she would start again at the top of the next row, as slow as a beet worker hoeing around each plant in a beet field. Occasionally her mouth formed the words.

"What is it you are reading?" I asked, but she did not hear me.

It's ten after four now and she has been asleep for about

half an hour with the magnifying glass in her hand. I am yawning and thinking of having a short nap too when the grating buzz of the front doorbell sounds. It's loud as a fire alarm. Uncle rigged it up in the kitchen, where Obasan is most of the time.

I peer through the living-room windows but I can't see who it is. The doorbell goes again and it's Mr. Barker at the door. I've rarely seen him since we left the farm. In the last several years I've not been home enough to see anyone except Uncle and Obasan and the people who might happen to be in the grocery store. Behind him, sitting in the car, is his new wife, whom I've met only once. The first Mrs. Barker died five years ago of cancer. Mr. Barker's second wife is much younger than he is.

"Hello, Naomi—Mrs. Nah Canny," he says, peering in through the doorway.

He must be dropping by to extend his sympathy. In a place as small as Granton, news spreads fast.

Mr. Barker hasn't aged since the last time I saw him three or four years ago. He has so many wrinkles his face is like an accordion.

I'm reluctant about asking him to come in, but he steps in unbidden, calling to his wife. She seems uncertain. "Come in, Vivian," he urges her.

She smiles a brief tight smile as she comes to the door. She is wearing a wine-colored pantsuit and when she greets me the small ruler of her mouth dips again into a rapid "V." Her light green-brown eyes remain unchanged, the pupils so tiny they seem like pencil dots. She is remarkably like the other Mrs. Barker, whom I was never able to approach. Once, when Penny brought me to their door, her mother said through her small precise mouth, "Penny, I told you. I told you," and closed the door, leaving me alone outside. Once, at night, I heard her singing the first few bars of "Love Is a Many-Splendored Thing" in a high tiny voice that seemed to come out of the tip of her tongue.

Obasan gets up off the couch and shuffles toward me, looking to me for guidance. "O," she says in her startled way.

Mr. Barker is so tall and the ceiling so low, his head almost touches it.

"Just dropped by, Mrs. Nah Canny," Mr. Barker shouts. "Very sorry today." His booming voice is not unkindly and he puts his thick hands over hers. Mrs. Barker stands beside him nodding, her hands cupped in front of her, whether to give or to receive I cannot tell.

"Thank you," Obasan says, and shuffles past into the kitchen.

We stand awkwardly in the living room, Mrs. Barker glancing around. Her eyes dart back and forth. I find myself donning her restless eyes like a pair of trick glasses. She must think the house is an obstacle course. There is barely room to stand. Cloth on cloth on cloth covers the chesterfield and armchair and footstool and shelves. Everything is protected. The patterns and colors all clash. A bright purple maple-leaf-fringed cushion rests on a green-and-gold throw. The footstool is covered with a blue wool crochet. The two window ledges are covered in plants, several of which rise to the low ceiling. Boxes of Japanese-language newspapers are tucked under TV trays and in corners. She must be wondering how any mind can rest in such surroundings.

"Please sit down." I pick up Aunt Emily's papers that are strewn on the chesterfield and make room for Mrs. Barker. Her thin eyebrows lift and fall like windshield wipers and she sits unsteadily, her pantsuit lifting and showing the tops of her nylon socks. She sits like a bird poised for flight.

"And what do you hear from Stephen?" Mr. Barker asks as he settles onto the sofa.

"Oh, well, he's . . . he's fine," I reply, trying to think of what else to say.

"He'll be coming to the funeral?" Mr. Barker says.

I nod.

"He's in Montreal these days? No more European tours?"

People in Granton are always asking about Stephen's musical career. But with the amount of correspondence we get from him, they know as much as we do.

The last time I saw Stephen was eight years ago when he came to Granton for a short afternoon visit with Claudine, a divorcée he'd met in Paris. She was trim and slight with deep shadows under her large brown eyes. She kept exclaiming in her mixture of French and English with her hands fluttering. "It is—how do you say?—like the Western movies?"

Stephen was obviously nervous having her in Granton. They were in the house less than five minutes. The rest of the time the three of us drove around the countryside. Obasan remained in the kitchen the entire afternoon preparing a meal that was as non-Japanese as she could manage but they left without eating. They have not been back since.

Last Christmas, according to Aunt Emily, the two of them were off on a cruise in the Mediterranean.

Obasan made some kakimochi—deep-fried and baked crackers coated with sugar and soy sauce—and packed them in an old Graham Wafers box. I mailed the parcel to Montreal but we never heard whether they received them.

Obasan shuffles back into the room, bringing a bowl of kakimochi and tea-stained cups on a chipped lacquer tray. The crevices of one of the fluted cups contains dark grease lines.

Mrs. Barker shifts uncomfortably. She puts her fists on

her knees and her eyes dart from the cup to Mr. Barker sitting beside her. She is breathing unevenly.

What is it she smells? What foreign odor sends its message down into her body, alerting her limbs? If only I could banish all that offends her delicate sensibilities. Especially the strong smell of miso and daikon and shoyu. Especially all the dust that Obasan and I are too short to see. Mrs. Barker's glance at Obasan is one of condescension. Or is it solicitude? We are dogs, she and I, sniffing for clues, our throats quivering with subliminal growls.

"Will Mrs. Nah Canny be all right here on her own?" Mrs. Barker asks me as Obasan pours the tea. She is staring at the cups.

I clear my throat and stammer. I lack communication skills.

Obasan hands me the bowl of kakimochi and I hold them out. Mrs. Barker is uncomfortable that I do not speak. She raises her hand to her chest and ignores the crackers, saying to Mr. Barker, "Sunnydale is a wonderful place, isn't it, Jack?"

The new Mrs. Barker is new indeed if she is suggesting that Obasan could go to the Sunnydale Lodge. Obasan would be as welcome there as a Zulu warrior. It's a white-walled, whitewashed, and totally white old folks' home.

Mr. Barker leans his head to the side in a noncommittal shrug as Mrs. Barker turns to face him. She sits straight as a flagpole. Her flag represents the Barker kingdom, a tiny but confident country. But momentarily she is planted here on this soil beside Obasan's own dark flag.

It's not what she is saying. It's the way she sits here, her fists held tight, as if desperate to stop something from gushing out.

Obasan is moving about deaf and impassive, unavailable

for questioning or their ministrations. Her land is impenetrable, so thick that even the sound of mourning is swallowed up. In her steadfast silence, she remains inviolate.

"Can she manage?" Mrs. Barker is asking me again.

Mr. Barker turns to Obasan. "You manage?" he shouts to her.

Obasan is startled by this outburst.

"Manage all right?" he says again.

Obasan nods politely and goes to the kitchen.

"She has what she needs," I say.

"You people very clever," he shouts after her.

He leans forward on the chesterfield and addresses me. "Sam, he was a clever man. Never once said a bitter word. Told me he used to be a fisherman. Lots of your people buried here in the prairies. Takashima, he was a fisherman."

Mr. Takashima, Mr. Yoshida. They certainly are disappearing. Uncle will be in good company.

The part of the cemetery that holds their bones is off by itself in the northwest corner of Forest Lawn. Perhaps some genealogist of the future will come across this patch of bones and wonder why so many fishermen died on the prairies.

I remember one time we drove up the mountainside near Sheep Creek and came across shellfish fossils. "Ha," Uncle said in awe, expelling his breath slowly, "the sea was here."

Mrs. Barker faces me with her whole body as if there are no independent joints. "A fisherman?" she asks.

"It was a terrible business what we did to our Japanese," Mr. Barker says.

Ah, here we go again. "Our Indians." "Our Japanese." "A terrible business." It's like being offered a pair of crutches while I'm striding down the street. The comments are so incessant and always so well-intentioned. "How long have you been in this country? Do you like our country? You speak such good English. Do you run a café? My daughter has a darling Japanese friend. Have you ever been back to Japan?"

Back?

Does it so much matter that these questions are always asked? Particularly by strangers? These are icebreaker questions that create an awareness of ice.

Where do any of us come from in this cold country? Oh, Canada, whether it is admitted or not, we come from you we come from you. From the same soil, the slugs and slime and bogs and twigs and roots. We come from the country that plucks its people out like weeds and flings them into the roadside. We grow in ditches and sloughs, untended and spindly. We erupt in the valleys and mountainsides, in small towns and back alleys, sprouting upside down on the prairies, our hair wild as spiders' legs, our feet rooted nowhere. We grow where we are not seen, we flourish where we are not heard, the thick undergrowth of an unlikely planting. Where do we come from, Obasan? We come from cemeteries full of skeletons with wild roses in their grinning teeth. We come from our untold tales that wait for their telling. We come from Canada, this land that is like every land, filled with the wise, the fearful, the compassionate, the corrupt.

Obasan, however, does not come from this clamorous climate. She does not dance to the multicultural piper's tune or respond to the racist's slur. She remains in a silent territory, defined by her serving hands. She serves us now, pouring tea into Mr. Barker's cup. She is unable to see and stops halfway before the cup is full.

35

Exhaustion since the Barkers' departure. Both Obasan and I have been dozing in the living room. It's almost seven. Aunt Emily and Stephen should be here by now. I hope they've eaten—I haven't thought about supper. There's Uncle's last loaf of everlasting stone bread, but neither of us is hungry.

I was having a nightmare just now. Something about stairs. Ah yes, and a courtyard. That's it. Stairs leading into a courtyard and the place of the dead. It wasn't at all a "fine and private place," that home beyond the grave. They were all there—my parents, the grandparents, and Obasan as well, small as a child. She was intent on being near me at the top of the stairs. And of course, there were soldiers. Always, I dream of soldiers eager for murder, their weapons ready. We die again and again. In my dreams, we are never safe enough.

In the courtyard, a flower ceremony was underway, like the one in my dream yesterday morning. Mother stood in the center. In her mouth she held a knotted string stem, like the twine and string of Obasan's ball which she keeps in the pantry. From the stem hung a rose, red as a heart. I moved toward her from the top of the stairs, a cloud falling to earth, heavy and full of rain.

Was it then that the nightmare began? The skin of the air became close and dense, a formless hair vest. Up from a valley there rose a dark cloud—a great cape. It was the Grand Inquisitor descending over us, the top of his head a shiny skin cap. With his large hands he was prying open my mother's lips, prying open my eyes.

I fell and cried out. I woke into the room where Obasan sleeps, her skin-colored mouth open—a small dry cave of a mouth. How unlike my mother's young heart-shaped mouth in my dream, her fingers deftly moving the long thread from knot to knot, drawing the flower closer to her lips.

Once I came across two ideographs for the word "love." The first contained the root words "heart" and "hand" and "action"—love as hands and heart in action together. The other ideograph, for "passionate love," was formed of "heart," "to tell," and "a long thread."

The dance ceremony of the dead was a slow courtly telling, the heart declaring a long thread knotted to Obasan's twine, knotted to Aunt Emily's package. Why, I wonder as she danced her love, should I find myself unable to breathe? The Grand Inquisitor was carnivorous and full of murder. His demand to know was both a judgment and a refusal to hear. The more he questioned her, the more he was her accuser and murderer. The more he killed her, the deeper her silence became. What the Grand Inquisitor has never learned is that the avenues of speech are the avenues of silence. To hear my mother, to attend her speech, to attend the sound of stone, he must first become silent. Only when he enters her abandonment will he be released from his own.

How the Grand Inquisitor gnaws at my bones. At the age of questioning my mother disappeared. Why, I have asked ever since, did she not write? Why, I ask now, must I know? Did I doubt her love? Am I her accuser?

> *Did you not know that people hide their love*
> *Like a flower that seems too precious to be picked?*

the Chinese poet Wu-ti asked.

My mother hid her love, but hidden in life does she speak through dream?

Her tale is a rose with a tangled stem. All this questioning, this clawing at her grave, is an unseemly thing. Let the inquisition rest tonight. In the week of my uncle's departure, let there be peace.

Obasan stirs and lifts her head, rubbing her eyes. She feels for the glasses dangling on her chest and attempts to get up. The rubber loops at the end of the chain that fit around the glasses are frayed and replaced by safety pins. When she has her glasses on she picks up the slippery blue pages from the coffee table and begins reading again.

36

I have gathered all the stained cups and dishes, the serving bowls and the teapot, and am cleaning them, removing the stains and grease, soaking them in a sink full of hot sudsy water. When I am halfway through I hear the sounds of two cars entering the driveway. The car doors close and there are voices in the yard. In a moment, there is a slow light rapping on the living-room door and Nakayama-sensei's voice calls "Gomen-nasai," announcing his arrival. He opens the door and calls "Gomen-nasai" again in a loud but gentle voice.

"O," Obasan says and begins to rise, holding the blue pages and the magnifying glass in her hands.

"Please, please." He comes into the room, removing his black felt hat and waving his hand in the rapid patting movement indicating she should not get up. His thin hair is so white it is almost luminous against his prairie-darkened face. Over the years, Nakayama-sensei has managed to visit Granton about once a month or so, when he is not traveling elsewhere.

Aunt Emily and Stephen are directly behind Nakayama-sensei. I am surprised at the amount of gray hair Stephen has. There is not so much that it streaks but the white is definitely visible as a light spray. He seems also to be slightly heavier than he was before, his face more full.

"Stee-bu-san?" Obasan says. She puts the papers and magnifying glass on the chesterfield and stands up tottering. With her two hands outstretched, she steps unsteadily toward him.

Stephen bends over and holds her hands with one hand as he removes his shoes with the other. He has just come in the door, and he already looks as if he would like to run out. His light black coat is pocked by large raindrops.

Aunt Emily also removes her shoes, then puts one arm around Obasan's shoulders. Obasan touches Stephen's coat where it is wet. "Is it raining?" she asks. Then she chuckles. "Even if there is rain or thunder, these ears cannot hear."

I take Aunt Emily's and Nakayama-sensei's wet coats and hang them on the hooks beside the kitchen, then pour water into the heavy kettle for green tea.

Stephen, still wearing his wet coat, is sitting in the armchair with his legs splayed out like splints.

"Everyone someday dies," Obasan is saying to him.

"What happened, Nomi?" he asks with his back to me.

"I don't know really," I answer. I am slicing the stone

bread to serve with the green tea. "I haven't got the details from Dr. Brace."

Aunt Emily puts her bag down behind the armchair and comes into the kitchen. She looks for a dish towel to wipe the teacups.

"The Barkers were here just a while ago."

"Yeah?" Stephen sits up and takes off his coat jerkily. He grunts as Obasan tries to help him with it. Stephen has made himself altogether unfamiliar with speaking Japanese.

Nakayama-sensei has picked up the magnifying glass and paper that Obasan left on the chesterfield and is glancing at the top page when Aunt Emily goes into the living room with the tray of teacups.

She stops short when she sees what Sensei is holding. All the rest of her papers are piled up on one edge of the coffee table.

"Everyone someday dies," Obasan is saying again, softly to herself.

Nakayama-sensei puts the papers and magnifying glass on the coffee table, then leaning back and with his mouth close to Obasan's ear, he says, "Should there be prayer?"

Obasan replies by bending forward in a prolonged bow.

I come into the room with the plate of buttered bread and kneel beside the coffee table. Everyone's head is bowed and we sit together in the stillness for a long time.

At last Nakayama-sensei stands up. He begins a long prayer of thanks in Japanese.

Stephen has his elbows on his knees and is feeling his chin lightly with his fingertips as he listens with his eyes fixed on the floor. I also have my eyes open. At one point, Stephen takes a corner of bread and breaks it off, then, changing his mind, he sticks it back on the slice. At the end of the prayer,

Aunt Emily says "Amen," and we sit together in the silence once more.

When Nakayama-sensei sits down, Aunt Emily opens her eyes, but Obasan's head remains bowed.

"It is good you are here," Nakayama-sensei says to Aunt Emily and Stephen. "You have come well."

Aunt Emily nods and takes her papers off the coffee table, making room for the teacups. Sensei leans forward to help and removes the blue papers and magnifying glass.

"Letters from a long time ago," Aunt Emily says to Sensei.

"Is that so?" Nakayama-sensei says, glancing down through the bottom of his bifocals. His lips gradually become pursed in concentration as he reads the top page. When he comes to the end of the page, he stops.

"About this, I had no knowledge," he says in a low voice.

"What is it, Sensei?" I ask.

He puts the first page aside and reads the next and the next, groaning quietly. When he is finished he puts the papers down and addresses Aunt Emily.

"Has there been no telling?"

"No," Aunt Emily says quietly.

"It is better to speak, is it not? They are not children any longer."

Aunt Emily nods slowly. "Yes," she says softly. "We ought to tell them. I always thought we should. But . . . kodomo no tame . . ." She fingers the buttons on her sweater and looks at me apologetically. "There was so much sad news. Mark was dead. Father was ill. The first time I came to Granton I brought the letters thinking we should tell them everything, but we decided to respect Nesan's wishes."

"Please, Aunt Emily," I whisper as she turns aside. "Tell us."

Aunt Emily takes the letters and reads the pages, handing them back to Sensei when she is finished.

"What is written?" I ask again.

"A matter of a long time ago," Sensei says.

"What matter?"

Nakayama-sensei clears his throat. "Senso no toki—in the time of the war—your mother. Your grandmother. That there is suffering and their deep love." He reads the letters in silence once more, then begins reading aloud. The letter is addressed to Grandpa Kato. It is clear as he reads that the letters were never intended for Stephen and me. They were written by Grandma Kato.

The sound of rain beats against the windows and the roof. The rain is collecting in the eaves and pouring in a thin stream into the rain barrel at the corner near the kitchen door. Tomorrow I will fill the plastic bucket and bring the soft frothy water in—use it to water the houseplants and wash my hair.

Sensei's faltering voice is almost drowned out by the splattering gusts against the window. I stare at the gauze-curtained windows and imagine the raindrops sliding down the glass, black on black. In the sound of the howling outside, I hear other howling.

Sensei pauses as he reads. "Naomi," he says softly, "Stephen, your mother is speaking. Listen carefully to her voice."

Many of the Japanese words sound strange and the language is formal.

37

There are only two letters in the gray cardboard folder. The first is a brief and emotionless statement that Grandma Kato, her niece's daughter, and my mother are the only ones in the immediate family to have survived. The second letter is an outpouring.

I remember Grandma Kato as thin and tough, not given to melodrama or overstatement of any kind. She was unbreakable. I felt she could endure all things and would survive any catastrophe. But I did not then understand what catastrophes were possible in human affairs.

Here, the ordinary Granton rain slides down wet and

clean along the glass, leaving a trail on the window like the Japanese writing on the thin blue-lined paper—straight down like a bead curtain of asterisks. The rain she describes is black, oily, thick, and strange.

"In the heat of the August sun," Grandma writes, "however much the effort to forget, there is no forgetfulness. As in a dream, I can still see the maggots crawling in the sockets of my niece's eyes. Her strong intelligent young son helped me move a bonsai tree that very morning. There is no forgetfulness."

When Nakayama-sensei reaches the end of the page, he stops reading and folds the letter as if he has decided to read no more. Aunt Emily begins to speak quietly, telling of a final letter from the Canadian missionary, Miss Best.

How often, I am wondering, did Grandma and Mother waken in those years with the unthinkable memories alive in their minds, the visible evidence of horror written on their skin, in their blood, carved in every mirror they passed, felt in every step they took? As a child I was told only that Mother and Grandma Kato were safe in Tokyo, visiting Grandma Kato's ailing mother.

"Someday, surely, they will return," Obasan used to say.

The two letters that reached us in Vancouver before all communication ceased due to the war told us that Mother and Grandma Kato had arrived safely in Japan and were staying with Grandma Kato's sister and her husband in their home near the Tokyo Gas Company. My great-grandmother was then seventy-nine and was not expected to live to be eighty but, happily, she had become so well that she had returned home from the hospital and was even able on occasion to leave the house.

Nakayama-sensei opens the letter again and holds it, reading silently. Then, looking over to Stephen, he says, "It is better to speak, is it not?"

"They're dead now," Stephen says.

Sensei nods.

"Please read, Sensei," I whisper.

"Yes," Aunt Emily says. "They should know."

Sensei starts again at the beginning. The letter is dated simply 1949. It was sent, Sensei says, from somewhere in Nagasaki. There was no return address.

"Though it was a time of war," Grandma writes, "what happiness that January 1945 to hear from my niece Setsuko, in Nagasaki." Setsuko's second child was due to be born within the month. In February, just as American air raids in Tokyo were intensifying, Mother went to help her cousin in Nagasaki. The baby was born three days after she arrived. Early in March, air raids and alarms were constant day and night in Tokyo. In spite of all the dangers of travel, Grandma Kato went to Nagasaki to be with my mother and to help with the care of the new baby. The last day she spent with her mother and sister in Tokyo, she said they sat on the tatami and talked, remembering their childhood and the days they went chestnut picking together. They parted with laughter. The following night, Grandma Kato's sister, their mother, and her sister's husband died in the B-29 bombings of March 9, 1945.

From this point on, Grandma's letter becomes increasingly chaotic, the details interspersed without chronological consistency. She and my mother, she writes, were unable to talk of all the things that happened. The horror would surely die sooner, they felt, if they refused to speak. But the silence and the constancy of the nightmare had become unbearable for Grandma and she hoped that by sharing them with her husband, she could be helped to extricate herself from the grip of the past.

"If these matters are sent away in this letter, perhaps they will depart a little from our souls," she writes. "For the burden of these words, forgive me."

Mother, for her part, continued her vigil of silence. She spoke with no one about her torment. She specifically requested that Stephen and I be spared the truth.

In all my high school days, until we heard from Sensei that her grave had been found in Tokyo, I pictured her trapped in Japan by government regulations, or by an ailing grandmother. The letters I sent to the address in Tokyo were never answered or returned. I could not know that she and Grandma Kato had gone to Nagasaki to stay with Setsuko, her husband, who was a dentist, and their two children, four-year-old Tomio and the new baby, Chieko.

The baby, Grandma writes, looked so much like me that she and my mother marveled and often caught themselves calling her Naomi. With her widow's peak, her fat cheeks and pointed chin, she had a heart-shaped face like mine. Tomio, however, was not like Stephen at all. He was a sturdy child, extremely healthy and athletic, with a strong will like his father. He was fascinated by his new baby sister, sitting and watching her for hours as she slept or nursed. He made dolls for her. He helped to dress her. He loved to hold her in the bath, feeling her fingers holding his fingers tightly. He rocked her to sleep in his arms.

The weather was hot and humid that morning of August 9. The air-raid alerts had ended. Tomio and some neighborhood children had gone to the irrigation ditch to play and cool off as they sometimes did.

Shortly after eleven o'clock, Grandma Kato was preparing

to make lunch. The baby was strapped to her back. She was
bending over a bucket of water beside a large earthenware
storage bin when a child in the street was heard shouting,
"Look at the parachute!" A few seconds later, there was a
sudden white flash, brighter than a bolt of lightning. She had
no idea what could have exploded. It was as if the entire sky
were swallowed up. A moment later she was hurled sideways
by a blast. She had a sensation of floating tranquilly in a cool
whiteness high above the earth. When she regained con-
sciousness, she was slumped forward in a sitting position in
the water bin. She gradually became aware of the moisture, an
intolerable heat, blood, a mountain of debris, and her niece's
weak voice, sounding at first distant, calling the names of her
children. Then she could hear the other sounds—the faraway
shouting. Around her, a thick dust made breathing difficult.
Chieko was still strapped to her back, but made no sound.
She was alive but unconscious.

It took Grandma a long time to claw her way out of the
wreckage. When she emerged, it was into an eerie twilight
formed of heavy dust and smoke that blotted out the sun.
What she saw was incomprehensible. Almost all the buildings
were flattened or in flames for as far as she could see. The
landmarks were gone. Tall columns of fire rose through the
haze and everywhere the dying and the wounded crawled,
fled, stumbled like ghosts among the ruins. Voices screamed,
calling the names of children, fathers, mothers, calling for
help, calling for water.

Beneath some wreckage, she saw first the broken arm,
then the writhing body of her niece, her head bent back, her
hair singed, both her eye sockets blown out. In a weak and
delirious voice, she was calling Tomio. Grandma Kato touched
her niece's leg and the skin peeled off and stuck to the palm
of her hand.

It isn't clear from the letter but at some point she came across Tomio, his legs pumping steadily up and down as he stood in one spot not knowing where to go. She gathered him in her arms. He was remarkably intact, his skin unburned.

She had no idea where Mother was, but with the two children, she began making her way toward the air-raid shelter. All around her people one after another collapsed and died, crying for water. One old man no longer able to keep moving lay on the ground holding up a dead baby and crying, "Save the children. Leave the old." No one took the dead child from his outstretched hands. Men, women, in many cases indistinguishable by sex, hairless, half clothed, hobbled past. Skin hung from their bodies like tattered rags. One man held his bowels in with the stump of one hand. A child whom Grandma Kato recognized lay on the ground asking for help. She stopped and told him she would return as soon as she could. A woman she knew was begging for someone to help her lift the burning beam beneath which her children were trapped. The woman's children were friends of Tomio's. Grandma was loath to walk past, but with the two children, she could do no more and kept going. At no point does Grandma Kato mention the injuries she herself must have sustained.

Nearing the shelter, Grandma could see through the grayness that the entrance was clogged with dead bodies. She remembered then that her niece's father-in-law lived on a farm on the hillside, and she began making her way back through the burning city toward the river she would have to cross. The water, red with blood, was a raft of corpses. Farther upstream, the bridge was twisted like noodles. Eventually she came to a spot where she was able to cross and, still carrying the two children, Grandma Kato made her way up the hillside.

After wandering for some time, she found a wooden water

pipe dribbling a steady stream. She held Tomio's mouth to it and allowed him to drink as much as he wished though she had heard that too much water was not good. She unstrapped the still unconscious baby from her back. Exhausted, she drank from the pipe, and gathering the two children in her arms, she looked out at the burning city and lapsed into a sleep so deep she believed she was unconscious.

When she awakened, she was in the home of her niece's relatives and the baby was being fed barley water. The little boy was nowhere.

Almost immediately, Grandma set off to look for the child. Next day she returned to the area of her niece's home and every day thereafter she looked for Mother and the lost boy, checking the lists of the dead, looking over the unclaimed corpses. She discovered that her niece's husband was among the dead.

One evening when she had given up the search for the day, she sat down beside a naked woman she'd seen earlier who was aimlessly chipping wood to make a pyre on which to cremate a dead baby. The woman was utterly disfigured. Her nose and one cheek were almost gone. Great wounds and pustules covered her entire face and body. She was completely bald. She sat in a cloud of flies, and maggots wriggled among her wounds. As Grandma watched her, the woman gave her a vacant gaze, then let out a cry. It was my mother.

The little boy was never found. Mother was taken to a hospital and was expected to die, but she survived. During one night she vomited yellow fluid and passed a great deal of blood. For a long time—Grandma does not say how long—Mother wore bandages on her face. When they were removed, Mother felt her face with her fingers, then asked for a cloth mask. Thereafter she would not take off her mask from morning to night.

"At this moment," Grandma writes, "we are preparing to visit Chieko-chan in the hospital." Chieko, four years old in 1949, waited daily for their visit, standing in the hospital corridor, tubes from her wrist attached to a bottle that was hung above her. A small bald-headed girl. She was dying of leukemia.

"There may not be many more days," Grandma concludes.

After this, what could have happened? Did they leave the relatives in Nagasaki? Where and how did they survive?

When Sensei is finished reading, he folds and unfolds the letter, nodding his head slowly.

I put my hands around the teapot, feeling its round warmth against my palms. My skin feels hungry for warmth, for flesh. Grandma mentioned in her letter that she saw one woman cradling a hot-water bottle as if it were a baby.

Sensei places the letter back in the cardboard folder and closes it with the short red string around the tab.

"That there is brokenness," he says quietly. "That this world is brokenness. But within brokenness is the unbreakable name. How the whole earth groans till Love returns."

I stand up abruptly and leave the room, going into the kitchen for some more hot water. When I return, Sensei is sitting with his face in his hands.

Stephen is staring at the floor, his body hunched forward motionless. He glances up at me, then looks away swiftly. I sit on a stool beside him and try to concentrate on what is being said. I can hear Aunt Emily telling us about Mother's grave. Then Nakayama-sensei stands and begins to say the Lord's Prayer under his breath. "And forgive us our trespasses—forgive us our trespasses," he repeats, sighing deeply, "as we forgive others . . ." He lifts his head, looking upward. "We are powerless to forgive unless we first are forgiven. It is a high calling, my friends—the calling to forgive. But no person, no people is innocent. Therefore we must forgive one another."

I am not thinking of forgiveness. The sound of Sensei's voice grows as indistinct as the hum of distant traffic. Gradually the room grows still and it is as if I am back with Uncle again, listening and listening to the silent earth and the silent sky as I have done all my life.

I close my eyes.

Mother, I am listening. Assist me to hear you.

38

Silent Mother, you do not speak or write. You do not reach

through the night to enter morning, but remain in the voice-

lessness. From the extremity of much dying, the only sound

that reaches me now is the sigh of your remembered breath, a

wordless word. How shall I attend that speech, Mother, how

shall I trace that wave?

You are tide rushing moonward pulling back from the

shore. A raft rocks on the surface bobbing in the dark. The

water fills with flailing arms that beckon like seaweed on the

prow. I sit on the raft begging for a tide to land me safely on the sand but you draw me to the white distance, skyward and away from this blood-drugged earth.

By the time this country opened its pale arms to you, it was too late. First, you could not, then you chose not to come. Now you are gone. Tonight, Aunt Emily has said a missionary found your name on a plaque of the dead. A Canadian maple tree grows there where your name stands. The tree utters its scarlet voice in the air. Prayers bleeding. Its rustling leaves are fingers scratching an empty sky.

There is no date on the memorial stone. There are no photographs ever again. "Do not tell Stephen and Naomi," you say. "I am praying that they may never know."

Martyr Mother, you pilot your powerful voicelessness over the ocean and across the mountain, straight as a missile to our hut on the edge of a sugar-beet field. You wish to protect us with lies, but the camouflage does not hide your cries. Beneath the hiding I am there with you. Silent Mother, lost in the abandoning, you do not share the horror. At first, stumbling and unaware of pain, you open your eyes in the red mist and, sheltering a dead child, you flee through the flames. Young Mother at Nagasaki, am I not also there?

In the dark Slocan night, the bright light flares in my dreaming. I hear the screams and feel the mountain breaking. Your long black hair falls and falls into the chasm. My legs are sawn in half. The skin on your face bubbles like lava and melts from your bones. Mother, I see your face. Do not turn aside.

Mother, in my dreams you are a maypole. I dance around you with a long paper streamer in my hand. But the words of the May Day song are words of distress. The unknown is a hook that pierces the bone. Thongs hang down in the hot prairie air. Silence attends the long sun dance.

Grandma sits at a low table in a bombed country writing

words she does not intend me to hear. "The child," she writes, "is not well." She does not declare her own state of health. The letters take months to reach Grandfather. They take years to reach me. Grandfather gives the letters to Aunt Emily. Aunt Emily sends letters to the Government. The Government makes paper airplanes out of our lives and files us out the windows. Some people return home. Some do not. War, they all say, is war, and some people survive.

No one knows the exact day that you die. Aunt Emily writes and receives no replies. All that is left is your word, "Do not tell. . . ."

Obasan and Uncle hear your request. They give me no words from you. They hand me old photographs.

You stand on a street corner in Vancouver in a straight silky dress and a light black coat. On your head is a wide-brimmed hat with a feather and your black shoes have one strap and a buckle at the side. I stand leaning into you, my dress bulging over my round baby belly. My fat arm clings to your leg. Your skirt hides half my face. Your leg is a tree trunk and I am branch, vine, butterfly. I am joined to your limbs by right of birth, child of your flesh, leaf of your bough.

The tree is a dead tree in the middle of the prairies. I sit on its roots still as a stone. In my dreams, a small child sits with a wound on her knee. The wound on her knee is on the back of her skull, large and moist. A double wound. The child is forever unable to speak. The child forever fears to tell. I apply a thick bandage but nothing can soak up the seepage. I beg that the woundedness may be healed and that the limbs may learn to dance. But you stay in a black-and-white photograph, smiling your yasashi smile.

Gentle Mother, we were lost together in our silences. Our wordlessness was our mutual destruction.

Nakayama-sensei is still praying softly, a long long prayer.

"Father, if your suffering is greater than ours, how great that suffering must be," he is saying. "How great the helplessness. How we dare not abandon the ones who suffer, lest we again abandon You." His voice rises and falls as it did when he was praying at Grandma Nakane's funeral in Slocan. "We are abandoned yet we are not abandoned. You are present in every hell. Teach us to see Love's presence in our abandonment. Teach us to forgive."

Obasan's eyes are closed and her hands are moving back and forth across the gray cardboard folder—to erase, to soothe.

I am thinking that for a child there is no presence without flesh. But perhaps it is because I am no longer a child I can know your presence though you are not here. The letters tonight are skeletons. Bones only. But the earth still stirs with dormant blooms. Love flows through the roots of the trees by our graves.

39

Five-thirty A.M. a hollow night's watching. I have lain awake on a mat beside Obasan, listening to the sounds of fitful sleeping in the house. Aunt Emily is in my room and Stephen is on the living-room couch. Obasan has been sitting up most of the night. She is kneeling on her bed, rubbing her hands over her knees, her nemaki half open.

By her pillow is her chocolate box of photographs. Uncle's ID card sits on top of the pile. She is shining her flashlight and looking at the pictures one by one—the photograph of Mother and me, Stephen with Claudine and Aunt Emily, Father and Uncle as young men, a picnic in Slocan.

"Samishi, Obasan?" I ask. "Lonely?"

She does not hear me.

Outside the heavily curtained window, the sky is flooded with night. There are no stars.

I am remembering a fugue Uncle used to love—a melody Father composed in New Denver which Stephen developed— a quiet light staccato, clear and precise with long pauses between the notes of the melody. Each time it was played it sounded almost as if it were being practiced for the first time. A light piece, more sad than happy, but quiet and dignified, as Uncle was, as Mother was. A gentle tune. How well they both hid the cacophony life wrote in their bones.

After the rotting of the flesh, what is the song that is left? Is it the strange gnashing sound of insects with their mandibles moving through the bone marrow? Up through the earth come tiny cries of betrayal. There are so many betrayals— departures, deaths, absences—there are all the many absences within which we who live are left.

Is it enough that we were once together briefly in our early Vancouver days? Is it enough that Obasan shared her lifetime with Uncle, and all these Granton years, through the long winters in the hut that could not be warmed, in the summer heat, her skin becoming the color of earth, through spring wind and chinook, through sleet and hail? They were constant together in all that shifting weather. They attended one another.

But now? Dead hands can no longer touch our outstretched hands or move to heal.

Obasan is small as a child and has not learned to weep. Back and forth, back and forth, her hands move on her knees. She looks at me unsteadily, then hands me the ID card with Uncle's young face. What ghostly whisperings I feel in the air as I hold the card. "Kodomo no tame—for the sake of the children—gaman shi masho—let us endure." The voices pour down like rain but in the middle of the downpour I still feel thirst. Somewhere between speech and hearing is a transmutation of sound. The rainlight drops to earth as salt. Obasan rubs her eyes and tries to speak but the thick saliva coats her throat and she does not have the strength to cough. Her round dry mouth is open. A small accepting "o."

What stillness in this predawn hour. The air is cold. In all our life of preparation we are unprepared for this new hour filled with emptiness. How thick the darkness behind which hides the animal cry. I know what is there, hidden from my stare. Grief's weeping. Deeper emptiness.

Grief wails like a scarecrow in the wild night, beckoning the wind to clothe his gaunt shell. With his outstretched arms he is gathering eyes for his disguise. I had not known that Grief had such gentle eyes—eyes reflecting my uncle's eyes, my mother's eyes, all the familiar lost eyes of Love that are not his and that he dons as a mask and a mockery.

This body of grief is not fit for human habitation. Let there be flesh. The song of mourning is not a lifelong song.

Father, Mother, my relatives, my ancestors, we have come to the forest tonight, to the place where the colors all meet— red and yellow and blue. We have turned and returned to your arms as you turn to earth and form the forest floor. Tonight we picked berries with the help of your sighted hands. Tonight we read the forest braille. See how our stained fingers have read the seasons, and how our serving hands serve you still.

My loved ones, rest in your world of stone. Around you flows the underground stream. How bright in the darkness the brooding light. How gentle the colors of rain.

.   .   .

Obasan's eyes are closed as she continues kneeling on the bed, her head bowed. In the palm of her open hand is Uncle's ID card. Her lips move imperceptibly as she breathes her prayers.

Through the open doorway I can see the faint shaft of light from the kitchen across the living-room floor, straight as a knife cutting light from shadow, the living from the dead.

I tiptoe out to the kitchen and put on my cleanly scraped shoes. Aunt Emily's coat is warmer than my jacket. I slip it on over my pajamas and step out to the car. The engine sounds loud in the predawn stillness. As I drive, the drops of moisture on the windshield skitter to the sides of the glass and disappear.

By the time I reach the coulee, the sky has changed from a steel gray to a faint teal blue. I park the car at the side of the road in its usual spot and wade through the coulee grass as I did with Uncle just a month ago. The stalks are wet with dew and the late-night rain. My pajamas and shoes and the bottom of Aunt Emily's coat are soaked before I reach the slope.

I inch my way down the steep path that skirts the wild rose bushes, down slipping along the wet grass where the underground stream seeps through the earth. My shoes are mud-clogged again. At the very bottom, I come to the bank. Above the trees, the moon is a pure white stone. The reflection is rippling in the river—water and stone dancing. It's a quiet ballet, soundless as breath.

Up at the top of the slope, I can see the spot where Uncle sat last month looking out over the landscape.

"Umi no yo," he always said. "It's like the sea."

Between the river and Uncle's spot are the wild roses and the tiny wildflowers that grow along the trickling stream. The perfume in the air is sweet and faint. If I hold my head a certain way, I can smell them from where I am.

Excerpt from the memorandum sent by the Co-operative Committee on Japanese Canadians to the House and the Senate of Canada, April 1946

It is urgently submitted that the Orders-in-Council [for the deportation of Canadians of Japanese racial origin] are wrong and indefensible and constitute a grave threat to the rights and liberties of Canadian citizens, and that Parliament as guardian of these rights and the representative of the people, should assert its powers and require the Governor-in-Council to withdraw the Orders, for the following reasons.

1. The Orders-in-Council provide for the exile of Canadian citizens.

The power of exile has not been employed by civilized countries since the days of the Stuarts in England. So seriously was it then viewed that the Habeas Corpus Act makes it a serious offense for any official to exile a British subject.

2. The Orders and the proposed exile of Canadian citizens constitute a violation of International Law and as Mr. Justice Kellock and Rand have stated, in-

volves invasion of another's territory, and the violation of sovereign rights.

The Congress of the United States has no power to exile citizens, and the British Parliament has not, even in the gravest emergency, found it necessary to assume such a power.

3. The Orders-in-Council put the value of Canadian citizenship into contempt. They cancel naturalization in a wholesale manner, and without any reason.

At this time when the Parliament of Canada will be considering legislation designed to enhance the value and dignity of Canadian citizenship, these Orders will have precisely the opposite effect.

4. The Orders-in-Council are based upon racial discrimination. Deportation on racial grounds has been defined as a crime against humanity, and the war criminals of Germany and Japan are being tried for precisely this offense, amongst others.

5. The proposed deportations are in no way related to any war emergency.

The necessity of removing persons of Japanese origin from the coastal regions during the war, was referrable to the emergency, but now that hostilities have ceased for some time, it cannot possibly be suggested that the safety of Canada requires the injustice of treating Canadian citizens in the manner proposed.

The Prime Minister has himself made it clear that no instances of sabotage can be laid at the door of Japanese Canadians.

If any of those concerned have been disloyal, there is ample power under the Immigration and Naturalization Acts for their deportation after proper inquiry into individual cases.

Many Japanese Canadians have already settled in the Prairie Provinces and in eastern Canada and have no desire to return to B.C. There is therefore no need for fear of concentration on the Pacific coast as in the past.

6. The Orders for deportation purport to be based on alleged requests to be sent to Japan. It is suggested that the signing of these requests indicated disloyalty. This is far from the truth. The signing of the forms was encouraged as an act of cooperation with the Government of Canada. The very form used implied that the Government approved and sought the signing of these forms. Those who refused to sign were described as uncooperative, and denied privileges accorded to those who did sign. For the Government, which through its agents obtained and sought the signing of these forms, to claim now that they indicated disloyalty, would be to implicate the Government itself in the encouragement of a disloyal attitude.

7. The Orders constitute a threat to the security of every minority in Canada.

8. The Orders cannot be enforced without grave injustice and inhumanity to innocent persons.

9. The effect of these Orders will be to cause lasting hostility to Canada throughout the Orient, where racial discrimination is deeply resented. The future of Canada's international relationship may depend upon the revocation of these Orders.

10. The Orders are directly in contradiction of the

language and spirit of the United Nations Charter, subscribed to by Canada as well as the other nations of the world, and are an adoption of the methods of Naziism.

Respectfully submitted,
James M. Finlay, Chairman
Andrew Brewin
Hugh MacMillan

If you enjoyed reading Obasan, Anchor Books *also publishes its sequel,* Itsuka. *The following is an excerpt from that novel.*

True to her energetic word, Aunt Emily has reached my un-reachable brother, and here we are in his expensive hotel res-taurant, Anna, me and Aunt Emily, with Stephen, his streak of white hair wider than before. He's put on some weight. His voice is still the rich baritone of a singer.

"Well, h'lo."

To most people our lack of expressiveness would seem pe-culiar. This is my one and only brother whom I haven't seen in over a decade and all I do is say "hello" and sit down. No hugs, no kisses, not even a handshake. We come from the territory of stone.

"So, Nome. Long time no see, eh?" He's in Toronto to judge a Mozart competition.

"How's Claudine? Are you still with her?"

"We survive."

I'm wondering as I sit here, opposite him at this square table, whether my heart has turned to stone, lava stone, rage grown cold. I'm Naomi Watcher Nakane tonight, hovering somewhere in the air, observing as I eat in this public place that my abdomen is in discomfort. I have a vague and general discomfort about everything and my appetite is dull.

What a long, long way we are from Granton, from Slocan, from the woods in the mountains and the sugar-beet fields. I glance at his face and find no clue to the pathway home. Stephen the celebrity beckons to waiters, orders wines. And there's not one pebble on the forest floor to guide us out of these woods. He'll be the guest adjudicator tomorrow for the piano sonatas and then he'll be gone.

I'm more at home in Chinatown than in this glitzy candlelit room of pink cloth napkins and waiters in bow ties. We've had crab and avocado appetizers, cold creamy soup. Next the entrées. Too much food. What must life be like for Stephen, who lives in hotels much of the time and eats like this often? No wonder he's put on weight.

There's a pianist playing light classics. Stephen says she's terrible. Some sort of business convention is on. We're surrounded by dark pinstripe three-piece suits, these suits of success, suits of armor, that declare down to the shiny shoes that here are today's knights, fighting the windy ways of Mammon with their ledger sheets and their wits.

Aunt Emily's mission tonight is clear. We need Stephen for the League. Whether he likes it or not, he's getting a short course on Japanese Canadian politics. It's like the old days in Granton when Aunt Emily would visit and they'd sit at the table arguing into the night. Stephen's been trying to change the subject.

"Really, your career is more important than all this redress stuff. Think about your future, Anna."

"Get thee behind me, Satan," Anna says and I smile, remembering her as a little girl defending Gaby and shaking her finger at Dog as she chanted the magic words.

"You can take the girl out of Granton," Stephen grins, "but you can't take Granton out of the girl."

"And you?" I ask. "Is Granton still in your veins too?"

"Not a drop." He flicks a non-existent piece of lint off his jacket.

When Stephen left Granton, he left. But his leaving goes with him. He's in perpetual flight. His eyes, even now, are wandering around the room.

For just an instant when I first caught a glimpse of him waiting in the lobby, I felt a flicker of something. I hardly know what the feeling was. But the sensation disappeared as swiftly as it arrived.

Neither Stephen nor I is fully here. He's walled away from Aunt Emily's insistent agenda, and I've fallen through my trapdoor into a room beneath the room where we sit. A bulletproof space.

Aunt Emily is intent on getting through to Stephen and she's being as patient and self-controlled as I've ever seen her.

"Tell me, Stephen," she says, "you surely do not agree with the prime minister. Tell me that you don't agree."

The prime minister's latest remarks have left people nonplussed. He, the man who speaks of "justice in our time," has dismissed our community, saying the "descendants of dead ancestors" are not deserving of either compensation or apology.

"Who's a dead ancestor?" Marion wanted to know. Ken said not only are we alive, but so are the perpetrators. And Sumi, smiling gracious Sumi who adores the prime minister, sat with her hands folded in her lap, saying nothing.

"So what do we expect of a man who thinks we're Japanese?" Anna asked.

It rankles people that the prime minister apologized to the Japanese in Japan for what Canada did to us Canadians. "Can you see him going to France to try to make amends to French Canadians?"

The report from Ottawa is that Government is prepared to offer its regrets, but there can be no further acknowledgment of the actions taken against us. The leaders of the past acted legitimately and their names are not to be tarnished today by an apology for their deeds.

"The Bundestag is supreme," Anna says. "We've got our Eichmanns in Ottawa, still defending the old laws of the land, and nobody twitches in bed."

Stephen recoils. "That's pretty offensive, Baby Anna."

"But don't you see her point, Stephen? If we're going to get anywhere with this obtuse government, we've got to pull together. We need our high-profile people."

"Look at it this way," Anna says. "What if one person from that elitist school, Upper Canada College—say Robertson Davies—what if the government took his house? See what I mean?"

"I get so tired of being used."

"Used?" Aunt Emily is getting fed up with the patient approach. "Used? The League doesn't use us! We use it!"

"Well . . ." Stephen looks away. "I've got better things to do. There's a broader picture out there."

"Good grief, Stephen!" Aunt Emily's voice is shrill.

The men at the next table glance our way. I nudge Aunt Emily to calm down, but she's getting geared up and nothing I know can stop Hurricane Em when she gets going. I can hear Stephen thinking, "Well, she certainly hasn't changed." He's embarrassed, but Anna's eyes are fixed on Aunt Emily in fierce identification.

"You can neutralize anything with the 'broader picture.' " Aunt Emily clutches his arm so that he's forced to look at her. "Listen to me. People need mud in order to see. You're living proof of that. If you don't get your hands in the mud, you won't get the eyes you need to see what to do about the broader picture."

In times like these, she says, a pristine name is like a lake killed by acid rain—beautiful but dead. He must, he must come down and join the struggle, because we, his family, his community, will never be at home, in this country or anywhere, unless we first achieve redress. This we must do for our psychic survival. This first, this basic thing. What heals people is the transforming power of mutuality. Mutual vulnerability. Mutual strength.

This is Aunt Emily of the Japanese Canadian Redress Crusade, reaching out to Stephen the Infidel. But he's not being persuaded. He pours wine into our glasses and sounds offhanded as he says we aren't realistic if we think we can attain mutuality. "Look at the facts," he says. He picks up a crumb from the edge of the bread basket. "Japanese Canadians count less than *this* in Parliament. You haven't a hope."

"You're wrong," Aunt Emily says. Her voice has quietened to the dead calm of conviction. "We're human, we're equal and we're coming through." She leans toward him and raps the table with her knuckles so hard the candle flame flickers. "Nothing in heaven or on earth can stop the labor of the heart, Stephen." She's preaching the Gospel according to Aunt Emily. The heart's power is greater than any power known.

Redress, she says, is a Canadian liberation movement. We're fighting the oppression of an entire Canadian minority.

"Oppression, now that's an abused word." Stephen hunches forward, leaning on his forearms. "You've got it all wrong. We're not oppressed. There comes a time when you've got to stand up and recognize that things have changed. Redress? Come on! The way everyone loves to play the victim. My God! Think what Japanese Canadian redress sounds like to the rest of the world. Can't you hear the false note in it?" He shakes his finger at us. "You're all suffering from a North American pathology. Do something useful, why don't you. Something for others."

Something for others! Has Stephen ever thought of anyone but himself? This is the man who never once condescended to visit and comfort the old woman who worshipped him. This is the man who will not stoop and lend his name to help his community. And he is blind to the fact that some of us do not feel as privileged as he now does.

"Your so-called little liberation movement . . ." He waves his hand, dismissing us. "A bunch of myopic crybabies."

Aunt Emily is taken aback for a moment, but she will not be dismissed by her nephew. "What an outsider's point of view that is. I'm telling you, Stephen, whether it's in suburbia or Ethiopia, when we fight oppression, we're fighting with the oppressed." She's carrying on doggedly, but I can see she cannot win. He's made his position totally clear. He won't be involved. Somewhere in all these truths lies a failure of love.

"I'm a minstrel," he says and shrugs. "I'll put the story to music if you want. Don't expect anything else from me."

He may well write a ballad, but the tune will be wrong. Stories without love are words without song.

Joy Kogawa was born in Vancouver in 1935. Like other Japanese Canadians, she and her family were interned and persecuted during the Second World War.

She is the author of two novels, *Obasan* and *Itsuka*. She has also written four volumes of poetry: *The Splintered Moon, A Choice of Dreams, Jericho Road,* and *Woman in the Woods.* She has received numerous awards and grants, and has contributed to many anthologies and periodicals; she has also worked as a schoolteacher, a writer for the Canadian Prime Minister's office, and is a member of the Order of Canada.